A CRUISE TO DIE FOR

ALSO BY CHARLOTTE AND AARON ELKINS

The Alix London Series
A DANGEROUS TALENT

The Lee Ofsted Series
A WICKED SLICE
ROTTEN LIES
NASTY BREAKS
WHERE HAVE ALL THE BIRDIES GONE?
ON THE FRINGE

A CRUISE to DIE FOR

AN ALIX LONDON MYSTERY

CHARLOTTE AND AARON ELKINS

THOMAS & MERCER

Text copyright © 2013 Charlotte and Aaron Elkins

Published by Thomas & Mercer
PO Box 400818
Las Vegas, NV 89140

ISBN-13: 9781477805077 ♦
ISBN-10: 1477805079

A CRUISE TO DIE FOR

1

Welcome to the Home Page of The Culture Guru
"Seen on the Art Scene"
by
I. Witt Ness

Word is that a multimillion-dollar painting proudly owned by the Greek tycoon-"art collector" Panos Papadakis is not quite all it's supposed to be, and if you don't believe me, you can ask Lyons' esteemed Laboratoire Forensique Pour l'Art, which has just finished subjecting two dozen of Papadakis's paintings to its fearsome array of tests. Twenty-three of them passed. The twenty-fourth? A dud. In other words, a sham. In other words, a FAKE.

Even your intrepid reporter's skills have not yet ferreted out just which one it is (stay tuned, but I have it on good authority that it is one of the gems of Papadakis's "collection" and set our boy Panos back something like $2,000,000 when he bought it in the mid 1990s—and that was before the explosion in art prices).

What makes all this especially titillating is that these particular twenty-four paintings were in the process of being readied for what has to be the glitziest and most exclusive art auction of all time. Strictly invitational, it is described in the auction catalogue as "Masterpieces of Impressionist and Modern Art from the Collection of Panos Papadakis," and it will be the highlight of a lavish Mediterranean cruise on megamillionaire Papadakis's mega-mega-yacht, the sleek, two-hundred-thirty-nine foot Artemis.

Some people in the know have begun to wonder if news of the fake will produce an epidemic of cold feet when it comes time to bid on the other paintings in the "collection." My guess? No problemo, señor. They'll be more eager than ever to be part of the occasion. Nothing like a touch of notoriety to add that delicious little hint of frisson to a society occasion. Especially when one can easily afford to lose a couple mill (as who cannot?).

Interested in securing an invitation to this fabulous junket on the bounding main? Not a problem . . . as long as you happen to be one of Papadakis's well-heeled financial clients with at least €1,000,000 invested with him. Oh, and to certify that you're willing and able to shell out at least the minimum acceptable bid on the least expensive painting. Anyone interested in a snazzy little Mihaly von Zichy (who?) with a reserve price of $980,000?

Know what your dauntless correspondent finds the most intriguing question about the whole affair? WHY is Papadakis putting a sizable chunk of his beloved "collection" up for sale? One can't help wondering if the mono-multi-mega-mogul's finances are in as much trouble as his native country's, so that—

.   .   .

Panos Papadakis slammed the iPad onto the slat-topped dining table hard enough to rattle the Armani-designed luncheon cutlery. "What the hell he means with all these, what you call them, quote marks?" He stared accusingly at Edward Reed, who sat beside him and had called the blog to his attention. "What, he's saying I'm not really a 'collector'? My collection isn't really a 'collection'?" He emphasized his points with sarcastic little air-quotation marks alongside his ears. "What, it's not good enough for him, the piker? What does he know? He don't even got the nerve to use his own name, the bum."

Suppressing both a sigh and a smile, but not quite managing to restrain one elegantly lifted eyebrow, Reed watched Papadakis stalk to the railing of the mountainside terrace of his enormous home above the posh seaside village of Gustavia on the Caribbean island of St. Barts. There he stood, the two-thousand-nine-hundred-and-fifty-eighth richest man in the world, muttering and staring down at the marina, squat, neckless, and incontestably toad-like. Thick-wristed, furry forearms stuck out of his short-sleeved sport shirt, from the open neck of which more wiry, dense hair sprouted like some black jungle growth struggling to get out into the sun. Although Reed knew for a fact that the man had shaved that morning, Papadakis's cheeks were blue-black almost up to his eyes and down to his collarbone. About the only place he seemed to have trouble growing hair was on his scalp, which got barer every time Reed saw him— so much so that, judging from today's coiffure, he had given up trying to make a comb-across work.

His anger had come as no surprise to Reed. An explosion was to have been expected, but not because of the quotation marks. To be honest, he hadn't thought that Papadakis would even notice them, let alone grasp their nuances. Once again, and not for the first time by a long shot, he reminded himself not to confuse the financier's natural coarseness with lack of intelligence.

On the other hand, it also wasn't the first time that Papadakis had been goaded by snarky observations about his collection, and the more of them there were, the more they seemed to get under his skin. The gist of them, generally speaking, was that his understanding of art was pathetic and his collection wasn't a collection at all, but a conglomeration, a mean-ingless potpourri, with no unifying principle underlying it. They were wrong, though; there was a powerful unifying principle, and it was called *profit*. The man had no emotional or scholarly interest in any particular artist, or period, or medium, or style. He bought paintings based purely on his estimate of their likely increase in value— a perfectly logical reason as far as Reed was concerned, and one for which he by no means shared the Culture Guru's contempt.

In Reed's opinion, in fact, regardless of all the high-sounding talk out there, there were only two basic motivations that drove today's art market—especially the Contemporary and Post-Modernist markets. One was to show off for one's peers: *You see, by paying millions of dollars for this stuffed shark or this collection of torn pieces of cardboard covered with unreadable graffiti written in chalk, I am demonstrating how very hip and avant-garde I am.* And it usually met its objective. Why else did auction audiences applaud so respectfully when someone paid an obscene amount of money for a preposterous pile of junk, or rags, or medicine bottles "artistically" lined up on shelving?

Reed found this motivation not only ridiculous but troubling. It did not bode well for the future of the market that he loved. The other motive, however—profit—had his wholehearted approval. After all, it was based on the same theory that successfully drove the stock market, the greater fool theory (otherwise known as the "dumber than thou" hypothesis): that is, you buy an object, regardless of its inherent value or lack thereof, in the expectation that someone dumber than you will eventually pay you even more for it.

And at that sort of predicting, Panos's record proved that he was very, very shrewd. He had sold pieces from his private collection for five and even ten times what he'd paid for them. And the art purchases for his investment business? Well, there Reed wasn't privy to the details, but it was no secret that they'd made him a millionaire many times over; some said a billionaire.

As Panos himself had once put it: "If I don't know nothing about the paintings I'm buying, how come I make so much money off them?"

But the man wasn't happy. He was no different from anybody else: The money was one thing, yes, but it was *respect* he ached for. He got it from the financial establishment, but to the snooty art world he was and always would be nothing but a vulgar, ignorant parvenu. In Reed's opinion, both points of view were correct.

Panos was still staring down at the bay and muttering. "Can you believe that guy!" Papadakis banged the metal railing. "A bum is what he is, the bum. I'll sue him. And how the hell this information got out? Myself, I just got the report this morning. I didn't even read it yet myself. I'll sue that goddamn lab too; who do they think they are?"

"Really, Panos, you shouldn't get so excited," said Reed with the leisurely British drawl—the sort of BBC accent you didn't hear very much anymore, even in England—that he'd brought with him when he'd come to New York twenty years before to open his Manhattan art dealership, and which he had worked hard to maintain. Sounding like Laurence Olivier to the American ear was no mean advantage in his world.

"Forget about suing them; what we really should do is give them a commission. That dreadful Culture Guru person as well. You know," he said, lifting his juice glass and scrutinizing it against the clear, bright sky the way a wine expert would study a *premier grand cru* from Château Haut-Brion, "this is really extraordinary. What in the world is in this concoction besides the blood orange juice? Bitters, of course, but . . . ah, is that juniper berry?"

"What, I'm supposed to know?" Papadakis grumped without turning around. "Ask her, the maid; Thea, or something. Tell me, why should I give them a commission?"

"Well, first of all I very much doubt that it's the laboratory that leaked the information, but whoever it was, we can thank them for stimulating gossip and speculation." Reed had a little more juice, decided he wasn't that crazy about it after all, and went to stand beside Papadakis at the railing, but quickly stepped back a little; the drop was steeper than he'd realized, and heights didn't agree with him. "I'm in the art-selling business, Panos. Trust me, in the end this will mean higher prices."

It was the selling of art that was Reed's connection to Papadakis, who had engaged him to curate his seagoing auction and handle all of the associated tasks, for which he was to collect three percent of the hammer price on each painting sold—only a quarter of his usual commission, but then how often did he hold an auction with total estimated selling prices of

CHARLOTTE & AARON ELKINS

thirty to fifty million dollars? How often did he hold an auction that required no sharing of his earnings with his staff? And how often did he hold an auction that had no expenses to speak of associated with it, no insurance costs, and just about no work?

Never, never, and never.

"Okay, okay, you're right, Edward." Panos grunted his disgust. "Ah, who got time to sue anybody anyway? Screw 'em."

Reed thought at first that it had been his smoothly worded reassurances that had calmed the other man, but now he saw that it was the prospect on which Papadakis gazed. Not the long row of luxury yachts lined up cheek by jowl in the marina below—seen from here, not so very different from a string of motor homes in an overnight trailer court—but further out to sea, beyond the harbor entrance, where boats too vast to moor in the marina were anchored. And there lay his pride and joy, the gleaming, blue-and-white *Artemis*, brilliant in the noonday sun and complete with a shiny new helicopter on a pad on the aft deck. But Panos's pleasure had been marred. A quarter of a mile beyond it lay an even bigger vessel, Roman Abramovich's monstrous *Eclipse*, the largest private yacht in the world at almost six hundred feet, bigger than a destroyer. When Abramovich had arrived in St. Barts that morning and anchored there, Papadakis, whose *Artemis* had been only a few hundred yards away, had moved his own vessel so that it wouldn't seem dwarfed by the giant. And he'd been grumbling about it ever since. To work well with Papadakis, one had to be aware of these little conceits. And Reed was.

Continuing to glower at the *Eclipse*, the financier-collector went back to processing his resentment of the Culture Guru's insinuations. "That business at the end—wondering if I still had any money, that part I really don't like. Who the hell is he to wonder? That's slander, right? For that, I could sic my lawyers on the lousy crumb, couldn't I? Am I wrong?"

"For heaven's sake, Panos, this is some sleazy two-bit blogger, not the *New York Times*. Besides, with all that's been happening in the world, who isn't wondering about everybody else's finances?"

6

Reed laughed as he spoke, but if there is such a thing as a mental wince, he was experiencing one. He was thinking about the sorry state of his own affairs since the weak moment when he'd let his wife talk him into bidding at that accursed Fairfield County estate auction.

And he'd actually, inexplicably, wound up winning the damn thing. So now he was the dazed owner—that is, mortgage holder—of a fifteen-year-old wedding-cake of a mansion that could have doubled for the east wing of Buckingham Palace (except that it was more elaborate), and the acre that surrounded it. It wasn't the price tag itself—$2,800,000, a "steal" (ha!) considering that it had taken $12,000,000 to build—that was the killer, it was what came with it. The property taxes ran $68,000, the once-extravagant landscaping ("a one-third-scale reproduction of Marie Antoinette's garden at Versailles") now looked like a random acre along the Upper Amazon, and his wife was already complaining about the dated bathrooms, of which there were a total of *seven*.

What had he been thinking? The thing was ruining him. He'd been trying to unload it almost since the day he'd bought it, and he was more than ready to take a loss, but it seemed that there weren't any other suckers out there; only him. However, if this auction of Panos's netted him as much as he was hoping for —three percent of thirty million was almost a million dollars, and that was the low estimate!—it would keep him afloat long enough to make something happen.

Both men returned to the umbrellaed table, where Papadakis absent-mindedly picked at his cooling lobster-and-avocado omelet. After a few moments of pushing pieces of it around on his plate, he finally got to the subject that Reed had expected him to erupt over.

"The truth is, Edward, what really bothers me, that a painting of mine, it's supposed to be a fake? That's impossible!"

"There's no 'supposed to be' about it, Panos. The *Laboratoire's* reputation is—"

"Yeah, yeah, I know, but I still don't buy it. And it makes me look like some kind of crook. Or a dope, which is worse."

"On the contrary, it's going to make you look like the most honest and forthright of men. Upon learning of the Monet's, ah, doubtful provenance, you immediately announce the fact and remove it from the auction, not wishing to give even the appearance of doing anything dishonest. You will do that, I trust?"

"Yeah, sure, sure, but I still don't buy it. I mean, how it can be a fake? You think I'd buy something without testing it every goddamn way there is? Listen, that Manet got certified not only by the lab in Geneva, but—"

"You mean the Monet."

"—by that big shot, what's his name, at the Museum of . . . what?"

"You said Manet. You meant Monet."

Papadakis stared uncomprehendingly at him for a second, then exploded with an agitated "Manet, Monet, what's the difference, goddammit! Don't keep interrupting me! I'm trying to think!"

Reed had all he could do to keep from shaking his head in wonderment. Admittedly, most people tended to confuse Edouard Manet with Claude Monet. Putting aside the similarity in names, both lived at the same time; both painted Parisian street scenes by the carload; both were cited by some as the father of Impressionism; both were snubbed by the critics and rejected by the Salon; both painted similar famous pictures called *Le Déjeuner sur l'Herbe,* and did many others with *Argenteuil* and *Seine* in the titles, and so on. So it was understandable that a lot of people couldn't keep them straight. Once, in the Musée d'Orsay in Paris, Edward had heard a man respond with some impatience to a question from his wife: "It doesn't matter. Either spelling is acceptable."

But such ignorance—such lack of concern—in a man blessed with the immense good fortune to actually own paintings by both these great masters? To be unaware of the differences in style, and technique, and even subject matter—Monet's joyful, animated, transitory "impressions" versus Manet's deeper, darker, less spontaneous explorations into personality and society—seemed to Reed to be emblematic of the sad level to which the once-refined culture of art collectorship had fallen.

On the other hand, there was a good side too. With speculation and ignorance rampant, there was more money than ever to be made (honestly, if not necessarily ethically), for less work than ever, and how could that be a bad thing? Various commissions from Papadakis had already earned Reed quite a sum, and the upcoming auction was a much-needed blessing. He looked with something like affection at Papadakis, who had his hands pressed to his temples and was rocking back and forth and groaning, "Oh boy, oh, boy, oh, boy."

Reed leaned forward over the table and peered at him. "Panos, are you well?"

. . .

Panos was not well. Panos felt like hell.

You don't get to be the two-thousand-nine-hundred-and-eighty-fifth richest man in the world by being stupid, and Panos Papadakis was anything but. It also helps if you don't mind bending the law a little, or even tweaking it, or even breaking it. He had, in fact, done a little of all three in relation to the auction.

For one thing, he had known full well from the beginning that there was a forgery among the twenty-four paintings. He knew because he'd put it there himself. Like several other fakes that he owned, he had commissioned it. As with the others, he had paid the forger $30,000 for it, an outrageous price, but he fully anticipated seeing it go for five hundred times that at the auction. And the original? That, he had other plans for.

The possibility of detection hadn't worried him. The forger was probably the best in the world at his craft, and he had justified his extraordinary fees by coming up with a clever and original means of making it virtually impossible for even the most stringent scientific tests to spot his fakes. And he had proven it; not one of the earlier ones had raised the least shadow of suspicion. Thus, Panos had been deeply shaken to learn that the *Laboratoire Forensique* had somehow spotted this one.

But that shock, unnerving as it was, paled to nothing when it turned out that they had *not* identified it. His forged Manet? That had indeed passed muster. The picture that had *not* passed muster was the *Monet*, a painting that he'd owned for more than ten years, that he'd paid a lot of money for, and in the authenticity of which he'd had absolute confidence.

How could this be? *Was* it a fake? What was going on? And the most important questions of all: If his painting was a fake, then where was his Monet, the real Monet? And . . . his eyes narrowed, his brain focused . . . *who had it?*

"Am I all right?" he said to Edward. "Yes, sure I'm all right, you just gave me a little shock, that's all. I'm fine." And he was telling the truth. Among the attributes that had gotten him where he was, was the ability to recover quickly from setbacks and disasters, to regroup his resources and go back on offense. He'd come up with no answers to his questions, but at least he knew where to start.

"Well, you just seem a little—"

But Panos had had enough of Reed for the time being; of his too-perfect manners, his fake concern, his barely disguised condescension, his stupid little mustache that he probably groomed with tweezers. "Edward, look, I got a lot of stuff to do. I need to talk to the insurance people about this, I need to get hold of Sotheby's, I need to . . . well, a lot of things. Do you got anything else we need to talk about right now that can't wait?"

"Well, you remember you were looking for someone who might serve as a sort of lecturer on the cruise? Someone who could speak knowledgeably about not merely the pictures, but the artists as well; someone the guests could come to with questions they might—"

Papadakis motioned with his hand: *Get to the point.*

"Well, I think I may have the perfect candidate for you. A young woman—"

Papadakis nodded. "'Young woman' is good."

"Quite pretty—"

"'Pretty' is good."

"Her name is Alix London. She's developed quite a reputation—"

"Wait a minute, this is the daughter of that Met crook? Went to jail for twenty years?"

"Yes, Geoffrey London. It was eight years, actually. But none of that reflects on her."

Papadakis frowned. "Wasn't she involved in a murder or something herself, not so long ago?"

"Yes, she was *involved*, but her own record is spotless, absolutely clean. That's what makes her so perfect. That murder got her a lot of publicity, you see, and my thought was that when that Culture Guru swine and the rest of the paparazzi get wind that she'll be aboard, it will provide a lovely dollop of excitement . . . cachet . . . ." He waved his hand expressively, seeking the word he was after.

"*Frisson*," said Papadakis and Reed laughed. "Okay, good idea, you see if she's available, but I'm not paying her nothing. She gets airfare and a free cruise, and she gets to meet a lot of important people. If that's not enough for her, forget it."

Reed stood up. "I'll see what I can do, Panos."

.   .   .

Two minutes after being dropped off at St. Barts' tiny Gustaf III airstrip, Reed was on his phone to the Federal Bureau of Investigation in Washington, D.C.

"May I speak to Ted Ellesworth, please?"

"Special Agent Ellesworth isn't available at the moment." The woman spoke with a twangy New England accent. "My name is Jamie Wozniak. I'm the operations specialist for the Art Crime Team. Can I help you?"

"Can you give a message to Mr. Ellesworth?"

"Of course."

"My name is Edward Reed. I'm a—"

"I know who you are, Mr. Reed. What is the message?"

"Tell him . . ." He peered around to make sure he wasn't being spied on. "Tell him Panos went for it," he whispered, feeling delightfully secret-agentish. "*She's in.*"

2

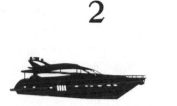

In Brooklyn's slowly gentrifying South Williamsburg neighborhood, on South Sixth Street, literally in the afternoon shadow of the Williamsburg Bridge, was an old bagel bakery, the loft of which had been outfitted as a four-room apartment. In the largest and airiest of these mostly featureless rooms stood its current renter, a tall man dressed in what would have been the height of fashion in men's at-home wear in eighteenth century Paris, London, or Rome. His normally longish hair had been shaved off, as it would have been on a gentleman of that era, to make the decorous wearing of a wig in public more comfortable and convenient, and on his head was a woman's bouffant shower cap, the closest thing to an eighteenth-century man's at-home "negligee cap" that was to be found in Williamsburg. He wore a richly textured morning gown— it would have been called a "banyan" then— of green silk damask with gleaming blue lapels over a ruffled white linen shirt and a fussy beige waistcoat. In his left hand, his thumb clamped securely through the thumbhole, was a traditional kidney-shaped artist's palette covered with daubs of mixed paint, and in his right, a delicate brush. A closer look would have shown that his morning coat bore its share of paint spots as well.

The shower cap had come from Walmart, the rest of the clothing from a costume store, and the brush and palette were his own, but all in all he'd done a good job making himself look as if he'd stepped out of a self-portrait by some well-to-do court painter of the mid-eighteenth century.

This was not by accident. The man's costume was based explicitly on the painter Georges Desmarées's 1769 *Self Portrait in Old Age*. Moreover, the loft was much as Desmarées's own atelier at the court of Maximilian III in

Munich would have been: roughly made wooden easels and low, three-legged stools that were used as tables for equipment and material; dozens of ceramic jugs containing hundreds of brushes, some made from stiff hog bristles, others, like the one in his hand, from soft, pliable sable; crude shelving on which pigs' bladders filled with pigments were stored; and paintings framed and unframed, finished and unfinished (or more likely abandoned), tacked to the walls or leaning against them. On the splintery wooden floors was the customary artist's litter of crumpled paper, discarded brushes, old props, and used-up paint receptacles, but the room itself was large and impressive, with beautiful velvet swags hung at the north-facing windows, and a great stone fireplace surmounted by an ornate oak mantel that had once decorated an even bigger stone fireplace in a Fifth Avenue mansion. The fireplace itself, long defunct, had come with the loft. The mantel had been rented for one month from an architectural salvage firm in Queens.

All these little conceits were helpful to the man who stood in the midst of them, lost in thought before a painting, a second brush clamped between his teeth. Christoph Weisskopf was an art forger, and among those few truly familiar with the profession, he was judged to be a master. He was also thought to be a little crazy, and this was equally true. The eighteenth-century trappings were not mere whimsy; they were necessities to him. In order to achieve his remarkable results, Weisskopf's method was to make himself believe for the time being that he truly was the artist he was imitating. The crazy part was that he generally succeeded.

His previous commission had been a Warhol, so he'd bought a straw-blond wig, dyed it even paler, and teased and sprayed it into what looked like an exploding haystack. For the month it had taken him to do the painting, he'd dressed in leather jackets, black turtlenecks, jeans, and high-heeled boots. He'd lived on pastries and tomato soup and pretty much convinced himself he was gay. Sometimes his neighbors didn't recognize him from one month to the next. Sometimes he didn't recognize himself and would be startled when he caught sight of his reflection in a mirror or a window. To switch personas from twenty-first-century New York to eighteenth-century Munich had taken more mental effort than usual, but for two days now, he had *been* Georges Desmarées.

Weisskopf was an exception to the general truth that the art forger's lot is not a happy one. The less able ones are constantly either in trouble with the law or one step ahead of it; their earnings are small, sporadic, and undependable; and the nature of the game requires them to associate with devious, unappetizing, and often dangerous types. Those with greater competence usually make better-than-good livings, stay out of trouble, and deal with an all-around better class of crooks. But they tend to be even more miserable, for they, almost to a one, are frustrated artists, angry with the prejudiced, know-nothing critics and dealers who dismiss or scorn the work they do under their own names, but are ever-ready to swoon over their "newly discovered" "Cezannes," "Chagalls," or "Picassos."

Not Weisskopf. Weisskopf was happy in his work. The fact that he had seen some of his own paintings, none of which bore his own signature, on the walls of the world's great museums didn't bother him. For one thing, he earned top dollar at his trade, being one of the very few with the talent and discipline to turn out—and get away with—*exact* copies of existing paintings, rather than the usual less demanding, less risky pastiches "in the style of" one artist or another. And unlike most of his ilk, he wasn't limited to one particular school or another; it made no difference, he could do them all. Donatello? Botticelli? Rubens? Miró? Kandinsky? Dalí? You name it; if you could pay his price he'd paint you one that'd fool any expert. His fee scale ran from $5,000 to $30,000 per picture, up to $1,000 of which was allocated to outfitting himself and his studio in the manner appropriate to the time, the place, and the painter. Each picture took a month to paint, usually followed by another month or so to properly age and dry it. He could easily work on two or three at a time and sometimes did, switching getups and altering his studio to put him in the appropriate frame of mind. His remarkable gifts meant that he didn't have to work on spec. His paintings were done on commission with fifty percent up front, no exceptions.

Last year his twenty-two commissions from thirteen clients had earned him $380,000 (tax-free, it need hardly be said), and things were looking even better this year.

The commission he was currently in the process of fulfilling was a 1760 portrait by Desmarées of Princess Maria Anna von Pfalz-Sulzbach of Bavaria. Desmarées was far from the most collectible of Rococo artists, but the person who had commissioned it claimed to be the husband of a woman who believed herself to be one of Maria Anna's descendants, and this was to be a present to her for their twentieth anniversary. As to whether this or any part of it was true, or whether some less innocent plan was behind it, Weisskopf had not inquired, as he never inquired. Unfamiliar with the monetary value of Desmarées's work, he had checked the auction prices for the artist's name before agreeing to take on the job and had found that a Desmarées portrait had recently gone under the hammer for $14,360 at Christie's in New York. Weisskopf, who enjoyed a healthy sense of irony, had set his price for the fake at $15,000.

The painting itself was done. Now he was about to apply the final touches of his peculiar craft, which in this case required creating the appearance of *craquelure*, the network of cracks that appears on the surface of almost every old oil painting. Most forgers accomplish this by rolling up the finished canvas, tying a rubber band around it, and sticking it in a warm oven for a few hours. Weisskopf, being Weisskopf, preferred the more delicate, elegant technique of applying two layers of varnish, the underlying one slow drying and the upper one fast drying. The upper layer thus contracts and hardens more quickly, forming a rigid skin at the surface. Then, when the lower layer eventually contracts in its turn, the by-now inflexible surface skin splits and fissures. The result, if properly done: an utterly convincing *craquelure*, at least to the naked eye.

He had just dipped his brush in the varnish when his phone (kept in the kitchen during his workdays) chirped. He grunted his annoyance and let it continue to ring away while he carefully made the first gingerly application of varnish. When the answering machine clicked on, all he heard at first was an unintelligible male rumble, but then it picked up in volume, a blast that couldn't be tuned out.

"You son of a bitch, Weisskopf, pick up the phone, you son of a bitch! I know you're there; you think you're fooling me? Pick up the phone!"

Papadakis, dammit. He gritted his teeth and continued to slide the varnish-laden brush over the painting.

"I'm waiting!"

That did it. The bastard wasn't going away. Anyway, the trance was shattered, probably for the rest of the day. With a resigned, lingering look at that first glistening swath, he laid his brush across the rim of the can (the can was one of his few nods to modernity) and went to the room that served as his kitchen, while Panos continued raving.

"You heard me, Weisskopf, I'm not—"

He picked up the phone. "Panos, no offense, but can this possibly wait half an hour? I promise to call you right back."

"No, it can't wait, you crook, you bum, you two-bit faker!"

"Look, Panos, I'm right in the middle of a delicate—"

"Don't give me delicate, you goddamn Nazi! How did your lousy Monet get in my collection?"

Weisskopf's jaw dropped. "*What?*"

"You heard what I said. How did—"

"Panos, I have no idea what you're talking about. How about—"

"What I'm talking about? I'm talking about my Monet isn't my Monet anymore. It's one of your fakes. You think I don't know your lousy style when I see it? How did it get in my collection? And where the hell is *my* Monet?"

"Panos . . . Panos, please—" Weisskopf, holding the phone a few inches from his ear to spare his hearing, was fumbling for words.

"You don't work for nothing. Somebody paid you to do it. Who?"

There was a tiny pause, as if for thought, and then the gravelly voice came down eight or ten decibels, so that Weisskopf had to put the phone up to his ear again to hear the menacing growl that ensued. "Or do *you* have it? If I find out—"

"Panos, listen to me. I swear to you on the life of my mother, if you've got a fake Monet in your collection, it's not my work. I've only done two Monets in my life, and that was years ago, and one is in a museum in Antwerp, and the other—"

"Christoph, *you* listen to me, and listen good. I don't give a damn about your other fakes, or your mother either. You can have this one back too, and I don't care what you do with it. But I want *my* Monet, you understand me? And I want it back now. I don't care what you have to do to get it. Otherwise—"

"Panos, will you *please* stop threatening me and listen to reason? Just think about it for a minute. How could I possibly—"

"You want reason? Okay, here's reason. If I don't have my own painting back inside of one week—*one week*—I'll have you put in jail for the next twenty years."

"But I'm telling you I had nothing to do with—"

"I'm not talking about the Monet now, I'm talking about a few other little things I happen to know about you."

Weisskopf was beginning to get a little hot under the collar, or rather under the shiny blue lapels of his banyan. "I don't like what you're insinuating," he said. "You're barking up the wrong tree now. I have never— *never*—knowingly participated in anything that was against the law. I take every—"

He was interrupted by a bark of derisive laughter. "Oh, really? That Hogarth in Gutterman's collection in Montreal? Tell me; you think he knows it's not a Hogarth?"

"Well, I admit, that's the way it turned out, but it was certainly no fault of my—"

"And that little so-called Pissarro of Mulas's, down in Lima? That wasn't your fault either?"

"I . . . I . . ."

"One week," snarled Papadakis and hung up.

Weisskopf put the phone down and stared at it for half a minute, the varnish forgotten.

Then, slowly, he picked it up again and dialed a number. It was answered on the third ring. "Hello?"

Weisskopf took a deep breath. "We've got trouble," he said.

3

Ted (Theodore Mark) Ellesworth was not your average FBI agent, and his work cubicle showed it. Where others might have criminal codes on their bookshelves and crime scene photos or Most Wanted posters on their walls, Ted's shelves were more likely to hold books on Titian, Rodin, or the Post-Impressionist painters, and the pushpins stuck into the partitions that served as walls held up museum posters of works by Rubens, Goya, Gustav Klimt, and Georgia O'Keeffe.

These fittings, which were a continuing source of ribbing from his friends in violent-crimes units, were there as much for work as for pleasure. Ted was a member of the FBI's seventeen-person Art Crime Team—three attorneys, an operations specialist, and thirteen agents, of which Ted was one of only two who specialized in undercover work. During his nine years on the team—generally referred to simply as the art squad, even by its members—he had posed as "bent" dealers, secretive or greedy collectors, and gullible, newly rich bourgeoisie looking to spend a million bucks, maybe two, on some culture they can flaunt. As undercover work went, it had a lot going for it—stays in expensive hotels, dinners in fine restaurants, sometimes a Ferrari or a Porsche to tool around in. And it certainly held none of the extreme physical hazards or other unpleasantnesses faced by undercover agents working drugs or organized crime. And most important, it was *interesting*.

But hazards there were. Undercover work, whatever the kind, put a huge strain on the memory, the psyche, and sometimes even one's moral core. On an assignment that might run months, one had to be on guard every minute. A single slip as to who you were supposed to be, or to your past, or what you were doing there, or anything at all you'd been telling people, and the mission was ruined, all hope of a bust gone. And there were hazards that filtered into your personal life too. You had to be dishonest with your friends and those you loved; not just the necessary sin-by-omission kind of dishonesty but outright lies or deceitful equivocations about what you were doing, and why you couldn't come over for dinner Friday night, and why you hadn't called or returned a phone call, and where the heck you'd been for the last two weeks.

And you had to *remember* all that. That took a toll on you. It made you closemouthed and evasive, and when it came to your feelings you learned that your safest bet was to keep them to yourself, to remain, using Ted's boss's word for it, "disconnected." And that, of course, was murder on your personal life. By anybody's measure, Ted qualified as an extremely eligible bachelor: thirty-three years old, educated, good-looking, funny, and an all-around likable guy. He liked women and they liked him, but since he'd taken on his undercover role, none of his relationships had had a ghost of a chance of panning out.

He'd met Alix London a few months earlier, when he'd been working a forgery case in Santa Fe. It was hate at first sight. She disliked him, or rather disliked his undercover persona, Roland (Rollie) de Beauvais, a foppish, faddish, not-too-principled Boston art dealer. He distrusted her because she was the daughter of Geoffrey London, a New York socialite and a respected conservator at the Metropolitan Museum of Art . . . until it turned out that he had a sideline: He was a serial forger and thief, for which crimes he'd deservedly served an eight-year prison term. Ted knew even at the time that it wasn't sensible to saddle the daughter with the father's reputation, but it was hard not to do so. Like him, after all, she was in the art world, and there she'd been in Santa Fe, "consulting," right in the thick of the illicit doings Ted was investigating. And who, it turned out, had arranged that consulting gig for her? Why, none other than the newly released Geoffrey London himself. So what else was Ted to think other than that she was in cahoots with the old crook in some reprehensible new scheme?

But she wasn't a crook—she was anything but—and he wasn't Rollie de Beauvais, and although it took them a few days to sort things out, they finally got them straight. Alix, he'd found, was not only straight as an arrow, she was a superbly trained art restorer and evaluator, and the possessor of a wonderfully keen eye, far keener and quicker than his, when it came to assessing the authenticity of a suspect work of art. So much so, in fact, that against all odds he'd gotten her interested in possibly doing some occasional consulting work for the squad. She'd filled out an application and come to Washington for interviews with his boss and the personnel people. Then she'd filled out more, lengthier forms, had been thoroughly investigated, and had been placed on the approved list.

The truth was, the problem he'd had to wrestle with the most when originally thinking about recruiting her, was that there was an unmistakable *something* in the air between them—he felt it, and he knew she felt it—and complications of that sort in his personal life were the last thing he wanted right now. In the end, however, he'd decided that her unique abilities were just too valuable to pass up and he'd advocated her hiring. But he'd been more relieved than disappointed when a job in Cincinnati had made it impossible for him to keep the dinner date they'd set for when she came to D.C.

The call he'd gotten from Edward Reed a little while ago signaled the start of what he hoped would be her first job, assuming that she wanted to do it. It was a case he'd been working on as lead investigator for months, so he would be her long-distance supervisor, although he didn't expect that there'd be any direct supervision involved. By telephone, Jamie had asked her to keep the third week in May open until she heard from them again, and she'd agreed.

Well, time for her to hear from them again. He pulled his chair up to the computer and opened his Contacts file.

. . .

The eleven-year-old Volvo that Alix's new budget had recently stretched for was pre-"hands-free telephone capability," so when the phone in the glove box warbled she had to find a spot to pull over, which wasn't that difficult on this dingy, depressing section of Alaskan Way South. Hard for a street not to be dingy and depressing, she supposed, when it lay under the Alaskan Way Viaduct—Highway 99—rumbling and shrieking overhead with the evening rush-hour traffic. Seattle's typical March weather didn't help either: temperature hovering in the low forties, a cold, penetrating rain coming down, and as black at five fifteen as it would be at midnight.

She was irritated as she reached for the phone; her father had a new habit of calling her a few minutes before she was due to pick him up, to tell her, "Alas, my dear, I'm so sorry. Something frightfully important has come up. You won't be very disturbed, will you, about waiting in the outer office with the boys for a few minutes?"

Damn wrong she wouldn't be disturbed. She flipped open the phone and snapped: "Okay, all right, tell me, what is it this time?"

Silence. Then, "Uh . . . Alix?"

It took a couple of seconds for the voice to register. *Ted.* The last time they'd spoken had been two months ago, just before she'd flown to Washington for her interviews, when he'd called to tell her she'd have to take a rain check on the dinner he'd promised. A couple of weeks later he'd telephoned to congratulate her on making it successfully through the hoops, but she'd been out so he'd left a message on her answering machine. He hadn't suggested—hadn't even implied—that he wanted her to call him back. She'd toyed with the idea of doing it anyway, but decided against it.

"I'm sorry, Ted; I thought you were someone else."

"Well, whoever it is, I'm glad I'm not him. Alix, I have some news. The job came through. It's been approved."

"Oh, good." She had yet to figure out if his blunt, impassive, get-to-the-point style was a locked-in part of his personality or just something that went with his kind of work. As usual, she decided with a sigh to simply follow his lead. "I *think*," she added. "Jamie didn't really give me anything in the way of details beyond asking me to make sure my passport was up to date."

"Oh, I think you'll like what we have in mind," he said expansively, and she could hear the smile in his voice. "How does a week-long, super-deluxe cruise through the Greek islands on one of the world's most luxurious megayachts sound?"

Frankly, not as wonderfully appealing as he apparently thought it would. Alix's mother had come from an old-money New England family, and Alix herself had been married (briefly) to the scion of another such family, so cruising and yachts were nothing new—she didn't know if they qualified as "mega," but they were big, fancy boats devoted to rich living—and the truth was that the experience hadn't been all it was cracked up to be. Too many self-important people, too much posturing and affectation, too much servile truckling to "celebrity" guests, too many amorous, sloppy drunks . . . and nowhere near enough interesting conversation.

As for the Greek islands, she'd experienced them too, and on a yacht at that, one belonging to her mother's black-sheep brother, Julian, who would earn his black-sheep status a few years afterward by divorcing his wife of twenty-two years to marry a Las Vegas dancer of twenty-two years, period. Alix had been sixteen at the time of the cruise, and one of the crew members had been a dashing Italian in his mid-twenties who had been the object of what she thought of as her first "grown-up" crush (in other words, one with fantasies that actually involved *S-E-X*). Fantasies they remained, however. Sergio was obviously willing enough, but her mother's eagle-eyed surveillance had put a stop to things before they got started, so what Alix took away from the trip was more along the lines of rueful, *if-only* memories of the gorgeous, smiling, bare-chested Sergio, than of dazzling beaches, quaint, whitewashed villages, and romantic ruins.

On the other hand . . . she looked out through the fogging windows at the wet, black, freezing pavement, and thought about wine-dark seas and

Greek islands: the Dodecanese, the Cyclades, the Aegean . . . the very
names warmed her. "Oh, I imagine I could handle it," she said.

"Well, if you prefer, I could get you something a little more exciting, a
little more 'real,' something in the seedy underbelly of art crimes, perhaps?
We have an opening for an operative to crack a gang of mob-connected
antiquities smugglers who operate on the Marseilles docks. Be glad to put
you in for it."

Alix laughed. He was so nice when he eased up. "No, thank you, the
Greek islands will do. But what am I supposed to be doing? Who am I
supposed to be?"

"You're you, Alix London. This isn't undercover work. And all you
have to do is keep your eyes open and give a few lectures about art."

"Lectures? I've never given a lecture in my life."

"Not *lecture* lectures, just, you know, schmooze with the guests, talk
about art, talk about painters. That, I know you can do. Oh, and be charming, which certainly won't be a problem for you either."

A compliment? And not about her abilities but about *her?* She waited
with interest for him to continue.

Nope, he was back to business on the next sentence. "Alix, have you
ever heard of a man named Panos Papadakis?"

"I think so. I know he's rich, anyway. And Greek, obviously."

"And a crook, though not so obviously. We think he gets most of his
income from a sort of Ponzi scheme he runs, where he invests his clients'
money and supposedly shares these huge profits with them."

"The operative word being *supposedly?*"

"Exactly. We've been on his trail for months, but this opening on his
cruise is the first chance we've gotten to insert someone right into his operation. And you're the perfect candidate."

There was something about the sound of being "inserted" into an
"operation" that she didn't like. For the first time she had a few qualms
about what she was getting herself into. "I see," she said, "but what am I
supposed to be *doing?*"

"Well, I told you. Give an occasional presentation—"

"No, I mean what am I supposed to be doing for the FBI? What does 'keep my eyes open' mean? Open for what?"

"Anything, anything at all that relates to his business or that makes you wonder if something not quite kosher is going on."

"But about what?" She was getting more confused, not less. "What *is* his business?"

"Mainly, he's an international financier—"

"Which is what, exactly?"

"Oh, a lot of things in his case—money manager, lender, venture capital bundler, investment adviser, and so on—but the main thing is he sells these fractional interests in paintings, and that's where the art squad's interest comes in."

"Mm . . ."

"Then when the paintings sell later for more money, everybody who holds a share gets a proportionate share of the profit. That's the idea, but we think our friend Panos is scamming the hell out of them. And *that's* what we'd like you to be especially alert for—anything that might relate to the fractional investments."

"Oh."

Pause. "Alix, you don't have any idea what I'm talking about, do you?"

"Not really." *Fractional shares of paintings? What did that even mean? How could you own a quarter or a twelfth of a painting?*

"Well, look, don't worry about it; Jamie will fill you in on the grisly details when you stop by DC on the way. In the meantime, I'm having her send you a list of the works that will be in the auction so you can bone up on them and look super-smart. You should get it tomorrow morning."

"Wait a minute now, Ted, you've totally lost me. What auction?"

"Oh, didn't I mention that? See, this is something that's not really related to the Ponzi thing. He wants to auction off some of his own private collection, and the way he's doing it is to hold it on a glitzy cruise aboard this sensational yacht he owns. During the cruise, he'll have the paintings on display for the passengers to get a feel for how it would be to live with them. This will be super-exclusive, an invitation-only group of his own highest-rolling clients, probably only half-a-dozen people. Then they'll hold the auction on the final night."

"I don't understand. Why would he want to limit it to six people? Wouldn't he be likely to get more for them if it was a regular wide-open auction?"

"Well, it will be. Catalogs will go out, the auction itself will be streamed online to a larger group, and people will be able to call in bids via iPhone, or iPad, or anything else that connects. But only the cruise passengers will have the privilege of being there on the scene."

"Oh, I see. And you think this auction is part of the scam? He's auctioning off shares of—"

"No, as far as we know, the auction itself is on the level. They're his paintings, and he's got the right to sell them. Of course, with our boy Panos, you never know, but it's being run by a New York art dealer, someone that—as far as we know—we have no reason to distrust, Edward Reed. No, you're there to just generally observe, to—"

"Keep my eyes open. And ears too, presumably?"

"That would be good."

"Ted, what do you suggest I tell people about this? Where I'm going to be that week? What I'm doing?"

"Tell 'em the truth: You're lecturing on a private Mediterranean cruise. Papadakis is paying your airfare back and forth, by the way, and you'll have the same privileges as any other guest while you're on the yacht. That's the deal from his side. And the Bureau will pay the regular fee you've agreed on with them, and cover any expenses Papadakis doesn't. That sound all right?"

"Yes, fine."

"Fine." There was a moment's pause. "Alix, we need to get something straight here. If any useful information comes out of this, great. If it doesn't, that's okay too; don't worry about it, all right? There's no need

27

to do anything beyond being your usual observant self. We're not asking you to *investigate*. Since all the invitees are in this investment club of his, I expect there'll be some talk about it, and all we're asking you to do is to be alert to the possibility. No horning in on other people's conversations, no subtle interrogations of fellow guests—or of Papadakis— no hiding behind potted palms to listen in on—"

"I don't think yachts have potted palms."

"This one does. I'm serious, so listen to me. Whatever comes your way that might relate to Papadakis's dealings, yes, we want to know about it, but we don't want you asking questions, probing, taking risks, understand? You're not trained for it, and if anything happened to you, Alix . . ."

Yes?

" . . . well, just think of the paperwork."

Sigh. "I'm touched by your concern, Special Agent Ellesworth. I gather, then, that I'll be reporting to you?"

"Technically, yes. I'm the lead investigator on this, but I'm expecting to be on another assignment most of that week. So it's Jamie you'll be contacting, if there's anything you need to contact us about during the cruise itself."

"And how do I do that?"

"Do you have a smartphone?"

"I do, yes, very high-tech." Not the kind of thing she would have bought on her own, it had been a thank-you gift from a Samsung executive for helping her "weed" an extensive but mixed-bag art collection she'd inherited from her mother.

"Good enough. You know how to lock it so no one else can get in?"

"Well, of course I do. God, Ted, what do you take me for?" *Note to self: how to lock phone.*

"Well, good. Keep it locked. You can just call her on that, but unless it's an emergency, don't call her from the ship, only when you're ashore. We don't know what kind of bugs or surveillance system Papadakis might have, but from what we do know, he's a little on the paranoid side—he once had some art pieces, Greek vases or something, stolen from the yacht, so there might be hidden mikes and cameras. Or you can e-mail her if you have any questions, or anything to report. *Do* you have any questions?"

"I guess not, for now."

"Good. If any come up, give her a call. She really knows more about it all than I do. And Alix?"

"Ted?"

"Glad to have you aboard." The phone clicked and went silent.

Glad to have you aboard . . . that was it? Not even a renewal of the aborted dinner offer when she'd gone to Washington the last time. Alix made a face at the telephone. This was starting to get old. She'd given more time than she should have to considering this guy as a potential romantic possibility. It was obviously headed nowhere as far as he was concerned. Maybe it was time to just cross him off the list. Not that there were any other possibilities in sight at the moment. She'd dipped her toe into the singles scene since coming to Seattle; not the usual bar scene, which repelled her, but the receptions put on by the symphony, or the Friday evening cocktail hours at the art museum that targeted twenty- and thirty-somethings. These had resulted in a few "dates." Her conclusion after a couple of months of trying: There sure were a lot of jerks in Seattle.

She had fallen into a bad mood as she re-started the engine. The cold and wet had seeped into the car and gotten through her sweater. And now *she* was the one who wasn't going to be on time to pick up her father. After all the times she'd chewed him out for being late, she knew she was going to get an earful about it.

Damn. For a woman who'd just accepted an invitation to go sailing in luxury on the sunny Mediterranean in a couple of months (and get paid for it), she was sure feeling grumpy.

4

She was wrong about her father, as she so often was. When she pulled into the parking lot of his seedy, drafty old warehouse-cum-living quarters—a dingy, brown-brick building with traffic-grimed windows, much like its industrial-district neighbors—he was pacing in slow circles, head down, hands deep in his pockets, shoulders hunched against the rain and the chill, his head encased in the ridiculous Russian fur hat (complete with earflaps) that he affected in the winter. In the sulfurous glare of a sodium street lamp, she could see that his face was folded into a frown. But the moment he looked up and recognized her car the frown vanished, to be replaced by a smile so filled with pleasure at seeing her that it could have lit up the parking lot on its own. One leather-gloved hand came from his pocket to throw her a kiss and a wave. When she drove up to him he pulled open the passenger door and squeezed in.

"So pleased to see you, my dear," he said in that plummy, jolly English accent that always made her smile, especially if she hadn't heard it for a few days. "Thank you for coming all the way down here to collect your poor old father." His hat and the black woolen overcoat he wore despite the wet weather were soaked. Water streamed down his cheeks from the hat. But not a word about her being twenty minutes late while he'd waited on the cracked and weedy asphalt of a desolate parking lot, in the murky, sodden misery of a "spring" night in Seattle.

"Sorry, Geoff, I had to take a call," she said, getting the Volvo rolling again.

He gave her a dismissive wave. "No matter at all." There were squishing noises as he shifted on the seat. "Oh, dear, I'm certainly giving your

30

nice new car a soaking, aren't I?" It was amazing how his voice brought back the cheery, laughing Geoff of her childhood, the doting father who'd taken her on so many visits to art museums and galleries; she'd loved them from the first. He didn't look the same, though. Back then, with his roly-poly body and twinkly eyes and his neatly trimmed graying beard and his all-around cuddliness, he'd been in demand as a Santa Claus at Christmas parties. Now, at seventy, his beard was more white than gray and no less neat, but no one would mistake him for Santa. "Cuddly" was a lifetime time ago. He was shrunken now, thin and worn. But then, eight years in prison could do that to you, she supposed.

Her heart took a dip. What a long way this horrible place he lived and worked in was from their old environs, the places where she'd grown up. "Home" had been an Upper East Side condo in a beautiful old brownstone just east of Central Park. From there, it was a two-block walk to his place of employment, the Metropolitan Museum of Art, where he would take her on fabulous private tours, off-limits even to visiting VIPs, through the treasures of the basement workrooms. She'd thrilled at being able to handle two-thousand-year-old Roman sculptures or silver tankards from Paul Revere's own hand, or Degas bronzes.

And then there was their summer home in Rhode Island, the rambling, comfortable old clapboard house in the exclusive enclave of Watch Hill, where they'd spent their Augusts among the New England elite (of which her mother's family, the van Hoogerens, were bona fide members). The young Alix loved the privileged life that had been handed to her, but, like all privileged kids, she took what came to her as natural.

Not anymore. Everything had changed. Her mother had died— blessedly, shortly before Geoff had brought their lovely world crashing down around them. The brownstone and the rambling, weathered summer home were long gone. Now he lived right here, in that ratty old two-story warehouse in one of the few areas of Seattle that could qualify as truly unattractive. The ground floor of the building was devoted to the surprisingly thriving business that he had started up less than a year ago, not long after having been released from prison. "The Venezia Trading Company," it was called, listing itself on its website as "purveyor of authentic, high-quality reproductions of fine objets d'art, in quantity and at reasonable prices."

In other words, Venezia's main business was to supply second-rate hotels with the pictures that were bolted to the walls of their rooms, the ornate lamps that were bolted to their tables, and the fancy ashtrays and other gewgaws that couldn't be bolted down but were cheap enough to replace without undue cost when guests walked off with them. One small Southern hotel chain with a total of only a hundred-and-twenty rooms, for example, ordered Venezia's "Aztec-style synthetic onyx soap dishes" four dozen at a time to make up for their popularity with departing clients.

The upper floor was where her widowed father lived, and although he'd been here in Seattle for almost a year now, she'd never been up there. Oh, he'd invited her enough times, but she'd always come up with excuses, some of them so ridiculous that he'd had to know they were pretexts. Being Geoff, though, there were no reprimands, no guilt trips laid on her. Just a soft, smiling, accepting "Perhaps next time, then."

Not bloody likely, as Geoff might say. The fact was she simply couldn't bear to see him in that environment—a man who valued and appreciated beauty more than anyone else she'd ever known. He lived for art, for elegance, and in the old days, thanks to his work at the Met and the near fortune her mother had inherited, he was surrounded by it, at work and at home. To think of him now, eating his canned and frozen meals alone—he was no cook—in a loft built seventy years ago to store metal piping, with the only "art" around him being the cheap knock-offs he dealt in . . . well, it hurt her just to think of it, and she would continue to put off seeing it for as long as she possibly could. It was just too, too depressing.

As for Alix's own living quarters, they were a far cry from the Upper East Side, but they were certainly nothing to complain about: a pleasant, six-hundred-square-foot studio apartment on a quiet, leafy street in the Green Lake district. And if her financial situation kept improving, she might soon move up to something a little roomier. It had come as a pleasant surprise that her budding career as an art consultant hadn't been damaged by her inadvertent involvement in a sensational art forgery case that had culminated in the murder of a well-known Santa Fe art dealer. On the contrary, her phone was ringing away now, not only with requests for advice on developing an art collection but with assistance determining if a work was the real thing. And then there was her new association with the FBI, a development that still had her shaking her head in amazement.

"I've got myself a pretty interesting job, Geoff," she told him brightly as she turned back onto Alaskan Way, then up the ramp to the viaduct, and headed north toward their destination, Sangiovese, an upscale wine bar in Belltown owned by Chris LeMay—a one-time client and now a good friend. It was largely on account of Chris—Chris and her wine bar—that Geoff was back in her life in such a big way. Her friend had taken to the old rogue, and his presence at the Thursday evening happy hours had wound up giving Sangiovese a new cachet and drawing an assortment of artists, art students, and anyone else who loved to talk about art. The sessions were certainly a wonderful tonic for Geoff, whose notoriety and genuine, wide-ranging art expertise—and of course that irresistible, twinkling charm of his—had quickly drawn a coterie of attentive, respectful admirers. They were good for Alix too, a chance to see him regularly and to chat on the drives, but not *too* much of a chance to be with him. It was a difficult situation. Their relationship, at least on her side, was complex.

Her father had reentered her life less than a year earlier, when he surprised her by moving to Seattle on his release from the federal minimum-security prison in Lompoc, California. At the time, she had been anything but pleased to have him in the same city. To say that she had "issues" with him was putting it mildly. Geoff's trial and conviction had virtually ruined her life. Their considerable family money had gone for attorney's fees and suits. Her own precious college fund, $60,000, had followed shortly (not that Geoff knew, or ever would know, that she had given it up for him), and she'd dropped out of Harvard in her junior year. Her relationship to him—the very name London—had made her the object of jokes and innuendo, an anathema in the art world she'd dreamed of entering when she graduated. His reckless, selfish actions had put a stop to those dreams, and although she'd come a long way back since then—years of dedicated apprenticeship with the great art historian and restorer Fabrizio Santullo in Italy had made her an expert in her own right—she was still angry with him over it. Despite that, over this last year she had almost unwillingly come to love him as much as ever. And if those emotions weren't confusing and contradictory enough, she was sad for him too, and filled with guilt for the resentment that yet remained, coiled in her chest, and sometimes boiled to the surface.

Complex was putting it mildly.

"A job?" he said. "Excellent. Restoration? Consultation?"

"Lecturing."

"Lecturing," he repeated with interest. "Well, this is a new path for you. Tell me more."

She began filling him in (everything but the FBI part), but only got a couple of sentences into it before he interrupted.

"Wait a moment—this yacht you'll be on—are you talking about the *Artemis*? Will you be lecturing on Panos Papadakis's auction cruise?"

She blinked. "You know about that?"

"Certainly I know about it. Don't you think I keep up with the Culture Guru?"

"The what? The who?"

He emitted a theatrical sigh. "My dear child, you have no idea how out of touch you are. I'm really going to have to introduce you to the blogosphere before it's completely hopeless."

Turning down off the viaduct as they neared the bar, Alix laughed, not without irritation. Her seventy-year-old father, having spent eight of the last nine years in a jail cell, was sitting there telling her that *she* was out of touch. He was right, of course, when it came to social media, or networks, or whatever they were called, which was exactly what made it so irritating.

"Panos Papadakis," he murmured. "My word, you're going to be moving in very high-powered company."

"You know him?"

"I know *of* him."

"I understand he sells fractional shares of paintings."

"Yes, I've heard that."

"I don't really know what it means, Geoff. Okay, I understand that if a painting sells for a profit, you get your percentage of the profit, but other than that, why would a collector want a 'share' of a painting? Is it like having a time-share condo? Does he get to hang it on his wall a certain share of the time, or what?"

"No, he does not. You're quite right, Alix. A truly serious collector would not be interested in owning a fractional piece of art."

"But people do— "

"Yes, but those people—" The corners of his lips turned down. "—*Those* people are not serious collectors. Genuine collectors are in increasingly short supply these days." He turned earnestly in her direction. "These people are *investors*. Speculators. Philistines. They don't know about art, they don't understand it, and they couldn't care less. They don't *want* the paintings hanging on their walls. They are perfectly happy to have them housed in some climate-controlled vault, for years if need be, or even for decades, as long as, in the end, their values rise enough for a healthy profit." He was talking himself into one of his rare fits of temper. He folded his arms and stared out at the oncoming headlights through the noisily scraping wipers. She'd hoped to make it through the winter without replacing them, but it didn't look like that was going to happen. "*Collectors*," he grumbled.

"I can understand why you'd be upset, Geoff. I am too. The idea of beautiful works of art sitting for years in the dark; unseen, unappreciated— that's awful, but still . . . well, people can do what they want with them. They own them, after all. It's not illegal."

"Oh? Whatever they want? So if they own a Rembrandt, they can burn it?"

"Well, no, there's a moral responsibility—"

"Oh, a *moral* responsibility," he said sarcastically.

"Geoff, I only meant that—and I'm talking about the shares thing now—that as long as what they're doing isn't against the law, which as far as I know it isn't, they have every right—"

"And if moral responsibility and the law are in conflict?" he snapped. "What then?"

Uh-oh, she'd stepped in it now. This was something she did not intend to discuss with him, and how like her father to bring it up when she was in the middle of driving on dark, rain-slippery streets, surrounded by impatient drivers honking their horns and cutting in, impatient to get home to their martinis and their white wine. Or had *she* brought it up? Hard to say, but why did she so often allow their conversations to get back to this raw, tender subject?

The thing was, it was the conflict between morality and legality that lay at the root of her father's undoing and the trauma that he'd brought upon them both. His crime had been to take a painting that had been entrusted to him for restoration or cleaning—these were not from the Met's collection, but from private clients—and use his meticulous skills to make an exacting copy of it. He would then keep the original and give the copy to the grateful collector ("What wonderful work, Mr. London! Look how bright it is! How crisp! Why, it's almost like new!"). Then, sometimes years later, he had quietly sold the originals, usually many thousands of miles away. His income from these illegal dealings had eventually gone the way of the rest of the family's money, to pay for lawyers and to settle suits. He'd been convicted on sixteen counts of fraud for this and had been locked up for eight years, a long, long time when you're sixty-one.

He had committed these criminal acts out of moral outrage over the way these exquisite eighteenth- and nineteenth-century paintings were being used by their owners. In every one of the cases in which he'd done it—and he'd proven this at his trial—they'd been given to him to restore in preparation for their sale to generate funds to buy ugly, late twentieth-century "monstrosities" that had inexplicably come to be worth more in money and prestige. The most egregious case, which he referred to in court and more than once in arguments with Alix, was that of the elderly couple who were selling a sublime and subtle Ingres charcoal drawing of a nude so that it could be replaced by a "political statement" made of wires and shellacked animal entrails. It was Geoff's position that he was rescuing these irreplaceable works from uncultured barbarians who couldn't tell the difference between art and garbage (and didn't care), and putting them under the loving stewardship of sensitive people who valued their beauty. The fact that he'd taken money, and plenty of it, for paintings that he'd stolen from clients who had trusted him was scoffed at, with considerable impatience on his part, as beside the point.

It was a position he'd taken under questioning in court, and a position he'd maintained to this day. "I didn't do anything *wrong*," he'd said to Alix the last time they'd talked about it. "I did something *illegal*. Can't you appreciate the difference?"

"You didn't do anything wrong?" she'd shot back. "You went to jail for eight years, for God's sake, and you're lucky they didn't give you twenty."

"And I deserved it," he said, "in terms of the law. But I did not do anything *wrong*."

"Well, you sure screwed up my life. And yours."

"Well, yes, perhaps I should have given more thought—"

"Of *course* you should have thought . . . !" she'd exploded in exasperation, and the conversation had gone downhill from there. She didn't mean to let that happen now.

"Geoff," she said with a placating smile as they pulled into Sangiovese's parking lot, "may I respectfully suggest that we save these philosophical meditations for when we get inside and you're surrounded by your groupies and your worshipful acolytes?"

He hated confrontation and argument even more than she did, and, as always, he was willing to suspend hostilities. "I was aware that I had worshipful acolytes," he said with his jolly laugh, "but I didn't know I had groupies. I wouldn't have thought that sixty-year-old women qualified."

"That's because you've been spending too much time reading blogs about the cultural scene and not enough time *in* it." She shook her head. "Really, Dad, you need to get out more."

Oh, sure, she thought wryly, *you're the one to talk. You're not even* reading *about it.*

His indulgent, knowing, fatherly smile indicated that he was thinking the same thing.

5

"Alix, you're kidding me!" Chris exclaimed. "Papas Papapapapuss's yacht—or whatever the hell his name is? The Greek islands? Mykonos, Crete, Corfu, Rhodes . . . *Whoa!*"

In any other public place, her full-throated whoop would have turned heads, but since they were in Sangiovese, Chris's own place, the regulars at the other tables were used to the proprietor's outbursts. Christine LeMay had many fine qualities, but ladylike restraint was not among them.

"I kid you not," Alix said happily. She sipped again from her glass of Chablis, thinking how strange it was that the woman sitting opposite her, whom she hadn't known existed six months ago, was now her closest friend.

It wasn't only the brief time they'd known each other that made it unlikely. It was just about everything. Alix, at a moderately tall five-nine, was quietly pretty, low-keyed, reserved, and traditional in her dress. More than once she'd been told she was conventional, or square, or out of sync with the times, with all of which she was happy to agree. Chris was the opposite: laid-back and flamboyant, given to jangling bracelets, cape-like shawls, and eye-catching colors that highlighted her strapping six-two frame. And Chris was a native Westerner, born in Tacoma into a blue-collar family. Her father had been a plasterer, and an alcoholic one at that, her mother a finisher at a second-hand furniture store. Alix, on the other hand, had been an advantaged New Englander, born into comfort and wealth. Chris had gone from poor to rich on her own merits as a systems analyst and software developer, along with a keen sense ("luck," according to Chris) of when to cash in on the stock options she'd earned from the high-tech company she'd worked for. Alix's fortunes had gone the opposite way (thank you, Geoff!), and only now was she beginning to turn them around.

They were similar in that they were both single, but Chris had recently gotten engaged to an old beau, while the way things were going for Alix, she was likely to stay single for some time, which didn't particularly please her, but didn't distress her either. And then, Chris was at home in the new world of high tech but only gingerly feeling her way into the less scientific but more impenetrable world of art and art collecting; Alix didn't know the difference between a megapixel and a gigabyte (*gigabit?*), but there was no questioning her knowledge of art, especially painting. Just about everything Chris knew about it—and she was learning fast—she'd learned from Alix.

And yet, with all that, here they were, one good friend unselfishly taking pleasure in the other's opportunity, the other taking pleasure in the first one's pleasure.

"So!" Chris said. "What are you going to do for clothes? Not that there's anything wrong with what you're wearing, of course." She paused, one eyebrow lifted, to take in Alix's workaday cold-weather outfit of comfortable, well-worn velour chinos and a roomy, cable-knit, cowl-necked sweater with its sleeves pushed casually up on her forearms. "But for this you might want something a little more, well, shall we say . . ."

"Flashy?" Alix suggested with an eyebrow lift of her own, at which she wasn't as good as Chris, and raked an eye over Chris's capacious red-yellow-and-purple starburst-patterned serape.

"I was going to say 'classy.' Chic. Au courant."

Alix sighed. "You're probably right. I guess I'd better see if it's not too late to get an appointment with my couturier."

That brought smiles to both their faces, knowing as they did that she was referring to her go-to source whenever upscale outfitting was needed: Blanche's Le Frock Vintage Clothing, an alarmingly cluttered consignment shop tucked under a highway overpass on Capitol Hill's down-market commercial fringe.

Chris lifted her coffee (she was a knowledgeable and appreciative wine drinker, but not when "on duty" at the wine bar) and let her attention wander to the *Sala del Caminetto*—the Fireplace Salon—a fireside nook that had been outfitted with low tables and arm chairs, and could hold a grouping of a dozen or so.

"Your father is in good form tonight," she said.

"He's always in good form here." Alix turned to look in that direction too. "Ah, Chris, you don't know how good it is to see him like this. I was afraid he'd be a broken man, all walled up inside his shell, when he got out of the clink, but just look at the guy."

"He's not in his shell, that's for sure," Chris said, laughing.

As usual, Geoff was holding his audience, mostly young, in thrall. "What do I think is the role of art criticism in today's world?" he said in answer to a question that had been put to him. He looked mischievously from face to rapt face, his eyes twinkling. "I believe it was Martin Mull who put it best: 'Writing about art is like dancing about architecture.'"

It took a second for them to process it, and then the burst of laughter practically rattled the glasses behind the bar. Geoff's pink cheeks glowed in the firelight.

"He's in his element, all right," Alix said, turning back to Chris. Then she turned for another longer look, a harder one. "Chris, that older woman sitting right next to him, the one with the pearls, hanging on every word, with that 'look' in her eyes? I've seen her here the last few Thursdays. Do you know who she is?"

"Oh, sure, that's Mrs. Prentiss. Widowed, well-connected in Seattle society, on the opera board, owns an upscale boutique hotel downtown here and another one in Bellevue. Other business interests too, I believe."

"Is she, uh, interested in him?"

"Romantically, you mean? Who knows? She's been through two or three husbands already, so she could be looking for another, but as far as I know it's strictly business. She was in here a couple of nights ago trying to pick my brains as to why she was having trouble talking him into moving up from his tacky old warehouse business—excuse me, those are her words—"

Alix shrugged. "Mine too."

"—and handling an interior remodel, very artistic and la-di-da, of the Bellevue hotel, with the Seattle one maybe to follow. I had nothing to tell her, though. I'd have thought he'd have jumped at it."

"Me too," Alix said pensively. Why *wouldn't* he jump at it? A chance to work among the genuine objets d'art he loved instead of the Aztec soap dishes and faux Carrara marble ashtrays in which he was knee deep now. "Maybe he's trying to get better terms out of her."

She glanced at her watch and then once again at the *Sala del Caminetto*, where Geoff was still holding forth, sprightlier than ever. "I think maybe it's time to get Mr. Wonderful out of there before his head swells up even more than it already has."

6

The return trip to the warehouse was easier than the drive to Sangiovese had been. The rain had let up, fading away to an on-again, off-again drifting mist, and the rush-hour traffic had slowed to what passed for normal. Geoff chattered away the whole time and was still bubbly when they pulled into Venezia's parking lot at seven forty.

"Oh, I've been meaning to tell you," he said—suddenly a little too casual, it seemed to Alix—when the car rolled to a stop. "After quite a bit of soul searching and exploration, I've decided to go in a new professional direction."

Ah, so Mrs. Prentiss had gotten to him after all. "Going into the hotel remodel business, are we?"

He seemed for an instant confused, then almost offended. "Certainly not, whatever gave you that idea?"

"Well, Chris told me about Mrs. Prentiss wanting you to—"

He waved the suggestion off. "No, no, no, no, I have no time for that, not with the exciting new venture I've embarked on."

"*New venture?* You're giving up Venezia?"

"Oh, no, not at all, certainly not. For one thing, it's doing very well. For another, I like being able to provide the boys with a rewarding source of honest employment. Oh, the boys are working with me on the, ah, new enterprise, and being very helpful there as well. I'm very pleased with how it's developing."

The "boys" were the two convicted felons who constituted Venezia's workforce. Like Geoff himself, each had served a lengthy sentence for one

43

variation or another of art fraud and both were old acquaintances of his. In what he referred to as his Old Cons Rehabilitation Foundation, he'd hired them when Venezia had gotten big enough to use a couple of employees. So far, it seemed to be working out for all concerned. The two of them—three, if you included Geoff—gave every indication of having left their problematic pasts behind them, at least on the surface. Alix fervently hoped that it was true, especially for her father. Indeed, she believed that it *was* true, but the men, otherwise not very similar in their personalities, shared a puckish rascality that sometimes made her wonder. And God knew, between them all they were a gold mine of skills, expertise, and experience in just about every form of art fakery ever devised. This "new venture" thing was making her nervous.

"Really. What is it, Geoff?" She was doing her best not to sound apprehensive.

"Well, I'd rather not go into the details yet, my dear. I simply wanted to forewarn you. Let's just say that it is a great deal better suited to my abilities and interests than running a hotel supply company."

Oh, great, she thought. "Well, what kind of business is it, can you tell me that?" What she really wanted to scream at him was: *Is it legal?*

"All in due time," he said calmly and then changed the subject. "Oh, look." He was pointing at two lit windows on the ground floor, which Alix knew to be the windows of the rudimentary break room that he had outfitted for his employees and himself. "The boys are still there, waiting up for you, I suppose you might say. Will you stop in and say hello? A cup of coffee, perhaps?"

Alix smiled back at him and opened the car door. "Sure, lead on."

Geoff unlocked the much-dinged, yellow-painted steel door that was the street entrance and they entered a short, depressing corridor with raw concrete walls and floor. He flicked a switch to turn on a couple of naked bulbs that hung from the ceiling and emitted a sickly light. As always, the cold that oozed from the naked concrete, whatever the season, sent a shiver down her back. She had told Geoff that a more inviting entry might be good for Venezia's business, but he'd laughed her off. Business was just fine, thank you, and anyway, "They like to see that we operate with low overhead. It makes them think that we must be charging less." Apparently, he was right, too; business was booming.

The corridor led to two wooden doors with frosted-glass panels and press-on signs. Once upon a time they'd said *Showroom* and *Offices*, but in the last month the lettering had begun falling off. Last week they'd said *Sho oom* and *Offi es*. This week it was *ho om* and *Of es*. Geoff, however, showed no inclination to repair things. Further proof of low overhead, she supposed.

The break room was at the back of the so-called offices, which were a collection of stark cubicles surrounding two pushed-together worktables in the center, where the packing was done. As they approached, she could hear conversation and laughter.

One of the two "boys" was someone she'd known a very long time, someone who went back so far she couldn't remember *not* knowing him: a gentle, slow-talking mountain of a man—over six-three and a good three hundred pounds—who now generally went by Tiny, but whom she still remembered as *Zio* Beniamino, Uncle Beniamino, from the days when he'd bounced her on his lap and sung sweet old Italian lullabies to her. He wasn't really a relative, but she hadn't understood that at the time, and even now she thought of him as her favorite of all her uncles.

Tiny had started out as a commercial artist, but in his thirties he had discovered that he was gifted at creating Monets, Picassos, Chagalls, and just about any other painter you could name. That faculty had made him a nice living for over a decade but eventually landed him in the clink, from which he'd emerged in his early sixties, chastened but not downhearted. Now his work entailed taking orders, maintaining their kitschy inventory, and packing up Aztec-style synthetic onyx soap dishes for delivery to Biloxi, Mississippi, or Winnemucca, Nevada. Being Tiny, he accepted it all with good humor and even gratitude.

The other man she'd met only a few months ago, after he'd come to work for her father. An ex-professor of art history, Frisby Macdowell had been, according to Geoff's admiring description, "the most skilled, dedicated forger of Neoplastic and Constructivist painting of the twentieth century." Unfortunately, Neoplastic and Constructivist art had gone out of favor in about 1965, so Frisby had switched to faking Dadaist art instead—Marcel Duchamp, in particular—for which, sadly for him, he didn't have the same knack. Hence, the journey through courtroom, jail, and redemption that eventually wound up with him working alongside Tiny and Geoff at the Venezia Trading Company. A small, quiet, bespectacled man, he too appeared to be resigned to his lot, if not quite as content with it as were his colleagues. Despite Frisby's pedantic, somewhat cranky exterior, Alix had taken to him from the first, charmed by the wry humor that often peeped through the cracks.

The two men were sitting on mismatched steel-and-plastic kitchen chairs at one of the two Formica-topped dinette tables (also mismatched) in the break room, sipping from their mugs and kibitzing when Alix and Geoff showed up.

As always, Tiny lit up at the sight of her. "Hey, look who's here—*la mia cucciolina!*"

La mia cucciolina. My little puppy. Tiny had been born above his cousin Marco's barbershop on 187th Street in the middle of the Bronx, but he enjoyed throwing in the occasional Italianisms of his Sicilian parents. Get a few glasses of Chianti or Barbera into him, and he even developed an Italian accent.

"So, take a load off," he said happily, indicating the two remaining vacant chairs. "How about some coffee?" Without waiting for their answers, he went to the Mr. Coffee and poured them a couple of cups. "It's fresh, sort of."

"I wouldn't advise it," Frisby murmured to the ceiling. A Lipton tag hung on a string from his cup.

"What's that supposed to mean?" Tiny asked. "I made it this morning. A minute in the microwave and you don't know the difference."

46

"Oh, I guess we'll chance it," Alix said. An electric space heater was going, but she was still chilled and having something warm to drink sounded good. She would have accepted hot water if that had been the offer.

They made small talk for a while and then Frisby, with an air of having restrained himself long enough, aimed a visual nudge at Tiny.

Tiny cleared his throat, clapped his hands once, and complied. "Okay, Alix, ready? Here's tonight's question for you. Ta-da . . . what famous artist forged his own paintings?"

Such questions were standard procedure for these post-Sangiovese get-togethers at the warehouse. For years after Geoff's self-induced implosion Alix's skin had crawled at the word "forgery," but as her rapprochement with him had developed, her attitude had changed. It still made her uneasy at times, but now she found knowledge of the subject to be not only helpful in her work but also fascinating. She had come to her own expertise through years of meticulous and painstaking study of *genuine* works of art. Santullo had been interested in teaching her (and she had been interested in learning) how to discriminate between good paintings and bad paintings, not real paintings and fake paintings. Of the techniques, materials, and history of forgery, she'd been taught nothing, she'd known nothing, and she'd wanted to know nothing. Now, with clients beginning to line up for her help in evaluating their paintings, she was making up for lost time, and Geoff, Tiny, and Frisby, experts if there ever were any, were providing the needed education.

"It beats me," she said honestly. "I don't understand how you can fake your own work. And if you did, well, by definition it wouldn't be a forgery, would it?"

They liked it when they stumped her, which was most of the time, so they sat grinning at each other for a few moments, and finally deferred to Geoff.

"Giorgio de Chirico," he announced.

"De Chirico? But how . . . I mean, how . . ."

As usual when the story was complicated, the explanation was left to Frisby, the best-organized lecturer of the three. And this was a complicated story.

De Chirico, the Italian Surrealist famed for his *Pittura Metafisica* pictures—strange, harshly evocative scenes of empty city squares, railway tracks, receding stone arcades, and blank-faced classical statues—decided somewhere around 1918 that, despite his fame and the healthy sales of his works, his talents were suited to more ambitious endeavors. Declaring himself the heir to Titian, he took to painting in a classical style, but his new paintings of nymphs, and naiads, and satyrs were unpopular; galleries didn't show them, buyers didn't buy them—

"Why not?" Alix asked. "Surely, he had the skill—"

"It wasn't a question of skill," Frisby said. "It was more . . . well, they were, how shall I put this? They were somewhat, ah—"

"They were crap," Tiny explained.

"Basically, they were simply ugly," emended Geoff with a smile. He generally left these sessions to Frisby and Tiny but commented if he thought a clarification might help. "Have you never seen any, Alix?"

"I don't think so. I know the *Pittura Metafisica* ones, of course—*Anguish of Departure, Melanconia*, and so on, but not the ones you're talking about. I don't remember seeing any de Chirico naiads."

"That's because no decent museum would have them, and the art history texts very properly turn up their noses at them," Frisby said. "At any rate, de Chirico's unsurprising reactions to his rejection by the establishment were seething resentment—a flood of angry critiques of Modernist degeneracy—and a stubborn sticking to his neo-Classicist guns. He continued painting in his new style for the rest of his life, sixty years. He even started signing his work '*Pictor Optimus*,' 'Best Painter.' But by then his paintings had become a joke and so had he."

"Yeah, but he got even," Tiny said with relish. "Come on, Frisby, get to the good part."

"Well, he started faking his own early paintings," Frisby said, mildly piqued at having his narration curtailed.

Alix shook her head. "I still don't understand. How can a painting be a de Chirico forgery if de Chirico himself painted it?"

Geoff interceded again. "Actually, whether or not they are technically forgeries remains open to question. But they are most certainly *fakes*."

Alix just shook her head this time.

Frisby took over again. "What he did," he explained, "was to paint a new picture in his old Surrealist style, say in 1950 or 1955, then date it '1914,' or '1915,' or '1916,' and then announce to the world that it was an old work he'd forgotten all about and just found in a closet or some old workshop cabinet."

"And they were accepted by the public? By the critics?"

"Certainly, why wouldn't they be? Until, that is, they began coming too thick and fast. Then people began to catch on to him."

Tiny laughed. "They had a saying going around that his bed must have been six feet off the ground to hold all this 'early work' he kept finding under it."

Alix laughed too, but she saw another, more serious side to it. "But doesn't that make it hard to determine what was done when? How can anybody know for sure now that a pre-1918 de Chirico is what it's supposed to be? Even experts."

"Well, they can't," Geoff allowed.

Frisby agreed. "Absolutely. Be assured, most of the ones you see hanging in museums—other than the Museum of Modern Art in New York—are not what they're purported to be."

"Right, and anyone who pays top dollar for what's supposed to be an early de Chirico is out of his mind," Tiny chimed in. "The guy screwed things up forever." He grinned. "But he did make good money at it while it lasted."

"But don't you think—" Alix, about to weigh in with something about the negative side of this—institutions being hoodwinked, unknowing

49

collectors paying for pictures that weren't really what they believed they were—held her tongue. The cheery, laughing faces of the three men told her that the prospect of stuffy museums and ignorant, greedy collectors being bamboozled was more amusing than anything else. *Well,* she thought with a sigh, *what the hell, these guys are what they are and I should be used to it by now.* Besides, the story really *was* funny. "Never mind," she finished weakly. "Nothing."

They must have had some idea of what she'd planned to say, because the aborted comment left a silence in its wake.

"Well," Frisby said. Tiny offered more coffee all around, was uniformly turned down, got some for himself, and sat down again.

"Did any orders come in while I was out?" Geoff asked.

"Only one sizable one," Frisby answered. "Log Cabin Inns finally decided on what they want in the way of guest room pictures for the new Iowa City place."

"Good. What?"

"Six of our mix-and-match Corot Collection; twenty-four in all."

At the mention of Corot, Tiny hooted. "Hey, Alix, did you ever hear the saying about Corot? 'Corot painted almost two thousand paintings just in the last ten years of his life. Three thousand of them are in the United States, a thousand of them are in Asia, and the rest of them are still in Europe.'"

"And how many of them are yours?" Frisby asked wickedly.

Tiny beamed and put on a New York accent that was even stronger than his ordinary one. "'Ey, I didn't do nuttin'. Dem guys, dey framed me."

"And Alix," Frisby said, "you know what the most delightful part of the story is? There were so many fakes out there after he died that they put out a picture catalog that would help people separate the originals from the copies. Excellent idea, correct? Except that most of the catalogs were bought by the forgers themselves, who used them to refine their work and make it harder than ever to identify the fakes."

Geoff, Tiny, and Frisby himself roared with laughter. *Trust these three to side with the forgers every time* Alix permitted herself no more than another little sigh.

"Well, everyone," Geoff said, stretching, "I suppose it's getting a bit late —"

"It is?" said Tiny, reaching into a hip pocket and pulling out an engraved gold pocket watch, much worn by the years and attached to his belt by an old-fashioned key chain. This was an object he took out of his pocket at every possible opportunity. When he pressed the button that opened the cover, a music-box tinkle of sweet Italian music floated into the air. "Eight fifteen," he declared, preening, if a lug that size could be said to preen.

Alix loved watching him do it. The watch was a gift she'd given him in appreciation for his help on some questions about that alleged Georgia O'Keeffe painting in Santa Fe. When she'd finally found it on *antique-watch.com*, it hadn't been working (probably since about 1900), but her father had put her in touch with one of his many expert if somewhat dubious friends, this one a skilled watchmaker, and he'd managed to bring it back to life for a modest fee. Altogether it had cost her less than $100, but it had taken a lot of effort to find it in the first place, because she'd been hunting for something very specific. The melody it played was *"Vieni sul Mar,"* one of the songs that Tiny had sung to her as a child. He'd known it from his own childhood, he'd told her, because his grandfather had owned just such a watch and Tiny warmly remembered his own joy when *Nonno* Luigi would allow him to "play" it.

He'd come near to tears when she'd presented it to him and he'd heard it for the first time, but now he just preened and grinned, which was preferable to her, if not to Frisby, who rolled his eyes; it was probably the dozenth time that day he'd heard the tune.

"That odious watch," he muttered. "How sweet my life would be if I were *never* to hear that vile melody again."

Naturally this prompted Tiny to start singing it, but Geoff only let him get through two lines before having mercy on Frisby. "Really, all, I do think we'd best call it a day. I haven't eaten yet, and I imagine you haven't either."

Ordinarily, this was the most uncomfortable part of their Thursday get-togethers, the point at which he invited her to come up for dinner and she manufactured some excuse. But, whatever the reason, sometime in the last few hours she had come around to thinking that she'd put off seeing him in his home environment long enough. Whatever it was, she might as well get used to it. So this time around, she intended to surprise him— astonish him, more likely—by taking him up on his offer and doing it with good grace.

"I have some reasonably fresh sourdough upstairs," he continued, right on cue, "and I'm sure I can find a can or two of soup somewhere. Tiny? Frisby? Would you care to join me?"

Before they could answer, he turned to Alix, who readied her smile. "I'd ask you as well, Alix," he said offhandedly, "but I know from sad experience that you'd only say no."

What? Her smile vanished.

He patted her hand. "Thank you so much for another *extremely* pleasant evening, my dear. Tiny, would you be good enough to see Alix to her car, please?"

"Certainly, boss, my pleasure," Tiny said gallantly.

"Please, let me," Frisby said, jumping up and taking her arm before Tiny could object. Alix was surprised. This had never happened before. Seeing her out to the car was long established as Tiny's job. The reason became apparent when they reached the car.

"Alix, please," he pleaded, clasping one of her hands in both of his, "next time you get Tiny a present, *please* make it one that doesn't make any noise."

• • •

She was still mulling things over when she got to her apartment twenty minutes later. *Why* had Geoff not extended his usual invitation? How much did it have to do with this hush-hush new "enterprise" of his? Why had he declined to tell her anything about it? What did it mean that he was "fore-warning" her? Had the "boys" been invited up—but not her—so they could continue with their clandestine plans?

Oh, please, she said silently, to whomever or whatever might be listening, *don't let them be doing something dumb again!*

7

Christoph Weisskopf, master forger, was not completely nuts. He only thought he was Georges Desmarées (or whomever) on weekdays, and then only until six p.m. At that time the alarm clock he'd set in another room went off, and after a momentary disruption of thought, he turned into Christoph Weisskopf again.

When it rang on this particular Monday in March, it took the usual few seconds to break through his daytime spell, but when it did he immediately stopped work, cleaned up, and put on everyday clothes. He had finished his Desmarées and was just starting on a Franz Marc hard-edged, semi-abstract painting of a tiger, so he was wearing an outfit based on a photograph of the artist: a green-collared, waist-length Bavarian jacket, a shirt and tie, and a gold-buttoned vest complete with watch fob and chain. The photo hadn't shown Marc below the waist, so Weisskopf, in his desire to be true to the place and time (Bavaria, 1900 to 1910) had opted for knee breeches—it had been either that or lederhosen. Thus, switching to passable everyday clothes required no more than taking off the breeches and putting on a pair of chinos.

In this case, however, he didn't bother. It would have been hard to find a more diverse piece of New York than this teeming, polyglot little corner of Brooklyn, and among the many religious sects was a population of ultra-Orthodox Hasidic Jews for whom the men's traditional costumes included knee breeches worn under a long coat, and high white socks. Thus, the sight of Weisskopf's pale, skinny calves peeping out from under his own dark overcoat would be nothing out of the ordinary.

He went to a window to check the night's weather. The twin arcs of blue and white lights on the cables of the bridge twinkled and glittered prettily, which meant there was no mist in the air, no muck, no precipitation. No wind, either, from what he could tell, and judging from what people on the street were wearing, not too cold. All in all, a fine night for March, almost springlike. That was good. What he liked to do, and he did it every night after work if the weather was amenable, was to pick up some carry-out food and take it to Grand Ferry Park, a tiny patch of green, not quite two acres, that sat on the East River a seven-or-eight-block stroll from his loft. It was the most peaceful, un-citified place he knew in Williamsburg, despite its being right up against the hulk of a nineteenth-century Domino Sugar plant, which didn't bother him very much, because you couldn't really see it at night anyway.

There were some dilapidated benches in the little park, but these he disdained. Among the big boulders at the water's edge was a grouping of them that was just right for a remarkably comfortable one-person seating arrangement: backrest, footrest, and even a flat little table-top rock on which you could safely put your drink without spilling it. And the seat angled you so that you looked diagonally across the river at the ever-changing colored lights of the Empire State Building and the midtown skyscrapers. He hated being in Manhattan, but he loved this shimmering, soundless view of it across the water's black expanse. And at least for the evening it helped cement him a little more firmly in the twenty-first century.

What with the bigger, grander East River Park less than a mile to the north, few others made use of Grand Ferry after dark (few others knew it was there at all), which made it a perfect place to unwind with a cup of Jägermeister, the German liqueur to which he was greatly attached, followed by a tranquil, leisurely dinner and perhaps another cup or two of the spirits and a short after-dinner nap, from which he would awake refreshed and relaxed.

His food-provider choices lasted about a week at a time, and this week it was Khao Sarn on Bedford Avenue, a few blocks from the park, and there he stopped for an order of vegetable spring rolls and a peanut noodle plate with fried red snapper. The white plastic bag that held them went into his shoulder pack along with the usual square green Jägermeister bottle and a mug from Heidelberg University. When he got to Grand Ferry, he was happy to find that "his" rocks were unoccupied, but not so pleased to see that a nearby bench was occupied by a bum in a hooded parka, talking to himself, hunched over and staring at the water. Weisskopf could smell his boozy breath and the moldy odor of his parka from ten feet away as he passed behind the bench, and he very loudly cleared his throat. He carried fifteen dollars in his pocket, a dollar or two of which were to be used if he were approached by a panhandler (which had happened a few times) and the rest to be held in reserve to placate a mugger who might choose him for prey (which had never happened, but this was New York, and you never knew).

The throat clearing was to alert the drunk to his presence so that the money transfer, if there was going to be one, could be gotten over with early and he could eat in peace. The only response, however, was a slight start and a grunt, as if the man had been sleeping, not staring, after which he lay down on the bench with a groaning sigh and settled on his side, facing away from Weisskopf's rocks. Fine. Even if he himself fell asleep after dinner, he'd be up and gone before this one awakened.

Weisskopf wriggled out of his backpack and arranged himself on the boulders. Out came the Jägermeister and the mug. He settled contentedly back with his feet up, embraced and supported by smooth hollows of rock, and with a sigh of his own, had his first long swallow of the bittersweet liqueur. This was the first night since Panos Papadakis's raving call four days ago that Weisskopf was truly able to relax. If what he'd been told today was true, and he thought it was, the problem was solved, over. He dipped one of the spring rolls in the tiny tub of sweet, vinegary sauce that had come with them, bit off half of it, and slowly, happily chewed.

An hour later, with his dinner leavings in the plastic bag for proper disposal and his third cup of Jägermeister warming him along with the previous two, he set the cup on the flat rock, turned up his collar and buttoned the coat to the top, stretched out just a little more, folded his hands across his belly, closed his eyes, and let the cool, gentle breeze carry sleep to him.

Five minutes passed. Ten. By the time the slumping figure on the bench unhunched and arose to move noiselessly toward him, Weisskopf was gently snoring. At one point, as if sensing something through the wall of sleep, he stirred. His eyelids fluttered but didn't part. He never saw the first flash, let alone the second and third, never heard the *pop pop pop*.

8

By hour nine of a sixteen-hour journey, unless one is lucky enough to be able to sleep on airplanes, one's mind more or less comes loose from its moorings and begins to wander. Thus, at a little past the halfway point between Seattle and Athens, Alix suddenly realized that she had no idea what was going on in the forgettable movie—the second forgettable movie—she'd been watching on the back of the seat in front of her, and very little idea where her mind had been for the last hour. Maybe she'd dozed without knowing it, but she was wide-awake now. She looked at her watch. It was 1:30 a.m. Seattle time, not a great time to be wide-awake, a little queasy, and restless, but with no place to go. The bright mid-morning European sunlight that was streaming in under the drawn shades only made things seem weirder, made her stomach more unsettled.

She turned off the video, tucked her earphones into the seat pocket, thought about pressing the button that would extend her seat into a reasonable approximation of a bed but, having tried it earlier, decided against it and turned on the call button. The French attendant was at her side in seconds.

"Madame?"

"Could I have some coffee, please? And perhaps a croissant?"

"At once, madame."

Alix stretched her arms and then her legs and then wiggled the kinks out of her torso before settling comfortably back. In Air France's business class she had room to do it without either poking her neighbors or getting poked, which was a blessing. Whatever else there was to be said about Panos Papadakis, no one could call him tight-fisted. He was treating her like royalty, providing her with a limo at each end of the flight, and with business-class seats every inch of the way. She'd checked the cost on the web: a whopping six thousand dollars. VIP treatment wasn't something she'd expected, and it was very much appreciated: Sixteen hours squeezed into a coach seat would have been a nightmare. Of course, a return to the lavish lifestyle she'd grown up with was hardly something she longed for, but, what the heck, there wasn't anything wrong with an occasional dose as long as you didn't let yourself get used to it.

When the pastry and the little pot of coffee came, she ate and drank slowly, mulling over some disturbing thoughts that had been on her mind since reading a book that Ted had sent her. The author was Robert Wittman, the man who'd founded the FBI's art crime team. Most of the book was given over to describing his many adventures, but every now and then there was a bit of introspection about undercover work, and it was one of those bits that was troubling her. Undercover work involved two basic steps, Wittman said. First you befriend, then you betray. And you either have the natural instincts and skills to do both . . . or you don't.

Did she or didn't she? It hadn't occurred to her to think about it until she'd been hit between the eyes with that brutal, honest word—*betray*. Could she "betray" someone whose hospitality and generosity she'd so readily accepted? He could have sent her coach tickets instead of business-class ones, and he could have skipped the limousines he'd arranged, but he'd done neither. He'd gone above and beyond what was required, and all the while she was planning to betray him in the end, if she could. But was what she was doing truly "betrayal"? She wasn't lying to him, she wasn't pretending to be somebody she wasn't, she was just . . . just . . . She grimaced. Yeah, "betrayal" was a good word for it. Watching him when he didn't know it, spying on him, informing on him when and if he had too much trust in her.

Still, she was helping the good guys, wasn't she? And Papadakis was one of the bad guys, wasn't he? Didn't he deserve whatever he got? Of course he did . . . and still her doubts nagged at her. She wondered how a truly decent guy like Ted handled this. She made up her mind to talk to him about it before she ever accepted another assignment. Until then, the best thing would be to put it out of her mind and do what she'd committed herself to doing. Besides, two o'clock in the morning was no time to ponder problems of morality.

She turned on the video again and scanned the movie offerings: ah, the latest installment of *Mission: Impossible.* Just what she needed. Something in which Tom Cruise and the good guys were a hundred percent good and the bad guys were thoroughly despicable nasties. Something completely unrelated to the real world.

•　•　•

If you'd asked her yesterday or last week or last year what the Greek isles smelled like, you would have gotten a shake of the head and a blank stare. What they *smelled* like? It had been thirteen years; why would she remember something like that? And at sixteen, why would she have noticed it in the first place?

Yet the instant she stepped out onto the portable stairs that had been rolled up to Olympic Air Flight 374, the last leg of the long trip, it came back in a rush. She would have known where she was if she'd had her eyes closed. Indeed, she did close them now, standing motionless at the top of the steps to breathe in the spicy, pungent air of the Aegean, a bouquet garni of juniper, oleander, sage, and sun-parched earth, and always underlying everything, never far away, the tang of the sea.

It was only when a woman behind her pointedly cleared her throat that she realized she was holding up the stream of exiting passengers. Quickly moving down the steps she went looking for the limo driver who would take her on the ten-minute drive to town.

At her request, he let her out at Mykonos's busy town center, Mando Mavrogenous Square, and continued with her luggage another few blocks to the small-boat pier, where the tender that would take her to the *Artemis* was waiting. The *Artemis* itself was too big to moor there and was anchored somewhere beyond the breakwater with the other larger vessels. She peered out at the ocean, but the only ships she could see were three cruise liners: two giant floating cities that carried two thousand passengers and more, and one relatively small one, the striking, upscale kind that held only a few hundred. No sign of the *Artemis*, which was probably hidden by one of the hulking leviathans.

When she looked around her, at Mykonos town itself, her initial impression was that the decade and more that had passed since her last visit had produced little change. The look of the city (cubical white houses, narrow, bewildering alleys, bustling streets, the famous, much-photographed row of the six squat, blindingly white windmills on the hill) and its smells (bougainvillea and frying fish) were much as they'd been before. But within seconds the changes started jumping out at her. The shops were as tiny as she remembered, virtual miniatures, but they'd changed from grocery stores and cheap souvenir shops into posh designer boutiques. And the people on the streets were different as well. The last time, there had been a dazzling jumble of clothes and lifestyles: elderly black-clad women hauling baskets of live chickens or rabbits or vegetables; men in traditional outfits of vests, sashes, ballooning knee breeches, and tasseled red fezzes; grungy backpackers and bicyclists; and even the occasional businessman or government worker wearing a suit and tie. Here and there a few wary tourists, usually in groups trailing behind an upraised red or yellow umbrella. Now the streets were no less lively, but the people had changed. Not a fez in sight, let alone a chicken, but plenty of baseball caps, tank tops, shorts, sneakers, and sandals. And a penetrating new smell too: sunscreen. The Age of the Cruise Ship had arrived in Mykonos, big time. Only the wandering backpackers seemed to have survived and even increased in number. Wherever the jet setting fashionistas who were supposed to hang out on Mykonos were, they seemed to be hiding out till after dark, when the cruise line day-trippers were safely gone.

Everybody seemed to be eating something as they walked or browsed, too—gyros, souvlaki, ice cream—and Alix's stomach, despite having gotten more than its fair share of good French food on the flight, started raising a fuss. She stopped at the sidewalk window of a taverna, where a vertical rotisserie was slowly roasting a cone-shaped column of sliced pork, and asked for a gyros.

"You want American gyros or Greek gyros?" the chef-hatted, white-aproned counterman asked.

Alix hadn't known there was a difference. "Greek," she said.

He approved. "Good. Greek is better."

The chief difference, it appeared, when she got her order, was that a serving of French fries, which sometimes came on the side back home, went right into the pita wrap along with the meat, tomato, onion, and *tzatziki* sauce. She couldn't really say that she preferred the potato in there getting soggy, but it hit the spot and she downed it with pleasure, along with a Coke, as she walked toward the boat dock.

With two months to prepare for the cruise, she'd boned up on more than the art and artists that would be in the collection. She'd researched Papadakis the man, megayachts in general, and the *Artemis* in particular, which had an entire long chapter to itself in a coffee-table book of photographic essays: *Amazing Yachts*. At 239 feet, it missed being in the list of the world's hundred largest yachts by only seven feet. When it was built in 1989 (for a Saudi prince; Papadakis had bought and refurbished it in 2006), it had squeaked in at number eighty-eight, and it was one of the first to boast a helicopter pad along with its own helicopter to go with it, but the big yachts were being built bigger every year, and grander too. Nowadays, in addition to the usual launches and tenders, they carried an abundance of high-tech gadgets with no purpose but to provide a few hours of fun: one-person devices that hovered just over the water, or flew a few feet above the surface, or skimmed just underneath it; high-speed boats (often two or three of them); even full-fledged, multipassenger submarines. In the language of yachting magazines and web sites, Alix had learned, these enormously expensive devices were universally referred to as "toys," which seemed to her a not-so-attractive example of coyly disingenuous modesty by the super-rich.

When she was a block from the pier, she saw that there were only two boats larger than rowboats that were pulled up to it: a boxy teak launch and a low, sleek cigarette boat, the kind of vessel that was sometimes called a "go-fast boat" and, once upon a time, for good reason, a "rum-runner's boat." At the sight of it, there was a catch in her throat. She'd always had a weakness for speed and would have given her eyeteeth for a spin in such a thing (she'd have thrown in a couple of molars as well, if a turn at the wheel were part of the deal). And now it looked as if she was going to get her chance and still keep her teeth. According to *Amazing Yachts,* a high-powered, thirty-foot cigarette boat capable of planing over the water at more than fifty knots was one of the *Artemis's* toys, and, what do you know, here it was, sent especially to fetch her.

The closer she came to it the more beautiful it got, a gleaming white hull with an arching red slash from front to back, so beautifully graceful and close to the water that even standing still it looked as if it were moving. As she came up to it, a man, his back to her, emerged into the open cockpit from the storage area in the boat's covered bow and folded back into place the steps that led down to it. He'd probably just deposited her luggage, brought by the limo driver.

"Hi, there," she said.

He turned. "Well, hello to you." The accent was Italian and elegant and the man himself looked as if he might have been made—manufactured—just to go with this boat. He was beautiful in the same way the boat was: handsome, smooth-skinned, ideally proportioned, and maybe a little (but only a little) too perfect.

"I'm Alix London," she said.

"And I—" He put a hand to his chest. "I am Michelangelo Benedetti." He smiled. Perfect teeth too, white and even and strong. At first she thought it was a clothing-store mannequin he reminded her of, but then she realized it was a doll, a doll she'd had as a child—Barbie's boyfriend Ken. He was even dressed like Ken in his yachtsman's phase: red-and-white striped polo shirt, sky-blue windbreaker and trousers, white deck shoes, captain's cap. The thought made her laugh, but he took it as the return of his own friendly smile. "And this," he said with pride, "this is *La Bella Vita*—in English, *The Beautiful Life*. Would you like to come aboard? I am about to take her out for a run, perhaps around Delos. You know Delos? I would have you back in an hour. It would be very exhilarating. So?" He offered a confident hand to help her on.

She stayed put. "Uh . . . you're not from the *Artemis*, are you?"

"*Artemis*? No, I am—"

"Madame, you are looking for *Artemis*?"

She turned. The voice came from the boxy launch, and the speaker was a slightly younger man, dark, lean, and fit—handsome, but in a wolf-ish way—in what she took to be a yachting crew uniform, spotless and crisp: white, short-sleeved, collared shirt with colorful epaulettes and a blue logo on the side of his chest that she couldn't read, and sharply creased white trousers.

"Yes," she said. "I'm Alix London. Are you here for me?" Her heart fell as she spoke. The launch, despite its shipshape condition, had more in common with the *African Queen* than with *La Bella Vita*.

"I come to bring you for the yacht, yes. I am purser of the *Artemis*." He pointed to the logo: *Artemis,* she saw now. "My name, Dionysodaurus Kyriakoulopoulos."

Gamely, she gave it a try. "Dio . . . Donosaur . . ."

He laughed. "Mostly, I am called Donny."

He took a step forward to help her over the gunwale, but, with a wry glance at Benedetti, she hopped onto the boat on her own. There was a bench around three sides, and she took a seat near the front. Donny deftly untied the mooring ropes, got behind the wheel, and gunned the engine.

Michelangelo Benedetti looked on with a smile both sad and ironic. "Does this mean you won't be coming with me?"

"I guess not. Sorry."

"Not as sorry as I am, signorina."

"That's what you think," she called back as the launch began to move out. That broadened his smile, but he would have been surprised to learn that it was the cigarette boat she was thinking of and not him.

.   .   .

The launch was anything but sleek, but nobody could complain about the furnishings. Alix was pleasurably surprised by how deeply she sank into the buttery white leather that cushioned the bench. She slipped on her sunglasses, tilted her head up to the sun, and stretched out her legs. She was wearing a simple, pale green linen sundress and sandals, and, with a sigh, she gave herself up to the caress of the warm Aegean sunlight—Apollo's gift to humankind—on her skin. With what struck her as a pro forma glance at her legs, almost as if he were simply doing what was expected of him, Donny started up the engine and began pulling away from the dock. Now the salt-laden breeze riffled her hair too.

Heaven.

She was startled out of a near doze by a sudden lurch of the boat. Her eyes popped open. "What—"

"*Figlio di puttana!*"

The oath came from Michelangelo Benedetti, to whose cigarette boat Donny had veered much too close. The furious Benedetti was leaning over the side and shoving on the launch's stern to keep it from swinging into his boat.

With a showily nonchalant spin of the wheel, Donny stopped the launch's forward momentum and sent it out of harm's way. "*Ante gamisou!*" he yelled back.

Alix had spent seven years in Italy, so she knew that Benedetti had called him a son of a whore, but Greek was a mystery to her. She had no idea what *ante gamisou* meant (other than being pretty sure it wasn't complimentary), and she had no desire to ask for a translation.

Benedetti just glared at Donny in response, then looked over at Alix with an expression that beautifully conveyed his sympathy over her being required to go off with this baboon in his bathtub of a boat, considering what might have been hers instead. With the launch safely out of reach and gaining speed, Donny raised his hand high without turning around and offered his farewell in the form of an extended middle finger, surely the world's most universally understood gesture.

Alix shook her head. She was going to have to get herself used to the various forms of Mediterranean machismo that she'd become acquainted with during her eight-year apprenticeship in Italy. They had struck her as flattering at first (for all of two days or so), then annoying, and finally boring. The never-ending flirting and strutting; the chest-puffing; the unsubtle hitting on any female who made the mistake of responding to a greeting; the strange sense of obligation, of duty, that seemed to require so many males to convince any passing woman younger than sixty (and often older if no young ones were available) that she had astounded them with her irresistible beauty. It was basically all showmanship. There was never any question that it didn't really have as much to do with *you* as it did with *him*. *Look at me,* he was saying, *how handsome I am, how manly. Have you ever seen such a smile, such a profile as this?* The whole boring routine was just plain silly, tiresome but essentially harmless.

Inside of five minutes, both Benedetti and Donny had demonstrated their inclinations in that direction. Benedetti had some things going for him—an attractive guy with an appealing, breezy charm (to say nothing of *La Bella Vita*)—but Donny gave her the creeps. It wasn't just that hungry, slinking air of his, either, or a simple absence of chemistry, although that was there too. Donny manifested another predilection of many males in this part of the world, and this one definitely made her want to steer clear of him. To men like Donny, every interaction with an unknown male was a challenge to his own manhood. It was necessary to demonstrate to anyone within range that he was tougher, or stronger, or more reckless, or more "connected," or more anything.

"You think that cigarette boat there was nice?" he asked contemptuously as they wove between the small craft that dotted the harbor. "Why, you like fast boats, huh? Wait, you see ours, the *Hermes*. Hermes, he was god of speed," he added for her instruction.

"I'm sure it's beautiful," Alix said politely.

"Not only it's beautiful. Fifty knots, she supposed to go? Me, I know how to get her up to seventy-five."

He seemed to expect a reply, so she said, "Really?"

"You bet, really. I drive her all the time. I am always taking out Mr. and Mrs. Papadakis. I'm only one he lets. He and me, we are good cousins, and I can drive it any time I want." He cleared his throat to make sure he had her full attention. "Pocahontas, she always likes for me to take her out two, three times when she comes."

"I'm sorry . . . you said—?"

He looked at her in surprise. "You don't know Pocahontas? The singer?"

"I'm afraid not."

"You never hear of Pocahontas?" He couldn't believe his ears. "'I Need It Now'? 'I'll Take It Either Way'? 'Rub Me the Wrong Way'?"

"Sorry."

"Come on, you know. 'I Gotta Get Me More'?" He launched into song, tacking what he must have thought was a white singer's version of an African American accent onto his already demanding Greek accent. Unfortunately, the words were still intelligible.

"Ah gotta get me mo',
Baby, Ah need it now.
But Ah ain't nobody's h—"

"Uh, Donny, shouldn't you be looking where we're going?"

He glanced forward long enough to adjust their course to avoid a fishing boat that was tooling in from a day at sea—apparently a good day, too; she could smell the fish. The two-man, rubber-aproned crew looked up from their work to grin in her direction, and one of them waved a fish at her.

She waved politely back.

"I thought everybody heard of Pocahontas," Donny said, still in semi-shock. "She's famous."

"I'll be sure to look her up."

"You don't got to look her up, she is right on board. I brought her over last night."

"She'll be on the cruise?"

"Sure. Hey, anything you want to know about her, you just ask me. You want to hear what her real name is? Isabelle Clinke." He snickered. "I call her Izzy. I know her real good. I know them all real well. Hey, maybe sometime, I can take you for a ride if you want, what do you say? In the *Hermes*. I could tell you some pretty wild stories. And we could stop somewhere for a picnic, you know? Some quiet island, maybe?" He turned his head and she could see the gleam of those wolflike teeth.

"Maybe," she said with a non-committal smile. *Maybe when hell freezes over.*

Under ordinary circumstances she would have been a good deal more committal than that, but the last thing she needed was to start cutting off her contacts. She was there for the purpose of getting information, and she anticipated that the crew would be a primary source of it. Especially this particular crew: Papadakis had made a practice of hiring only people he knew, mostly from his own ancestral village of Karavostassis on the nearby island of Folegandros, and most of those, like Donny, were his cousins or nephews or nieces. He had paid to have them taught English and to attend training that met international requirements for the crew of a yacht the size of the *Artemis*. They were, so it was believed, an extremely tight-knit, loyal group—no outsiders allowed—which was why the FBI had never been able to get any of their own aboard until the opportunity for Alix London had come along.

So she simply smiled and let him continue to swagger and brag about the intimate terms he was on with the guests, and how close he was to his cousin and great friend Panos, and how much Panos depended on him for advice. He also managed to let drop that he was a sometime swimsuit model, that he spoke four languages, and that he had been the marathon-swimming champion of the Cyclades in 2010. At one point he did make a passing remark that perked up her ears as being of possible interest— something that implied that all was not well between the Papadakises—but following up on it too obviously was out of the question, so she let him meander on to something else.

"You need anything, anything at all," he said as they came within a hundred yards or so of the smallest of the liners, an almost aerodynamically beautiful four-decker with an impossibly spotless, smudgeless, dingless, Prussian-blue hull and white superstructure, "you come to me."

"Thank you."

The sounds of an on-deck cocktail party reached her as they swung even closer: music, tinkling glassware, chatter, and shrill, slightly false laughter. She looked up toward the open deck near the stern and saw that it was filled with people, most of whom had glasses in their hands.

She also caught a glimpse of the silvery, foot-and-a-half-foot-high lettering on the hull. *Artemis*.

Alix was amazed. She'd known the *Artemis* was big, and she'd even seen pictures of it, but somehow the actual physical hugeness of the thing had never quite penetrated. She just hadn't expected that a two-hundred-and-thirty-nine-foot yacht would be so *long*, that it would loom over her like this, that its broad, clean side would be so intimidatingly massive.

And here she'd always thought her Uncle Julian's eighty footer was something.

Wow.

9

Entry to the yacht was midway down the port side, by means of a bay door hinged at the top so that it swung upward, allowing a small floating dock to be extended from the entry and laid down on the water. Alix was assisted onto this by a hand from a capable-looking young woman in a snappy tailored uniform—short-sleeved white cotton blouse with gold buttons, epaulets, and a trim blue skirt—the same Prussian-blue as the hull—that came down to just above her knees. As with Donny, the shirt bore a discreet *Artemis* logo in woven blue script.

"Welcome aboard, Ms. London," she said. "My name is Artemis."

"Artemis? Really?"

"Yes, really. Sometimes I think it is why Mr. Papadakis hired me," she said with a smile, although it must have been a pretty tired joke with her by now. "I am the chief stewardess."

As expected, her accent was Greek, although her syntax, unlike Donny's, was flawless. If she and Donny really were relatives of Papadakis's, then the Papadakis gene pool was awash with DNA for good looks, of which poor Panos had missed out on his fair share, assuming the photos she'd seen were accurate.

She moved aside to let Alix precede her into a simple foyer. "Mr. and Mrs. Papadakis have asked me to apologize on their behalf," she said smoothly. "They would have liked to greet you personally, but they are occupied in hosting a pre-launch reception on the aft deck for island dignitaries and friends. And for those of our cruise guests who wish to attend, of course. They are hoping that once you have had a chance to refresh yourself and see your stateroom, you will want to join them."

"Of course." *Stateroom*, she thought. *Well, that's another good sign.* Originally she hadn't been sure whether she'd be treated as one more member of the crew or as a bona fide guest. But now—stateroom, the VIP treatment in general—it was clear that it was to be the latter. Good, that was going to make her privy to more of the information she was supposed to be keeping her eyes and ears open for, and, what the hell, admit it: It was going to make the whole enterprise a lot more enjoyable.

Artemis led the way into the yacht's main atrium, of which the centerpiece was a four-story spiral staircase with veined marble steps and dark, richly polished wood banisters and support columns. The walls were done in tones of rust and sand, with accents in the same exotic wood that was on the staircase. Evenly spaced along the walls were eight fluted, shoulder-high marble columns (with capitals of the Ionic order, as Alix dimly remembered from some long-ago art history class), each one supporting a Classical bronze or marble head. Greek sculpture was something she knew little about, but these beautiful and evocative fragments struck her as being of museum quality. The teakwood floor had been so freshly sanded that its earthy fragrance still hung in the air.

Artemis took her up one flight of the spiraling stairs, paused at the top, and surprised Alix by saying, "This is Miss London," to the smooth wooden post around which the staircase wound. "She will be one of our cruise guests and is entitled to full freedom of the ship."

After a moment the pole said, "*Efkharisto,* Artemis."

"I know *efkharisto* means 'thank you'," Alix said, "but I never heard it from a pole before."

Artemis pointed to the recessed junction between the pole and the sixth step upward. "Video camera," she said, "and speaker."

Alix peered. "I still don't see it."

"That's good; you're not supposed to. There are many of them on the ship, in all the public areas. Mr. Papadakis is a cautious man."

Alix frowned. The idea that she and the other guests would be under continual surveillance for the next week struck her as being closer to the paranoia that Ted had mentioned than to caution, even considering the multimillion-dollar cargo they were carrying. All of the cruise guests, after all—and there were only six of them, five collectors and herself—had been personally invited by Mr. Papadakis. What did he imagine could possibly happen? Did he really think one of them would walk off—swim off? Jet boat off?—with a Renoir?

Artemis saw what she was thinking. "They will not be operational during the cruise, Ms. London. It is only for this afternoon's occasion with so many people aboard, not all of whom are personally known to Mr. Papadakis. There are almost one hundred of them. They have already seen the pictures and had their tour, and now that food and drink are available, they have been asked to remain above deck, where the reception is underway. That is why the cameras are operational."

"I see. Where *are* the paintings, anyway?"

"Why, right here. In the music room. Behind you. And others on the walls of the main salon, just beyond."

Alix turned to look. The digital auction catalog that Edward Reed had e-mailed her was divided into two sections, Impressionist and Modern, and it was immediately obvious that the music room had been given over to the Impressionists. There they were, hung on the ash-paneled walls of a thickly carpeted room that spanned the width of the yacht, a glorious cross-section of the art of painting as it was in France in the final quarter of the nineteenth century. From the catalog she recognized the Degas, the Manet, the Renoir, the Cézanne, the Gauguin, beautiful paintings all. . . .

"Wow," she breathed, taking a step toward them without consciously intending to, almost as if the pictures were powerful magnets and she was an iron filing that couldn't help itself. On her second sleepwalking step she came smack up against a distinguished-looking man who had stepped into her path from the side.

"Oh, I'm sorry," she said. "I wasn't—"

"No, don't apologize. My fault entirely. I should have been watching where I was going."

"Distinguished looking" didn't begin to do him justice. In his fifties, slim and elegantly tuxedoed, very erect, with a pencil-thin mustache that belonged on a thirties' matinee idol, his longish but carefully styled dark hair made even more perfect by the wings of silver that swept back from his temples, he radiated civility and good breeding. His accent, much like her father's but more la-di-da, completed the picture.

"You're Alix London?" he asked.

"I am, yes. And you're—?" There was something familiar about him, she thought.

"My name is Edward Reed." Nope, nobody she'd met before. "I'm curating the auction—"

"Of course, " she said, holding out her hand. "You're an art dealer in Manhattan."

"A gallerist, yes," he said, gently correcting her.

She'd heard that some high-end dealers, feeling that the term "dealer" implied that they practiced a low form of trade or were in it for the money (surely not!), now preferred to be called "gallerists," but this was the first one she'd actually met. Until now it had struck her as a silly affectation, but on Edward Reed it was a good fit.

"Miss London—"

"Alix."

He acknowledged this by dipping his chin. "Alix, I was just in the process of looking things over down here. The hordes were driven through earlier and left only a few minutes ago, and I wanted to make sure everything was in order, which it seems to be. But while we're both here, it would be my privilege to introduce you, shall we say, to the collection," He smiled invitingly.

And the smile made her realize why she'd thought she knew him. Edward's smile, his aristocratic bearing, his flawless grooming, his polite, cultivated speech—all brought back memories of the patrician collectors and connoisseurs she'd met through her father in the pre-*Venezia*, pre-prison days when Geoff was a welcome regular at society events, at the Met, at the Frick, and in the elite condos of the Upper East Side. These people were cordial, considerate, perfectly mannered, and unfailingly polite. And yet, without their being openly supercilious or condescending, you were always aware of a subtle dismissiveness just below the surface, a cool, objective distance they preserved between themselves and others who were not of their own exalted breed. It was a type that sometimes fascinated, sometimes repelled her. Which it would be with Edward she didn't yet know, but so far she found him agreeable enough.

"Oh, I'd like that," she said. "I'm very eager to—" She suddenly remembered Artemis, who was standing politely by. "But Artemis was just taking me to my room, and I don't want to hold her up."

Edward flashed his smile at Artemis. "Oh, but I'm sure the lovely Artemis would allow us a peek. Just the gem of the collection, its shining jewel, perhaps?" His eyebrows lifted. "Yes?"

Artemis glowed. "A few minutes won't hurt."

"No more than five, I promise. I want the pleasure of being there when Alix sees it for the first time."

The gem of the collection (she wondered uncharitably if he might be referring to the super-high estimated sale price that had been set for it) hung at the front of the room. Edward smiled at it as if at a precocious child of whom he was particularly proud. *"Luncheon at the Lakeside."*

The simple four-by-six card beside the painting agreed with him. *Édouard Manet, 1861, Le Déjeuner au Bord du Lac.* An engraved brass plate nailed to the bottom of the gilt frame simply said, "Manet, 1832–1883." The canvas was fairly large, about three feet by four.

Edward sighed. "I *love* Manet."

Alix nodded. Manet was one of her favorites too. One of the two men most often credited with being the father of Impressionism (the other being Claude Monet), he was a lifelong individualist, a man who rejected labels, refusing to refer to himself as an Impressionist or as anything else. Besides which, in her opinion, some of his paintings were among the most beautiful and appealing artworks that had ever been created.

Le Déjeuner au Bord du Lac was a handsome early work, a quiet pastoral scene showing a decorous middle-class family of three—a man, a woman, a girl of eight or ten—picnicking beside a lake with their beached rowboat a few yards behind them. Alix had been taken with its photograph in the catalog and had looked forward to standing before the real thing, as she was doing now.

But as she took it in, she felt the beginnings of a fluttery, uneasy feeling in her stomach, and she knew what that implied. She stared harder at the painting, almost scowling at it.

"Is something the matter?" Edward asked.

"I don't . . . I'm not . . . there's something . . . Edward, does this look all right to you?"

"All right?" He paled, literally paled. "My God, did they do something to it?" She could see his eyes dart wildly over the surface.

"No, no," she assured him, "I don't mean it's been damaged. No, the condition looks perfect."

He wasn't much soothed. "Then *what*?" His voice shot up to an unbecoming near-screech.

"Well, I don't know," she said lamely. "It's just that something doesn't seem right about it. I can't put my finger on it—yet."

"Alix, you're making me very nervous here. What do you mean, not right?"

"I'm sorry, Edward. Look, I was probably just imagining it. Something must have hit me wrong. It was an overnight flight, you know . jet lag . . I don't know. Please, forget I said anything. Just ignore it." She finished with an apologetic shrug.

Edward remained decidedly unsoothed. "I'm trying to see what it is about it that disturbs you, and frankly . . . " He shook his head.

Alix caught a glimpse of Artemis stealing a discreet glance at her watch. "Oh, Artemis, I'm sorry. Why don't you show me my stateroom now? Edward, I'll see you up at the reception?"

"Yes, yes, I'm going there now," he said absently, continuing to stare moodily at the painting. *I've offended him*, she thought. *That didn't take long. A mere five minutes aboard the ship, and I've already antagonized my first person.*

But that didn't change the feeling in her stomach. *Something wasn't right.*

10

She followed Artemis down the forward corridor, over more of the same ultra-soft beige carpet that had been in the salon, to a door on the port side, which Artemis opened for her.

"Whoa," Alix murmured. She'd known to expect something spacious and well appointed, but this place was the size of her entire apartment in Seattle and outfitted like a layout in a designer showroom.

"I hope you'll be comfortable here," Artemis said with a perfectly straight face.

"It seems quite nice," replied Alix with what she hoped was an appropriate nonchalance.

Artemis presented her with the key card, offered to help her unpack, told her that she could be called upon at any time for anything Alix needed or desired, wished her a memorable journey and left, softly closing the door behind her.

Memorable, Alix thought with a wry laugh. It was already memorable, and it hadn't even started. That sense of something being "off" about that Manet was still with her, but maybe she was better off leaving it till morning when she'd be rested. After all, she probably *was* jet-lagged and was certainly sleep deprived, and maybe the only thing that was "off" was her nervous system.

What she should do right now, she knew, was to forget about it for the time being and go on up to the reception as requested. She moved decisively toward her luggage, which had been set on a long, low table at the foot of the bed. A quick wash was in order, a change of clothes, and then she'd go up and meet her hosts.

Except that she knew she wouldn't, not quite yet. What she *would* do was go back to the music room and spend a little more time with Monsieur Manet and see if she could resolve what it was that was nagging at her about his painting. And she figured the Papadakises could bear to wait another twenty or thirty minutes for the pleasure of meeting her.

She did pause to perform the quick wash, and then she was out the door in a flash, practically trotting down the passageway, the lush carpet completely muffling the sound of her feet, and pausing only for a smile and a wave at the spot where the sixth step of the spiral staircase joined the central post. As she'd hoped, Edward Reed had gone; she had the music room to herself. She went at once to the Manet, which was at the front, behind a low stage that held a grouping of musical instruments—a full-sized Steinway concert grand piano with a bright red shawl laid across its closed lid, a harp, and a cello on a stand. The Manet was hung in pride of place, centered over the piano. She leaned back against the piano to study it from five or six feet away and opened her mind to it.

Nothing popped out at her, or at least nothing pertinent. What a long way this *Déjeuner* was, she thought absently, from Manet's more celebrated *Déjeuner*, now in Paris's Musée d'Orsay. That painting, *Le Déjeuner sur l'Herbe*—the Luncheon in the Grass—had made him both famous and notorious, scandalizing the Parisian public with its depiction of three people, two men and a woman, lazily enjoying what looks like a lovely nineteenth-century French picnic in a Paris park. The painting is prettily done and the scene was commonplace enough in the art of the time— except that the two men, a pair of dandies, are fully clothed and the woman is stark naked, every inch of her. Her discarded clothing lies in a heap on the grass beside her. The nude woman, oddly enough, is being treated as if she weren't there, the men apparently absorbed in lazy conversation with one another. The painting, now much admired, ignited an uproar at the time, French standards of propriety being stricter than they subsequently became.

But that wasn't to happen until 1863, two years after the *Déjeuner* before Alix was completed. This painting, *Déjeuner au Bord du Lac,* was painted when he was still an unknown artist (not a starving one, however; his father had been a judge, his mother the goddaughter of the Swedish crown prince), and his work hadn't yet developed its mature style. The style . . . she frowned; was it something about the *style* that was bothering her? She moved in for a closer look.

. . .

Two decks below her, in the closet-like security command center next to the engine room, twenty-year-old Yiannis Alexopolous sat before a console of six color monitors on two levels, each screen divided into four quadrants showing four separate locations on the yacht. He set down the empty plate that had held the best *keftedes* he'd ever tasted—the meatballs ground as fine as custard, the tomato sauce as thick and sweet as honey—licked his lips, and took hold of the tray filled with little squares of baklava, lemon cake, walnut cake, and half a dozen other desserts he didn't recognize. He didn't need to recognize them; he knew they'd be delicious. Yiannis ate like this only two or three times a year, when his third cousin twice removed, Panos Papadakis, hired him to put in an evening's security duty for a party. The incredible food alone would have been enough to make him jump at the chance—all he wanted to eat, plus whatever he could get away with stuffing in his clothes—but the money, as much for three hours of sitting there doing not much of anything as he got for two full days' work in the butcher shop, made it the best job he ever had or ever would have.

The only problem, if you could call it that, was that it was boring to stare and stare and stare at six television screens showing twenty-four different passageways or stairways or public rooms in none of which anything ever happened or even moved. Not that he was complaining. He moved the tray to his lap, leaned back and popped a square of baklava into his mouth, closing his eyes to savor the taste: super-sweet and sticky. Perfect. When he opened his eyes he thought he actually saw something move on one of the screens. He quickly swallowed what was left of the baklava and rose halfway out of his chair, the better to see what it was. No, not movement, but a change. The lower right quadrant of the screen had gone a strange, fuzzy gray. He checked the location key posted below the monitors: aft stairway, deck three.

He hesitated. His instructions were to call Mr. Christos, the security chief, at once if anybody who hadn't been cleared was spotted below decks, but this was different, probably just a glitch in the system and he was reluctant to—

But now it was the lower *left* window of the monitor—the music room—that was affected as well. Horizontal streaks of gray spread rapidly across it and in one second it was as blank as the other one. No, something weird was happening. He was all the way out of his chair now and excitedly punching the telephone button for security. "Mr. Christos—"

.   .   .

Even from six inches away, Alix couldn't figure out what it was. Now, to take it in again from further off, she backed away until her hips bumped up against the grand piano, folded her arms, and let her intuition go to work.

Alix's reputation for assessing and authenticating works of art was well deserved, but she wasn't the conventional kind of expert, the sort who examines a questioned painting and says, *Aha, the draperies of that purported Velasquez do not fit his technique with fabrics,* or *I'm sorry, but I don't see how this can possibly be a Gauguin. The pigment in this lemon is surely lead-tin yellow, and since lead-tin yellow was not available between 1750 and 1941 and Gauguin's paintings were all made between 1873 and 1903, certainly you can see . . .*

Oh, she knew such things, and better than most experts did, but her particular gift, and a rare and controversial gift it was, was what is called a "connoisseur's eye," the ability to tell almost instantly, without thinking about it—to *feel* rather than to *know*—that a particular painting was or wasn't what it was purported to be. The absence of lead-tin yellow or the presence of a few incongruous drapery folds might well be what she was picking up, but she was picking it up subliminally. That sort of conscious analysis would come later—sometimes a long while later— and serve as a source of confirmation rather than the starting point.

In this case, whether viewing the painting from a distance of six inches or ten feet, her intuition was the same: *Something was definitely not right.* She realized suddenly that her stomach wasn't the only part of her that was trying to tell her something. The back of her neck prickled. There was someone else in the room. . . . She turned—

And ran into a wall, a soft, giving wall that first blinded and suffocated her and then tightened around her head. She thought for a second it was a blanket, but the texture, the dusty smell of it, told her it was the shawl that had been lying across the piano. Panicked, thinking she was being smothered, she flailed blindly against whomever was there. Her fist found what she thought was a shoulder and she tried to claw at where she imagined the eyes would be, but she was spun roughly around and then shoved so that she stumbled. Her elbow cracked into something. Her ankle caught in something else and she lost her footing entirely. She lifted her arms to try to protect her head. She—

11

Somebody had her by the shoulders. "Miss London—"

She swung at him and contacted a face, a cheekbone. The result was a grunt, more of annoyance than of pain. She swung again but her wrist was grabbed and held.

"Please stop hitting me, you are all right, you are safe."

"What? I thought—" She swam back up toward awareness and opened her eyes. She was flat on her back on the carpet, lying at the base of the piano. Her head felt like a soccer ball, a dangerously overinflated one. A man was kneeling behind her head and bending over her—she could see only the top half of his face, and that upside down. He had both her wrists now.

"I am the chief of security for this boat, madame, Yiorgos Christos by name." He let go of her wrists and held up one of his hands a few inches from her eyes. "How many fingers do you see?"

"Two. What happened to me?"

"This, I think." He very gently touched a spot above her ear, and the soccer ball exploded.

"Ouch!"

"I'm sorry. Follow with your eyes my hand."

She did, trying to keep her throbbing head steady. "What happened? How did—" Then it came back. "He threw something over me, he threw me down, I must—"

"'He'? You saw who it was?"

"No, I was looking at a painting. I didn't see him coming."

82

"But you believe it was a 'he,' a man?"

"No, I can't say that either. He—" She stopped to wriggle herself into a more comfortable position on the floor. The security chief helped her to get her back against one of the piano legs, so she was more or less sitting, then stood up himself. Now she could see him right side up, all of him, and he was colossal, the shoulders of his blue blazer straining across his back, the sleeves bulging with muscle. The face went along with the frame too, big, beefy, and ornamented with a prodigious black mustache, an honest-to-God handlebar mustache, waxed so that it curled up at the ends. A long-forgotten image popped into her not-yet-altogether focused mind, a vintage Barnum & Bailey Circus poster that an old roommate had had up on the wall: ÖZBEK, THE TURKISH GIANT, THE WORLD'S STRONGEST MAN. Put an over-one-shoulder leopard skin on this Christos guy, and he might have posed for it.

"No, it could have been a woman, I suppose," she finished. Her voice seemed unconnected to her, hollow and far away. She wasn't altogether back from cloud-cuckoo land yet. "He seemed pretty strong, but I didn't see him. He threw something over my head."

Christos nodded. "It was this object, I think, yes?" He held up a corner of the red shawl, now caught on the jutting edge of the music support stand above the keyboard, torn almost in two.

"It probably was," Alix said. Her head was calming down and she began to rise.

Christos leaned over and placed a soothing hand on her shoulder. "No no no no no. A moment longer, sit, stay a minute, what's the hurry?"

She settled back against the leg of the piano. "I was unconscious, wasn't I? For how long?"

"Not so long," said Christos, "a few seconds, no more. Maybe less. Maybe not at all, really." He smiled reassuringly, a kindly giant.

"But why would someone do that to me? What was it all about; do you know?"

"Oh, yes, we know." He pointed to the wall. "That."

To see what he was pointing at she had to twist her neck, which shot a wrenching stab of pain through her head—skull, teeth, eyes, everything— as if it had been thrust into a giant electrical socket.

"Ai!" The worst of the pain was quickly over, but it made her eyes tear, so it took a few seconds before she could focus on what it was that Christos was talking about.

"The Manet," she breathed, her still-pulsating head forgotten. "Oh, no."

A ragged, two-foot-long gash ran obscenely down the middle of the canvas, separating the man and the woman and bisecting the long-haired little girl who sat between them eating a roll. Both canvas and lining had been ripped clear through; the edges had curled back, so the wall behind was visible through the laceration.

"Oh, how awful," Alix said. "Shouldn't someone tell Mr. Papadakis?" Something began niggling at her fogged mind, something important about the painting, but she couldn't put her finger on it.

"I have sent Dionysodaurus for him. He will—ah, he is here."

A close-bunched crowd of people, four of them, was clacking down the marble steps. Donny was in the lead with Edward Reed, looking stricken, on his heels. The other two she recognized from photographs. Behind Edward was Gabriela Papadakis, a jowly woman of forty, prematurely aging and growing plain, but still recognizable as the beautiful American opera star who had been a darling of the paparazzi a dozen years ago, regularly photographed on the arms of movie stars or princes. She had ruined her voice with poor role choices before ever making it to the top-most rung, however, and then—obviously—she'd put on weight, and now other faces looked out at you from the magazines when you were on the grocery checkout line.

Bringing up the rear, red-faced and puffing, two decades older than his wife (his third), was the Man himself, Panos Papadakis.

Donny moved respectfully out of the way and the other three stared disbelievingly at the scene. Like Edward, Papadakis was in a tux, but it was too tight for him. He looked like an uncomfortable sausage about to burst its bun. Mrs. Papadakis wore an emerald-green cocktail dress that was as classy as they came, but didn't do her any favors by drawing the eye to her freckled, plump shoulders.

Edward was the first to find his voice. "Oh, dear, how very terrible."

Panos was sucking air noisily in through his nose and huffing it out almost as loudly. His face seemed to be swelling up before Alix's eyes. It wouldn't have surprised her to see steam hissing out of his ears.

Of the three, only Mrs. Papadakis wasn't caught up in the painting. "Oh, no," she said softly, fingering the torn shawl. "Look what they did to my—"

Panos jerked it out of her hands and flung it to the floor. "I just lose fifteen million dollars and you're worrying about a lousy shawl? What the hell is wrong with you, for Christ's sake?"

Mrs. Papadakis said nothing, just stared stonily at the floor. Alix saw tears welling in her eyes.

Panos lost interest in her and turned to Christos. "How you could let this happen? How anybody could even get in here? Who the hell was it?"

"Hey, Panos, it just happened. Give me little time."

"Time! What about all those expensive television sets that are supposed to be so great according to you, what about that damn kid who was supposed to be watching them? This is your job, your responsibility!" He was standing almost on tiptoe, trying to jut his chin into Christos's face but got only as high as his collarbone.

Christos, a foot taller and a hundred pounds of muscle heavier, was uncowed. "It wasn't the kid's fault. Whoever it was, he sprayed the cameras, so the kid, he couldn't see anything. He called me right away."

"I don't care; I want him fired. He never works for me again, understand? And what's it supposed to mean, he sprayed the cameras? What, with paint? Where the hell he could get a can of paint?"

Christos used his thumb and forefinger to smooth his mustache, but it was clear that he was doing it to hide a smile. "Not paint, Panos. Whipped cream." And then, after a pause, "Myself, I tasted it."

Whipped cream? Still dopey, Alix had to stifle her own giggle.

Not Panos. "He uses *whipped cream* to ruin a fifteen-million-dollar painting, and you think it's funny? What am I paying you for? I find him," muttered Panos to himself, fists clenched, "I kill the son of a bitch, I rip his ears off, I send him to jail for the rest of his miserable life. Somebody I invite on my own yacht, somebody I trust, a wolf in sheep's clothing, a snake in the grass, a . . . a . . ."

Alix was getting a little annoyed with the way things were going. Certainly a slashed Manet was no small matter, but what about her? None of them had asked what she was doing on the floor or asked if she was all right. Did they think she was sitting there because she found it comfortable?

It was Mrs. Papadakis who finally took notice. With tears over the ruin of her shawl still glimmering on her eyelids, she bent over Alix. "Why, you're Alix London, aren't you? What's wrong? What happened to you? Yiorgos, is she all right?"

"Yes, I believe so," he told her. "She suffered a bump on her head and fell." And then to Alix: "Would you like to try getting up now? Give me your arm."

Alix nodded and started to rise but had to stop when a wave of wooziness billowed over her. Mrs. Papadakis was quickly at her other side. "Here, let me give you a hand."

"Thank you," Alix said as the dizziness faded. Mrs. Papadakis's face was close to her own. Alix got a whiff of gin and saw that the woman was less steady than she'd first appeared to be. Her makeup had been applied with a heavy hand. It had caked and fissured in the creases alongside her nose and along her softening jawline, and her mascara had run when the tears had started. Even her lipstick had gotten smeared. *Her life is unhappy,* was Alix's immediate thought. She might live among surroundings like these, but things had not turned out for her as she must have hoped, back when she was Gabriela Candelas, the beautiful and sought-after young mezzo-soprano.

Once Alix was solidly on both feet, the two people on either side of her relaxed their hold. Alix, not quite fully stable, leaned back against the piano. If Panos had yet taken any notice of her he gave no sign. He was glaring accusingly at the painting as if the whole thing was its own fault, and muttering to himself in Greek.

"But Panos," Mrs. Papadakis was saying, "after all, it's insured, isn't it?"

He glanced disgustedly at her. "Yeah, sure, for what it cost me fifteen years ago, not what it's worth now." He had simmered down to grumbling rather than yelling. "Besides, the money is just money, but to destroy great art like this, it's a crime against humanity. It belongs to the world. It's the principle of the thing, you know what I'm saying?" He must have realized how dubious this sounded coming from him, because he looked angrily around, as if to challenge anyone who might doubt him.

"You're probably right about the insurance, Panos," Edward said, "but look at it this way: The picture is far from a total loss. Yes, it looks just awful now, but it's certainly reparable, and I would have every expectation that your insurance would cover the cost of repair."

"Every expectation," Panos grunted sourly.

"Now look, Panos. As a conservator of some repute, Miss London here would know about such things."

At the mention of her name, Alix jumped. What had he been saying? "Well . . ."

"Wouldn't you say it's reparable, Miss London? Couldn't a good restorer make the damage hardly noticeable?"

For the first time Panos seemed to be aware of her. He stared at her with suspicion, as if to say, *Who the hell are you? What are you doing on my boat?*

"Hardly noticeable? Yes. Unnoticeable, no I don't think so, not without a great deal of overpainting that would greatly decrease its artistic standing." *Hey,* she thought, *that was pretty coherent. I think my mind's working again.* She had edged nearer to the picture as she spoke. Whatever was down there nagging her about it was bubbling closer to the surface.

"Hardly noticeable," Panos said dismissively, "artistic standing. Yeah sure, but what about the value? All of a sudden that's hardly noticeable too."

"Well, the value, of course . . . ," Edward said with a shrug. "That's another story."

"Yeah, suddenly it's three million, maybe four, not ten or fifteen."

"So you'll be withdrawing it from the auction?" Edward asked.

"Of course I'm withdrawing it," Panos snapped. "What, are you nuts? Who's gonna buy it like this? And I'm sure as hell not giving it away for peanuts."

Edward flushed and then showed a discreet little flare of pique. "Panos, I was merely ascertaining . . . no matter. We'll withdraw it."

Christos had been eyeing Alix. "Ms. London, you don't look so hot. We got a couple of doctors at the reception. I think maybe we should get one of them—"

"Thank you, I don't need a doctor."

"She don't need a doctor," Panos said, barely looking at her.

Alix was liking him less by the second. It was one thing for her to decline medical assistance, but where did Panos come off declining it for her?

He was talking to Christos. "Put it in the storage room, the secure one. I'll go down with you to open it."

"Okay, give me a minute to turn off the alarm system so we can take it off the wall."

Panos had shown signs of calming down, but now he exploded again. "Alarm system! That's another thing—what the hell good is an alarm system if this can happen? I thought this was the best one money could buy, no? You told me that yourself, no?"

Christos, who had yet to display trepidation in the face of Panos's wrath, now showed some annoyance of his own, quiet but trenchant and pointed. "Don't talk to me like this anymore, Panos. I don't like it." *No love lost there*, Alix thought.

Panos's eyes popped. He wasn't used to being spoken to like this by a member of his staff. "I . . . you . . ."

Christos stared him into silence, but once having gotten his message home, shifted gears and shrugged sympathetically. "It is the best, Panos," he said, smiling. "Remember, you are the one who said no touch detectors, no invisible walls—you don't want bells going off every time somebody got too close. You said these people knew enough not to touch. Well, no bells went off."

"All right, all right," said Panos, now thoroughly deflated. "It's all my fault. Isn't it always my fault? God damn it," he tacked on, as if to prove he was still in command.

He looked so downcast that Mrs. Papadakis came closer to him and took his hand. With a disgusted glance at her and a grumbled, "Aagh," he jerked it free. *What an unpleasant man,* Alix thought.

Morose silence took over for a few seconds.

"Wait a minute!" Alix exclaimed so abruptly that every face turned toward her. She'd continued to stare at the painting, and the elusive recollection that had been knocked out of her head had suddenly come rushing back. "I don't think that *is* a Manet."

Panos's brow beetled. He glowered at her. "*You* don't think it's a Manet! And who makes you such an expert, better than the scientists?"

Alix had wanted to take her words back the millisecond they were out of her mouth, and now she regretted them even more. Now she'd antagonized Panos too. She should have kept her mouth shut until she'd figured out exactly what it was that was bothering her—or until she'd decided that her connoisseur's eye had played her false this time, which didn't happen often, but did happen. It wasn't magic.

"Mr. Papadakis, I'm sorry, I should have—"

Edward smoothly cut in. "Miss London flew all night to get here, Panos, and now she's taken a pretty severe blow to the head. I say we allow her a little—"

"What's wrong with it?" Panos demanded.

"Um . . ." She dithered, pretty sure that "my stomach tells me" wasn't going to do the trick. "I'm not sure. I may have spoken too quickly."

"I think you just might have, Alix," Edward interceded, smiling. "Perhaps it would help you to know that we have the stamp and seal of the *Laboratoire Forensique*—which, as I'm sure you know, does *not* make mistakes—on the back of the painting; we have two authentication letters from two different experts, both of them incontestable, here on the yacht—you're more than welcome to see them; we have an impeccable catalogue raisonné—"

She was seeing a less appealing side of Edward now, condescending and superior. The innate dismissiveness that seemed to go along with his kind was now apparent, and she warned herself to watch her tongue before she said something else she'd regret. But she didn't have the meekest temper in the world, and he was definitely getting under her skin, not only with his manner but also with what he was saying with so much assurance. Surely he knew that only in dreams did such things exist as a lab that made no mistakes, or an incontestable letter of authenticity, or an impeccable catalogue raisonné (a supposedly complete and faultless catalog of an artist's works and their history). All were based in the end on human judgment— even the laboratory results—and letters of authenticity were written by very human experts, the majority of whom were honest but understandably preferred to provide results that would please whoever was paying them for their services.

"More than that," Edward went on, "*Déjeuner* has an absolutely unassailable provenance that traces it back more than a century and a half, back to the year of its creation. How much more do you want?"

An *unassailable* provenance—that took the cake, but, fortunately for her, Panos started yelling again before she could say anything.

"What is this? Everybody shut up! Who cares about all this stuff— catalogs, letters . . ." He shook his head. "To think such a thing . . . I invite them here, they enjoy my boat, they eat my food, they drink my liquor, they smile and bow . . . and then *this*." He had wound down again and now looked simply poleaxed, standing there slumped, staring mournfully at his ruined treasure.

Christos took advantage of the hiatus. "Panos, this can surely be discussed more beneficially tomorrow. I would like to get this young lady in bed now."

Under ordinary circumstances that would have brought smiles, but only Christos himself showed any reaction to what he'd said. Under the great mustache his mouth twitched, and when he caught Alix's eye he winked, but not in a way to make her uneasy. Alix, exhausted as she was, smiled back.

With no protest from anybody, he escorted her to her stateroom, offered to get her something to help her sleep, which she declined, and departed. She could barely move, but she did manage to undress and get into her pajamas, thought about brushing her teeth, decided that she had earned the right to give it a skip, and slipped into bed. In seconds she was spiraling down into sleep.

12

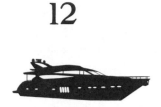

It was the trembling of her eyelashes that woke her, reacting to the morning light that was pouring through the big windows and wheedling its way through the slits between her eyelids. She shifted a few inches to get her face out of the sun, briefly cranked open one eye to look at the watch she hadn't gotten around to taking off when she'd fallen into bed, and saw that it was 7:10. Had she really slept for fourteen hours? She lay with her eyes closed, assessing her condition. Her head ached, no surprise there, but the throbbing was gone and the pain wasn't enough to require anything more than a couple of ibuprofen, if that. And they could wait. Not bad, all things considered. For the moment just lying there, deeply rested, relaxed and unmoving, feeling the sun on her, was lovely, too perfect a state of repose to disturb. But there was nothing she could do about her mind, which swarmed with questions . . . conjectures . . . .

The Manet—why would anyone do that? Jealousy, resentment of the brazen showiness of all this wealth, this opulence that was on display? Maybe. She had no trouble understanding someone's harboring those feelings. Or perhaps it was more personal—antipathy toward Panos over some wrongdoing, real or perceived? *Le Déjeuner* was the painting for which he'd reportedly paid the most and the one that was likely to bring the highest price, so, yes, that had something going for it as an explanation.

Or had Edward Reed been the target? After all, relatively speaking, he had more to lose than Panos did. At least Panos would recoup something from his insurance company, but for Edward it meant the entire loss of his commission. Assuming the painting went for eight or ten million—a conservative guess from what she understood, as it was considered the gem of the collection—and even if he was getting an extreme low-end commission of 2 or 3 percent, that slash had cost him many thousands of dollars.

Except that *she* knew it wasn't the gem of the collection. It wasn't even a real Manet. Could the slasher have known that too, or was it mere coincidence that it was the one painting about which she'd expressed her doubts? No, forget the mere-coincidence hypothesis. Miss Bigmouth here takes one look at the painting and blurts out, in front of Artemis and Edward, that there was "something wrong" with it. Twenty minutes later, maybe less, she's lying under the piano hearing the birdies tweeting, and the painting has been hacked. That'd be some coincidence. But what would be the point of slashing something you knew to be a fake?

And why had the creep, whoever it was, found it necessary to knock her senseless in the process? What was the rush? Couldn't he have just turned around and tiptoed away when he saw her and come back later? Well, there, at least, there were possible explanations that made sense. The obvious one would be that it was someone who was aboard just for the reception, for whom there wouldn't be any "later." The other, less obvious but no less likely, was that it was someone who wanted it to *look* as if it had been someone who was aboard just for the reception. Explanations, yes, but what did they explain?

Where the Manet itself was concerned, though, her uncertainties had diminished. She was more positive than ever that there *was* something wrong with it; she just couldn't say what. Her brain had apparently been plugging away at the problem while she'd slept because she could practically feel the answer nudging away at the undersurface of her consciousness, trying to break through. And when it did, she'd keep it to herself this time instead of instantly announcing it to everybody in range. My God, where had her mind been last night? She'd blabbed it to all of them outright: Papadakis, Mrs. Papadakis, Edward Reed, the security guy. Even Donny had been there. The only person she should conceivably have

93

informed was Ted, back in Washington. He would have had some ideas about where to go with it from there. Talk about a lousy start to undercover work. She didn't know whether to blame it on jet lag, or getting knocked on the head, or inexperience, or opening her mouth without thinking first (she'd heard that one before), or just plain naïveté—

No, beating up on herself wasn't going to get her anywhere. *Okay, you, that's it, knock it off right now*, she commanded her brain, and when that didn't work she pulled herself up against the padded leather headboard and opened both eyes to give herself something else to focus on.

"Whoa," she said softly.

It was the first time she'd really taken in her stateroom beyond goggling at its size when Artemis had first brought her here. That time, she'd been all in a lather about the Manet, which she'd just looked at with Edward, and was in a hurry to get back to it. When Yiorgos had delivered her back to it, she'd been in no shape to notice anything. But now she noticed; she couldn't help but notice.

To start with, its size was the least of it. One curving wall was all glass, three huge, floor-to-ceiling windows—through which she could now see that the yacht was underway, with no land in sight. On two of the other walls hung fragmentary marble reliefs—two muscled warriors' torsos on one, and on the other, three splendid battle horses in profile, their necks arched, their nostrils dilated; they looked to Alix as if they must have come from the same Greek temple. The fourth wall held an extraordinary two-foot section of Roman floor mosaic that showed a lion pouncing on a deer. She placed it somewhere in the first century, about the time that Pompeii was flourishing. She wouldn't have been surprised to learn that it was *from* Pompeii. How it had come into Panos's hands was probably something she didn't want to know.

The walls themselves were paneled with something like cherrywood, but with a subtle pattern that looked like veins of gold. Placed around the room, seemingly at random but not really, were leather armchairs, several low tables, two sofas, a desk with a laptop set up on it, and a flat, wall-mounted TV screen that must have been six feet across. In a niche a few feet from the bed, wedged between two interior walls, was a vanity table made from a single five-foot-wide block of honey-colored, rough-worked stone, probably the remnant of yet another ancient Greek ruin. On its top, beside the hollowed-out sink, was a square-cut crystal vase with what must have been two dozen perfect white roses in it.

The flowers truly were perfect: not a spot of brown, not a wilted petal, not even a misshapen leaf. *Everything* she'd seen so far was perfect and, frankly, it was starting to irritate her. No corners had been cut anywhere, in cost, in craftsmanship, or in maintenance. She'd grown up in a rich environment (not like this, but plenty rich enough), so mere wealth didn't faze her. But the New England blue bloods her family had lived among had conscientiously practiced a kind of conspicuous non-consumption—threadbare (if once costly) rugs, pitted old wooden floors, worn furniture, ultra-nontrendy cars—and she had come to respect its restraint. What she was seeing here was not only conspicuous consumption but conspicuous, if not obscene, opulence. The gleaming wooden banisters on the spiral staircase had shown not a fingerprint or a smudge; the carpets all looked as if no one before her had ever trodden on them; her bed, when she'd first seen it the day before, might have been some contemporary art piece cast in porcelain, so very perfectly had it been made up. Even the launch, now that she thought about it, looked as if it had been bought new that morning, in anticipation of her arrival.

She couldn't really say that there was anything wrong with all this. It was Panos's money and Panos's world, and he had the right to make of it what he wanted. There was nothing wrong with a little more beauty in the world either, and the *Artemis* and all that was in it were certainly beautiful. And of course keeping it the way it was gave employment to craftsmen and artisans and cleaners. All the same, there was something so flagrant about it, so self-congratulatory . . .

Was she envious? Was that at the bottom of it? Did she think *she*, and not people like Panos Papadakis, deserved to have Seurats and Renoirs and Pissarros on her walls? Had her current state of relative impoverish-ment turned her into a knee-jerk malcontent in need of vilifying the super-rich for the sole reason that they were superrich?

She suddenly laughed. Her frown disappeared. No, that was *not* what she needed. What she needed was a giant cup of coffee; that was all. Surely in a place like this there was a way to get it. This looked like a job for Artemis & Co. On the bedside table was a telephone and she was in the act of reaching for it when it softly chimed. *My God,* she thought, *do they even know when I need coffee before I know it myself?*

But it was Mrs. Papadakis on the line. "Alix, good morning, this is Gaby Papadakis. I hope I didn't wake you."

"No, I'm up."

"You're feeling better?"

"Much, thank you."

"Oh, good. I'm not sure if you've had a chance to look at the guest booklet yet, but we don't offer a set lunch or breakfast in any of the dining rooms on the *Artemis*, we leave it up to our guests to order their own when-ever and wherever they feel like it. I was hoping you might like to join me this morning—on the main deck, by the pool? It's a gorgeous day."

"I'd love to, thanks. Which one's the main deck?"

Alix was pleased at the invitation. Her opera-loving mother had been a fan of Gabriela Candelas's, and Alix remembered a performance of *Aida*, seen at the Met in her mother's company, in which Gaby's sensuous, pas-sionate voice had turned even the poisonous Amneris into a tragic figure. Alix's mother had wept, and Alix herself had been impressed.

More recently, in researching the Papadakises for this cruise, she'd learned that she and Gaby shared similar family histories. Gaby's father had been in jail too; was still in jail as far as Alix knew. In the 1970s Peter Candelas had been a mob accountant in New York, first for the Gambino family and then for the Gottis. The suspicions were that his assignments had extended beyond keeping the books, but all the FBI, the New York Police Department, the U.S. Attorney and the New York County District

Attorney were able to make stick were various customs, fraud, and tax manipulation charges. One of her father's brothers and several cousins were in prison on more serious mob-related charges, including homicide. Another of Gaby's uncles had been charged with two murders but remained unconvicted. There was another uncle who had been assassinated by mob rivals. Only two or three years ago, the D.A. had described the whole Candelas clan as "a murderous cancer, not part of the human race." So Gaby had had to cope with a bloodline that made Alix's look like a royal lineage, and she'd done it with great success. All in all, an interesting and unusual woman. Alix looked forward to getting to know her.

"It's the one where the reception was last night . . . oops, I forgot. You didn't make that, did you?"

"I was unavoidably detained."

"I'm glad you can laugh about it," Gaby said. "It's the third deck, the one above you. Nine o'clock, shall we say?"

"Fine. Gabriela . . . uh, Gaby? Did anything interesting happen after I left last night?"

"No," was the answer, accompanied by a deep-throated chuckle. "Everything interesting happened before you left."

"I mean, did they find out who slashed it?"

"No, they haven't found out, but Yiorgos—you remember Yiorgos?"

She thought for a moment "With the mustache. And the muscles."

"That's him, our security chief. He interviewed last night's temporary staff before we left this morning, and now he's talking with the regular crew to see what they might know. He's also supplied the Hellenic Police with a list of last night's guests and they're looking into them all. Yiorgos was a lieutenant colonel with them, you know. It's a high rank, so he still has plenty of clout."

"You're pretty sure it was one of the people here for the reception, then?"

"Of course." She sounded surprised at the question. "Who else? The people here for the cruise are all collectors themselves; they'd never do such a thing. And the crew . . . they're almost all relatives of Panos, and to these Greeks, loyalty to family comes before everything else."

"Yes, you're probably right."

"Panos is furious that someone he invited, someone he trusted, would do this to him. And to *you*." *Oh, sure,* Alix thought sourly. *That was why he'd been so terribly concerned for my welfare last night.* "And let me tell you, my husband, when mad, is something to reckon with. When they find whoever it is, he'll see that they throw the book at him and then some."

"I'd like to throw a book at the guy myself," Alix muttered, fingering the lump above her ear.

"Oh, listen, I almost forgot, there's something Panos wanted me to ask you," Gaby said.

Alix sensed a hesitance, a false brightness, as if Gaby were pretending that whatever it was had just occurred to her.

"It's just that, you know, getting the painting slashed was bad enough, but when you started saying it might not even be real, that kind of upset him. So he asks . . . he asked me to ask you to, well, unless you have something more to go on than just a feeling, to, well . . ."

"To shut up about it."

"That's about it. I'm sure you can understand."

"Tell him not to worry, Gaby. I'm done talking about it, believe me."

She didn't think it would make much difference what she did or didn't do anyway. With the motor-mouthed Donny having been there, she'd be surprised if the whole ship didn't know about it by now. "So is Mr. Papadakis thinking about bringing in another painting for the auction, or just leaving it at twenty-two?"

"Honey, you're asking me questions I don't know the answers to. I'm not exactly privy to everything that goes on around here. I'll see you at nine, yes? Oh, I might have somebody else there that I think you'd enjoy meeting, if that's okay."

"Sure, I'll be there. What do I do to get a cup of coffee before then?"

"You pick up the phone, you dial 'three,' and you say 'coffee.'"

13

The coffee came in a small pewter serving thermos brought by a smiling young stewardess, and of course it was perfect. The two croissants that were delivered with it were also unfaultable: beautifully shaped, warm and buttery, flaky and tender. Not that Alix would have complained if they'd been otherwise. She'd had no dinner the night before, and she was ravenous. In three minutes everything was gone. Another telephone call brought a second pot of coffee, which she consumed in a more civilized fashion, appreciative and reflective. As she did, something new popped into her mind. Why was she assuming that the Manet was the only fake? For all she knew, they could all be fakes. She didn't really think that, but then she hadn't checked, had she? She hadn't "checked" the Manet either; it had just jumped out at her. Well, there was something for her to do today: go through the collection and see if any more jumping-out occurred. Not that she was expecting anything to.

She showered and changed to a tank top and Bermudas, which she was pretty sure would pass for daywear on the *Artemis*. That took her to eight o'clock. With an hour to go, she had time to browse through the rest of the collection to see if there was anything else that didn't seem right. And if anybody was around, it would be a chance to start fulfilling the twin responsibilities she'd signed on for: schmoozing with the other guests for Papadakis, and inconspicuously trolling for fractional investment tidbits for the FBI.

At this early hour she had the music room, where the Impressionists were displayed, to herself. She moved quickly from painting to painting, partly because after last night, she was a little edgy about standing in one place for too long, but mostly because she wasn't "studying" them; she was just seeing what might catch that celebrated—or bogus, depending on whom you talked to—connoisseur's eye of hers. Nothing did. Nice to know, but no real surprise there.

Generally speaking, all seemed as well as could be expected in the room; no further slashings, anyway. The torn Manet had been removed and the remaining paintings on that wall had been redistributed over-night, so one couldn't even tell where it had hung. The ash paneling looked as flawless as ever, not a spackled hole, not a sign of repair. It was if the Manet had never been there. Would she have an opportunity to look at it again and see if she could determine what it was that was wrong with it? She was pretty sure Panos wouldn't give her the chance, and she was in no position to press. That wouldn't stop her from chewing it over, though. She remembered it well enough, and if cogitation and research could do the job, she'd figure it out. It wasn't Edward or Panos she'd tell about it, though; it was Ted, and he could take it from there.

Gaby's shawl no longer draped the piano, and there was one painting that was supposed to be there that she didn't find, by Claude Monet, one of his extraordinary, light-flooded studies of Rouen Cathedral. She made a mental note to ask Edward where it was hung.

On into the salon, where the Contemporary paintings were displayed. This room was about the same size as the music room, but with walls made of three-foot squares of glossy brown granite flecked with yellow and orange. The carpet was a pale tan with a mazelike pattern that she sup-posed might represent the Minotaur's lair at Knossos, on the island of Crete, toward which they were at this moment headed. The pattern was repeated on the fabric of the half-dozen armchairs that were scattered about. On the walls, in addition to the paintings, were a few more tasteful Greek and Roman reliefs. It was altogether another quite splendid room, but Alix was starting to succumb to splendor burnout. Besides, she was more interested in the people in the room.

There were two of them, a tall, bony woman with an extraordinary mop of frizzy, orange hair that surrounded and stood out from her head like a thick cloud of dandelion seed, and a shorter, rounder man, both standing in front of what Alix recognized as the Rothko. Like most Rothko's, it was big, about six feet by five. This was Rothko as he had painted in the 1950s, a vertical stack of fuzzy, irregular rectangles in warm, earthen colors. She wasn't ready to admit him to her pantheon of the Greats, but she did find this period of his work pleasing in an interior-decorator sort of way. The stacked rectangles seemed to breathe, to go in and out of focus, in a way that soothed and relaxed.

As she got closer, she heard the woman say: "I *need* this painting, Durward. It's terrific." The woman's gaze wandered lovingly over it. "It has everything I look for in a work of art. Everything."

Alix stopped where she was to listen, partly because she was curious to hear what this woman liked so much about the picture, but mostly because she was already relishing Geoff's reaction when she informed him that he'd been his usual high-handed and judgmental self in writing off these people as philistines who neither knew nor cared anything about art beyond its investment potential. At least some of them (at least one of them) were genuine lovers of art who knew what they were looking for and why.

"I know just what you mean, Miss C," the young man said, his voice thrumming with excitement. "It's just beautiful. The colors are amazing. They leap off the canvas at you in great swaths—"

"Control yourself, Durward," Miss C said dryly. "You're trying too hard again. That is *not* what I mean. What *I* see leaping off the canvas at me is liquidity, security of principal, proven record, and a practically guaranteed return on investment along with a huge growth potential in a market that's only now beginning to find its feet."

Alix managed not to break out laughing, but only with an effort. *Good old Geoff,* she was thinking. *There wasn't too much he got wrong.*

"Good morning," she called before they found her eavesdropping on their own.

Miss C turned and stared coldly at her. "Yes?" The woman had a determinedly off-putting glare. "Is there something I can do for you?"

A little civility would be a good start. "No. I was just having a look at the paintings," she said, smiling. "I'm Alix London."

The woman thought for a moment and then finally showed some interest. "Oh, you're the lecture lady."

"I guess that's me, yes. Happy to meet you."

"Yes, I was planning to stop by your session this afternoon and say hello."

"My session?"

"'Informal chat session,' it was called. You're supposed to be making yourself available to edify us on the paintings, didn't you know? From three to five on the days we're at sea, I think it is. It's in the guest booklet."

"No, I haven't had a chance to look at that yet." She was pleased. *Chat session* sounded a lot more up her alley than *lecture.* If that was all that was expected of her, she was going to do just fine.

"So, Alix, the word is that you had yourself a little excitement last night. Tell me, did he truly wrap you up in that shawl and fling you bodily down the steps?"

"Not down the steps, no, it wasn't quite as exciting as that, thank goodness. Awful about the painting, though."

"But he knocked you out, didn't he, or is that just a rumor too? How are you feeling now?"

"Oh, I'm fine. Could have been a lot worse."

"Well, that's good. Too bad we can't say the same for the Manet."

"Yes."

There was an awkward pause during which Alix waited, expecting her to introduce herself, but it didn't happen. "And you are . . . ?" she asked.

The woman blinked. "Are you serious?"

"Well . . . yes. I'm sorry, have we met?"

"You *are* serious. Damn. I'm Izzy Clinke."

"Izzy . . ." Alix echoed. After a second, it came to her. This gangly, quietly sardonic woman who loved Rothko because his paintings provided security of principal was the famous pop singer Donny had been raving about? The words *I gotta have mo'* suddenly took on new meaning. "Pocahontas?" she asked hesitantly.

"I should say so," said the man, his first words to Alix. He was a blinking, spreading, soft-looking young guy in serious horn-rimmed glasses, the sort of person, she thought, who should have been wearing a short-sleeved white shirt and tie, with a pen holder stuffed with ballpoints in the pocket. When she took a second look, she saw that, with the exception of the tie, he was.

"This is Durward," Izzy said.

"Durward G. Sternberg," said Durward, shaking hands with Alix. The handshake was firm, but the hand itself was as squashy as Alix expected it to be.

"Durward is my factotum," Izzy said with a perfectly straight face.

He nodded his agreement.

Alix laughed, thinking that a joke was being made. Who seriously calls somebody else a "factotum"? And does it right to his face? And has it promptly acknowledged? But neither of them returned the smile.

"You certainly laugh easily," Izzy said. "You must have a very happy life." The rueful implication seemed to be that she herself had anything but. It was hard to tell, though. Izzy had a curious way of speaking, halfway between supercilious and self-mocking, that gave much of what she said a wry tinge of irony, as if she were an observer taking in everything she saw, including herself, with tolerant, faintly cynical amusement.

"I'm not complaining," Alix said. "Well, it's a pleasure to know you, Izzy. I'd better go. I'm supposed to be meeting somebody by the swimming pool."

"Which one?"

"There's more than one swimming pool?"

"Well, of course. I mean, you really can't expect people not to go swimming just because it's raining, can you? Or snowing, for that matter. But I suspect you mean the one on the main deck, aft. Would it be Gaby that you're meeting, by any chance?"

"It is, yes."

"Well, so am I. I guess we're a threesome. I'll walk with you, then. Durward, have you dealt with my e-mail? Taken care of the Sony cover letter? Asked the Bellagio what the hell they want from me? Straightened out the mess with Ralph Lauren?"

Each of these questions was answered with a self-satisfied little simper.

"Good. Go forget about me for a while, then. Be bold. Take what comes to you. Enjoy life."

After she and Alix had gone a few steps, she called back to him: "You've got your pager, right?" He tapped his belt to show that he did.

Alix smiled as they started again. "That makes it a little hard for him to forget about you, doesn't it?"

"Oh, it does him good. He lives to please. You know, Durward may not look like much, but the man is a jewel. Not only is he totally devoted to me, he is the world's most efficient person, whereas I am the world's most disorganized human being. I'd be totally lost without him. I don't go *anywhere* without him."

They walked a little farther and Izzy said, "Alix, I'm sorry I was so stiff at first. I thought you were one of the crew and you were going to ask me to autograph your forehead, or babble about how much you love my stupid songs, or something, and that's what I'm here to get away from. I just want to be Izzy Clinke for a week. Well, that and to come away with that gorgeous Rothko if I can."

"Well, I can't do much to help you with the Rothko, but I can certainly promise not to bring up Pocahontas again." That would take no effort at all, since she'd pretty much exhausted her knowledge of the singer, all of which had come from Donny, and of popdom in general.

As they walked through what seemed to be the ship's library, lined by shelves filled with flawlessly lined-up books that looked as if they'd never been opened, and a few window alcoves that held two or three armchairs, Alix heard her name called.

She turned, thinking someone was trying to get her attention, but she saw that it had come from a couple of breakfasting men in one of the alcoves with their chairs angled toward the sea. One of them was Edward Reed. The other was someone she hadn't seen before.

"Alix London?" the one she didn't know repeated even more incredulously than he'd said it the first time. "*That's* the lecturer you've chosen; that's our expert?"

"Yes, Alix London," was Edward's measured reply. "I gather you've heard of her, then?"

"If it's who I'm thinking of, I have. But surely you don't mean the daughter of that—"

"Well, yes, that's right, but she's not her father, and, you know—"

"And wasn't she in the middle of some sordid affair in Santa Fe, where—"

"Well, yes, she was, but really, Emil, she has firmly established her credentials as a legitimate and bona fide authority on—"

"Credentials!" The Danish pastry he'd had in his hand was tossed contemptuously onto his plate. "Edward, I know all about this person. I still have my contacts at Harvard—my second doctorate is from Harvard, you know, the first being from Oxford—and I happen to know—as you certainly should have known—that she dropped out of school there . . . in her *junior* year. The woman never earned a degree. She *has* no credentials! What she has, as I understand it, is a 'connoisseur's eye.'" His tone left no doubt about his opinion of connoisseurs' eyes.

"I fully understand your point, Emil," Edward said, "but, er, Panos settled on her, and . . . well, you know what Panos can be like."

"Unfortunately, I do."

Alix, her curiosity naturally aroused, had slowed her step to get a look at the new man as she and Izzy climbed the aft stairs to the main deck. Like Edward, he was in his mid-fifties and had probably been good looking as a young man, but he was one of those people (unlike Edward) to whom age had not been kind. His hairline was receding now and he was running to fat, with a defeated, hangdog look to his sloping shoulders. His criticism of Alix had been not so much blustery as put-upon, as if her presence aboard was a calculated personal affront to him. He spoke with one of those very slight, hard-to-pin-down Continental accents.

"And now—" he was still at it "—she's been on the *Artemis* not even one day, and already . . ."

But Alix and Izzy were out of earshot. Izzy grinned another of her taut smiles. "Looks as if I'm not the only celebrity aboard."

"Oh, I'm used to it," Alix said resignedly, but she was pleased to see a distinct change in Izzy's manner, as if her notoriety made them comrades in arms. "I'd hoped maybe it wouldn't come up, but I can't say I'm surprised."

"Well, I wouldn't take anything Emil Varga says personally. It's just his way. Faultfinding, nit-picking, they come naturally to him. You name it, he'll pooh-pooh it. You'll see."

"Sounds like you know him pretty well?"

"I don't know about 'pretty well,' but, sure, we all know each other. We may not all be friends, exactly, but all of us have been on Panos's cruises before, and nobody's killed anybody else. Yet. Give it a little time, you'll understand the guy better."

"Yes, but will I like him any better?"

Izzy grinned. "Hasn't worked for me."

"He has some kind of accent, doesn't he? Russian or something like that."

"Yeah, he was born in Lithuania, or Bulgaria, or one of those. I don't know, Macedonia? Came over when he was a kid."

The stairwell opened onto the main deck, and they were drawn to the handrail to get the full benefit of the wonderful blue expanse of cloud-flecked sky and calm sea, and the sweet, fresh morning air that went along with them.

"Beautiful," Izzy sighed, looking out over the Aegean and sucking in a couple of deep breaths, but she was still thinking about Emil. "See, what his problem is, is that he thinks he's some kind of intellectual giant. You heard all that crap—Oxford this, Harvard that—and yet he's stuck in some rinky-dink art museum in Maine or someplace, and the only reason he's the director there is that he inherited the job from his wife's uncle, whose collection started the place fifty years ago. He can't get his head around how that happened to him.

"And then there's the wife, Maddy." Izzy shook her head. "She's all over him every minute, correcting his grammar, telling him his shirt's buttoned wrong, criticizing his table manners, contradicting him every chance she gets. If he says, 'I like quiche,' she says, 'No, you don't, you hate quiche.' And I'm not making that up, that's an exact quote. I was there. If she's that way in public, you can imagine the way she is at home."

"I can hardly wait to meet her."

"You won't get the chance. She stayed home this time. I don't have a clue how he managed that, but all I can say is, thank heaven for small blessings. Oh, listen, there's something else you probably should know about Emil to understand him. He's not poor—he couldn't be and still be in the fractional investment consortium —but he's not in the same league as the rest of us high rollers, and anyway, the money is hers, not his. I think that makes him a little defensive too, you know? Insecure."

"Interesting." Alix paused for a moment. A chance for a little trolling, she thought. "Fractional investment plan?" she repeated innocently. "What exactly is that?"

But Izzy was peering over Alix's shoulder. "Hey, there's Gaby, waiting for us by the pool. Shall we join her?"

14

Only there wasn't any pool, not this morning. Alix had read in *Amazing Yachts* how the *Artemis*'s main-deck swimming pool, considered a marvel when the yacht was constructed, was a triple-duty affair. Most of the time it functioned as a roomy, six-foot-deep pool, but if there was to be dancing in the evening the water would be drained and the faux mosaic floor, with its larger-than-life image of the famed Minoan bull-leapers fresco, would be raised flush with the deck to provide a dance floor. And if a helicopter were expected, the raised swimming-pool floor could then be covered with a portable landing pad.

Apparently, a helicopter was expected today; a three-man crew was struggling to get the bulky, folding pad in place.

"We anticipating company?" Izzy asked as they reached Gaby, who was in a straight-backed deck chair over near the railing, sipping tomato juice. *Or was it a Bloody Mary*, Alix wondered.

"Yes, our final guest should be landing shortly."

"Oh, right, our own touch of royalty, Saskia, hereditary Countess of Brabant, or so she claims. I wondered why Her Majesty didn't make her usual regal appearance at dinner."

"No, Saskia's not coming. She stepped off a curb the wrong way in Antwerp a couple of days ago and tore up her knee, so she's sending a nephew in her place, with full authority to act as her proxy in the bidding. I understand they left Athens with him an hour ago, so he should be here pretty soon. Hey, pull up a chair, you two. I see you've met without my help."

They sat down with her around a small table, and Izzy immediately squinted and put up her hand to shade her eyes. The sun was very bright. Alix was wearing a visor and was getting out her sunglasses, and Gaby already had both on. Izzy had come out with neither. She opened her telephone and hit a button. "Visor," she said into it. "And sunglasses. No, Durward, I do not care what color."

While she was speaking, Gaby had nodded at someone over Alix's shoulder, and Alix turned to see Panos Papadakis approaching, topped by a broad-brimmed straw hat and casually dressed in polo shirt and Bermudas, but looking even more bulgy and uncomfortably stuffed into his clothing than he had in a tuxedo.

"Have you ever noticed," Izzy whispered sidewise to Alix, "how many fat people seem to think tight clothes make them look thinner? Doesn't work, does it?"

"Not too well in this case," Alix whispered back.

"Good morning, good morning, ladies!" Panos sang, whipping off his hat.

"Good morning, dear," Gaby replied. "You're very cheerful this morning."

"And why I shouldn't be cheerful when I step out on my deck and the first sight that greets my eyes is three such beautiful ladies? I must be in heaven, ha-ha-ha."

Gaby smiled in return but was glancing around as if she were looking for someplace to hide.

"And you, dear lady," Panos said to Alix, "how you are feeling this morning? Better, I hope? I'm *so* sorry for what happens to you last night. What a terrible, terrible thing."

"Thank you very much, Mr. Papadakis, I'm just fine."

"Panos! You must call me Panos," he said with an expansive gesture. "Please!" He placed his hand over his heart.

"Thank you. I wish I could have done something to protect your painting, though."

"Poof, as long as you are not hurt, that is the important thing."

The jovial, expansive, geniality-oozing Panos who now smiled so broadly down on her was like a completely new person, someone she hadn't met before. All things considered, she thought she might prefer the other persona: abrasive, inconsiderate, and overbearing. If nothing else, it was more natural on him.

It occurred to her that the befriend-and-betray quandary that she'd been fretting about might be moot in Panos's case. His oily, unconvincing bonhomie this morning served to accentuate the nastiness that had poured out of him last night: the brutal way he'd treated Gaby, the vulgar emphasis he'd put on the Manet's market value (despite his cringingly insincere "principle of the thing"), and his crude arrogance and undisguised disrespect for everyone around him. Add to all that the fact that he himself was befriending and betraying his investors, and the idea of betraying him, if that's what it was, was no longer so troubling. Befriending him—that would have been the hard part.

"Gaby, my darling wife," he said, redirecting his smile to her and lowering his voice, "you spoke with Alix about that matter I asked . . . to keep to herself what she . . . yes?"

"Yes, and she will."

"Keep what to yourself?" Izzy asked Alix with interest.

"Oh, it's just something that Mr. Papadakis . . . Panos . . . felt—"

"What, that the Manet is a fake?"

Panos's good humor swirled away like water down a drain. Down came his eyebrows. Down turned his mouth. "Where did you hear this? Who was it who told you this?" He turned his scowl on Gaby and then on Alix, trying to decide which of them was the guilty party.

"For heaven's sake, Panos," Izzy said, "don't get so excited. It's all over the place. Everybody's talking about it."

"I didn't say it was a fake," Alix said, trying both to smooth the waters and to set the record straight. "I said there was something about it that didn't seem right to me. But it was just an impression at the time, it doesn't mean—"

"Dionysodaurus," Panos uttered in a low growl. "Bastard. I should know . . . I should . . ." He kept the rest of the thought to himself, but it was obvious that this wasn't going to be a good day for the purser of the *Artemis*.

"I must leave you now," Panos said abruptly and stalked grimly off.

"*Was* it Donny?" Gaby asked Izzy.

"No, actually, it was one of the stews. She was talking about it in the lounge last night. But I asked her where she heard it, and she said she got it straight from somebody who was there—"

"Donny," Gaby said with a nod.

"Right. This is a guy who doesn't know the meaning of keeping something to himself. Believe me, I learned the hard way." Izzy grinned. "I heard some pretty good stories about you too, Gab."

Gaby took this seriously. "About me? Like what?"

Alix could see that Izzy was sorry she'd said anything. "Oh, hell, nothing, just stupid stories, nothing embarrassing, nothing you have to worry about. Still, if Panos didn't want people to know about last night, it's Donny he should have told to keep his mouth shut, not you, Alix. You'd think he'd know that."

"He did," Gaby said. "He asked *everybody* to keep quiet about it. Well, except Alix. I got that job."

"Gaby," Izzy said, "does it seem to you that Donny's getting worse? I don't know, more devious, more of a gossipmonger, a scandalmonger, maybe a little too big for his boots?"

"All of the above. Alix, he brought you over on the launch, didn't he? He behaved himself, didn't he?"

"Oh, he didn't do anything I can complain about, but . . . well, I can't say that he inspired a lot of trust in his judgment."

"You really ought to talk to Panos about doing something about him, Gaby," Izzy said.

"You know, I just might do that. After all, I have so much influence on him." She gave an almost imperceptible nod in no particular direction and a male steward materialized at her side, awaiting instructions.

"I'll just have fresh fruit and yogurt this morning, Takis," she said, "and pastries and coffee for all." And to Alix: "As Izzy already knows, just ask away, whatever your heart desires. Our chef's a genius; he can do anything. If you want something simple, you couldn't do better than one of his Greek omelets."

"A Greek omelet sounds wonderful," Alix said, and Takis, nodding, murmured, "Greek omelet." He was as spick-and-span as every other crew member whom Alix had seen so far (including the three wrestling with the landing pad, who were apparently not permitted to sweat).

"And for you, madame," he said to Izzy, "a plain egg-white omelet made with two eggs, accompanied by sliced cucumbers and one Rye-Krisp cracker, dry. And a glass of cranberry juice."

"Whoa, there, Takis," Izzy said, "that's some memory you have."

"You are hard to forget, madame."

Izzy smiled her response but as he left she screwed up her eyes. "Was that a compliment, or wasn't it?"

"Of course it was a compliment," Gaby said. "They're programmed to provide nothing but what guests want to hear. You should know that by now." She closed her eyes and turned her face up to the sun. "You know I ordinarily go for a bigger breakfast than fruit and yogurt," she said lazily. "Well, not bigger, but more protein rich. You know—food. But this morning . . ." She shook her head. "I'm not feeling all that spunky. I drank a lot more than was good for me last night. If either of you see me doing that again on this cruise, kindly shove me over the railing. But you won't. See me doing that."

Alix believed her. Gaby was looking a lot more put together and a lot less pathetic than she had the night before. Seen like this, in brilliant daylight, sober, and with no makeup other than lipstick, there was something stable and reassuring about her, something resolute. There was a subtle overlay of sadness too, or regret, but who wouldn't regret being married to Panos? She wasn't really as overweight as she'd appeared last night either; it had been the puffiness of too much alcohol too quickly consumed that had made her seem that way—that and her softening jawline. She was still quite attractive, really, but in a more mature, almost motherly way.

"So, ladies, what shall we—" Izzy began, but Gaby interrupted.

"Wait, before anything else, I want to apologize to you, Alix."

Alix was getting a little uneasy. Why was everybody apologizing to her?

"That scene I made last night?" Gaby said. "You must have wondered why I got so upset about that old rag that had been on the piano."

I sure did, Alix thought. "Not at all, Gaby."

"You see, that was my *Carmen* shawl. I wore that at La Scala, at Covent Garden. . . ." She smiled. "I wore it at the Met, with Domingo as my *Don José* . . ." For a moment she appeared poised to float off into the past, but she caught herself. "It's one of the very few mementos that I kept from those days, and it held a lot of good memories for me."

"But surely you can have it repaired," Alix said.

"I suppose so, but now somehow it's been, I don't know, defiled . . . tarnished . . . now it's a reminder of something I *don't* want to remember."

"You know what you need?" Izzy said, slapping the table. "You need to come shopping with me. Remember that wonderful little street in Corfu? Let's go buy some stuff when we get there. There are very few upsets in life that a few pairs of shoes and a couple dozen scarves and four or five new bags won't cure."

"Maybe," Gaby said without conviction, "but you know, possessions—*things*—don't mean too much to me anymore. I already have tons of stuff, more than anybody has a right to have, but " She hunched her shoulders. "—in the end, it's nothing. It's meaningless. It's worthless. The shawl was different. It meant something. It meant something good that I don't have anymore." She smiled at Alix. "Anyway, that's why I was being such a crybaby about it."

"I understand completely, and there's absolutely nothing to apologize for." Alix couldn't help noticing that there was a beautiful burgundy-red leather satchel tossed carelessly at Gaby's feet, the way you see them in those full-page Louis Vuitton ads. Three thousand dollars, minimum, Alix thought. *Meaningless*, maybe, but not exactly *worthless*.

She sensed someone zip by, and when she looked up she caught sight of a man speeding away from them, elbows churning, not technically running in that both feet were never off the deck at the same time but moving at a hell of a clip all the same.

"No, that was not an errant ballistic missile," Izzy told her. "That was the famous man of mystery, Mirko Koslecki. Have you met him yet?"

"No, I haven't. Why is he famous? And what makes him so mysterious?"

"Mirko's the Man Without a Country," Gaby explained, "the Homeless Billionaire."

"Come again?"

"You haven't heard about the Homeless Billionaire? Come on, everybody's heard of the Homeless Billionaire."

"Everybody's heard of me too," Izzy said, laughing. "Not Alix, though."

"I heard of Gaby," Alix said in her own defense. She thought it best not to mention that she'd first heard of her from her mother, who had been such a big fan.

"He's coming around again. He always does a few turns. I'll introduce you," Gaby said, "assuming I can get him to slow down," and a few seconds later: "Hey, Mirko!"

The man braked and guardedly approached. "Good morning, Gaby. Izzy." He spoke with another one of those hard-to-place Continental accents: a compact man, long-necked, small-headed, alert, and darty. It seemed to Alix that there was something nervous and furtive in his manner, something . . . well, weasely. He eyed the three women the way you might look at a trio of hungry lions from whom you were separated by a set of bars that didn't look up to the task. He was very short, no more than five-five, with tiny, delicate, graceful hands.

"Mirko," said Gaby, "I'd like you to meet Alix London. Alix, Mirko Koslecki."

Mirko offered a precise half bow, so crisp that his lank, straight, black hair flipped down over his forehead and then back up again when he straightened. If he'd been wearing shoes instead of sneakers, Alix thought, she would have heard his heels click. "A pleasure, good morning." And off he went, having barely come to a complete stop.

"Not exactly what you'd call Mr. Conviviality, is he?" Alix said.

"He's not the world's biggest talker, no," Gaby agreed, "and he tends not to spend much time standing in one place. No moss grows on Mirko."

"Which, essentially, is why they call him the Man Without a Country," Izzy put in. "A fascinating guy, really. I'm not sure he's really up in Billionaireland, but he must be close. As for not having a country, though, that's way off base. The man has more of them than he knows what to do with. He was born in the United States and his mother was from Hungary and his father was from, I forget, Macedonia, or Herzegovina—"

"Montenegro," Gaby contributed.

"Right, and so that gave him three passports right there, the day he was born. And then, later, he put a lot of money into some resort in Aruba, or maybe it was the Bahamas, or one of those places down there—"

"St. Kitts," Gaby said.

"Okay, whatever, and they gave him a citizenship in return, and then I know he's got at least one more from New Zealand, I think it is—" She paused, awaiting Gaby's interjection.

"Australia," Gaby said on cue. "I know because I've seen it, but don't ask me how he got it. Anyway he's got six in all."

"But seriously, he has no home?" Alix asked.

"Hence the name," Gaby said. "What he does have is a chain of five-star hotels all around the world, and he keeps a permanent suite in each one, and those are basically where he lives, but only a couple of weeks at a time and then he moves on. He doesn't own a car, either, or a television set, or even a wristwatch."

"You really know a lot about him," Izzy said.

"Well, we were pretty good friends at one time," Gaby said, dropping her eyes. Alix saw splotches of pink jump out on the sides of her throat.

Oho, there's a history there, Alix thought, pretending not to notice. "But if he doesn't own anything, what's he doing at an art auction? What would he do with a painting? Or is he just here for the cruise experience?"

"He's not here for the cruise experience, I can tell you that much. He once rented the *Christina O,* Onassis's old yacht, for a week when he felt like a cruise—at seventy-five thousand dollars a day, plus running expenses, and, believe me, the *Christina O* makes the *Artemis* look like a tugboat. No, he's here for the auction. He's got a fabulous art collection, but he doesn't *own* it in the usual sense. Couldn't be bothered with maintaining it, so the whole thing—every painting, every sculpture—is on loan to one museum or another whose board he's on, or to one or another of his hotels, where they keep it on display except when he comes to visit, when they put it up in his suite."

Alix just shook her head. It was hard to associate the jumpy little man she'd just been talking to with the romantic, larger-than-life—if terribly isolated—person she was hearing about.

"Really," Gaby continued, "in the sense that we usually mean 'own,' the one thing he has is this beautiful little Learjet—well, not so little—for getting around from hotel to hotel. He only has one personal employee—"

His factotum, Alix thought with a smile.

"—his pilot, who also buys him a few days' worth of clothes when he needs them—which eventually get left in one of his hotel rooms. He claims he doesn't even own a suitcase."

"I can confirm that," Izzy said. "Donny picked us up together yesterday, and he had all his stuff in a couple of grocery bags, one of which was pretty small. Compared to my two big trunks. Mirko's one unusual guy."

Alix laughed. "I'd say 'unusual' doesn't even come close. I'd say he sounds, well . . . weird."

Gaby gave it some thought. "No, I wouldn't say that. Unique for sure, but not weird. He's just got this aversion to baggage, real or emotional, and he's got the resources and the *cojones* to gratify it. Never raised a family, never been married, never linked to a woman, or to some other guy, for that matter, always a step ahead of whoever's badgering him. Just completely his own man."

"You sound almost envious," Alix said.

"Alix, I almost am."

"I know I am," Izzy said. "And there's no 'almost' about it. I kid you not."

The two older women smiled wistfully at each other, and Gaby added, "Maybe someday."

The exchange made Alix uncomfortable and she looked for something else to talk about. "Okay," she said, "I've met Mirko, and you, of course, Izzy, and I've seen the man from Maine, Emil Varga, and then there's the Belgian lady, or rather her nephew, who hasn't shown yet. That's four. Aren't there five altogether? Who am I missing?"

To her surprise they both laughed. "His name's Lorenzo Bolzano; he's a collector from Florence."

"And what's he like?"

Izzy and Gaby looked at each other and laughed again.

"Well . . ." Gaby said and let it hang.

"Let me put it this way," Izzy said. "Let's just say he's indescribable. You'll have to see for yourself."

"Now I'm really intrigued."

"Oh, you'll enjoy him," Gaby said. "He's good fun . . . as long as you don't have to take too much of him at a time. Wait'll you hear him talk. It's amazing."

"Yeah, but have you ever understood anything he said?" Izzy asked.

"Never; not a word." And to Alix, who was looking puzzled, "Don't worry, you'll see."

Durward showed up with Izzy's visor and sunglasses. "Here you go, Miss C."

Izzy stared incredulously at them, one in each hand. "You got me a *mauve* visor and *green* sunglasses?"

Durward looked stunned. "But you said I should—"

"Oh, hell, it doesn't matter, forget it."

He reached for them. "I'll go and—"

Izzy pulled them back. "*Forget* it, Durward, I'll deal with it."

Durward left, his shoulders drooping, and Izzy said, "I hate to do that to him, I really do, but it has to be done occasionally so he doesn't think he's perfect. I'll make it up to him later. Anyway, you know those inflatable punching-bag clowns—you knock 'em over and they bounce right back up? That's Durward."

The steward brought the coffee and pastries and poured cups for each of them.

"Alix," Gaby said, adding cream to hers, "have you really never heard of Izzy? That is, of Pocahontas? She's on TV all the time."

"I thought I was impossible to escape," Izzy agreed. "I don't know how you managed to get away with it."

Gaby laughed. "Pay no attention to her. She's incredible. You've never seen anything like it. You'd think she didn't have any *bones*. And that weird expression, like she's a million miles away on some other planet—"

"That part's easy," Izzy said. "Comes naturally."

"No, really," Gaby persisted. "You can't take your eyes off her. It's as if she's in some kind of trance, and then after a minute you're in one too. Somehow, watching her is relaxing and stimulating at the same time, it's—well, you really have to see for yourself, Alix. Look at one of her videos and you'll see what I mean." She'd been leaning enthusiastically forward, and now she sat back and picked up her coffee.

Izzy smiled faintly over the rim of her own cup. "Is that it?"

Gaby looked puzzled. "What do you mean? Did I miss something?"

Izzy arched one tweezed eyebrow. "I notice you made no reference to my vocal qualities."

"Your vocal qualities!" Gaby shifted into a plummy English accent. "Oh, very nice, indeed, my dear, but personally, I prefer singing."

She accompanied this with a deep-throated, melodious laugh straight out of her old Verdi repertoire, and that made all three of them laugh like old friends. Alix had warmed up to both of them more quickly than she usually did with strangers.

"Oh, just put me down as jealous," Gaby said, sobering. "Izzy, you were so damn smart to stick with your career instead of . . . ah, what the hell, it's too late now."

"Well, it's not like I had a lot of choice in the matter, Gaby. The guys chasing me weren't exactly the cream of the potential-husband crop. There weren't any fairy-tale gazillionaires who came to me on bended knee wanting to turn me into a princess." She raised one eyebrow in thought. "Well, there was one, but he was too bizarre, even for me. Anyway, why would I want to get married? Durward provides everything I need from a husband, and he doesn't bother me with all the sex crap. I'm happy."

"Fairy tale," Gaby said. "Yup, that's my life in a nutshell. Princess first, and then a wrinkle or two turns up on your face, and poof, you're a pumpkin." She smiled. "Except that if Panos had gotten down on bended knee, he wouldn't have been able to get up again." She tossed her head and turned to Alix. "Ever been married, Alix?"

"Briefly," she answered and then seized on the opportunity to change the subject that Takis's arrival with their breakfasts offered. "Wow, that smells wonderful."

As they ate, the conversation turned to the usual safe female topics—food, fashion, travel. The omelet she'd ordered really was worth talking about, wonderfully fluffy and quiche-like, cooked in olive oil and filled with melting goat cheese and chives. And after the subject of food was exhausted, she was able to hold her own in the fashion talk. Before hanging out for those weekly happy hours with Chris at her wine bar, she'd have been at sea. Until then, what she'd known about fashion had been ten years out of date. There had indeed been a time when she'd worn outfits straight from the designer showrooms, but dear old Dad's debacle had put an end to that. And afterward, in those years of dedicated art restoration study with Santullo, she'd totally lost interest in the subject and never regained it. A good thing, too, given her current economic status. But Chris had made the fashion reeducation of Alix one of her objectives, on the simple grounds that any fully formed woman of today should know such things. Alix didn't quite agree, but she seemed to have absorbed a lot of information, mostly by osmosis.

Sitting there, Alix was struck by the fact that she was somewhere between the two women at the table, metaphorically as well as physically. Careers and marriage had become more complex in today's world, and both were littered with land mines. Gaby had apparently walked into her minefield willingly, but Alix was in no position to feel superior. She herself, after all, had once been married to Paynton Whipple-Pruitt, of *the* Whipple-Pruitts (of Boston, Watch Hill, and Palm Beach), patrons of the arts, society-page regulars, and stalwarts of New England's inbred, old-money elite. And first-class prigs, one and all.

How she'd gotten herself into that situation in the first place was something she was trying to forget and certainly had no desire to talk about. With anybody. Suffice it to say that it had happened at a bad time, the most susceptible and insecure time of her life. Geoff's self-destruction had just occurred and with her college savings, along with the family money, gone, she suddenly had no family, no money, and no future. Bereft and adrift, she'd accepted Paynton's noblesse-oblige-motivated proposal of marriage. It hadn't taken her long to get a grip, though, and to comprehend the enormity of her mistake. On day number eleven of their wedded life, she had begun the process of filing for divorce—this despite the prenuptial agreement drawn up by the Whipple-Pruitt attorneys that allowed her nothing at all if the marriage lasted less than a year. That had been fine with her; she'd had no interest in contesting it or negotiating something less draconian. She just wanted out.

That put her more in Izzy's camp than in Gaby's, she supposed, although her choice of a career—could you call art consulting a career?— had proved a pretty rocky road so far. But as she'd truthfully told Izzy a little while ago, she wasn't complaining. She was where she wanted to be, things were looking up, and life could hardly have been more interesting.

The clatter of an approaching helicopter brought her from her thoughts, and suddenly everybody was rushing around. Stewards and stewardesses descended on them to usher them safely away from the landing pad and to clear away the table and chairs. The two- or three-passenger helicopter—white with Prussian-blue detailing (she was starting to think of it as Papadakis blue)—hovered directly overhead, a few hundred feet up, and the clatter grew deafening. It got even worse as the big machine descended, and Alix had to cover her ears, as did Gaby and Izzy.

Then came the terrific wind from the rotor blades. "Damn!" Izzy exclaimed as it tore the visor from her head and sent it sailing into the sea. "Well, at least it was the mauve one," she muttered. Gaby and Alix managed to grab and hold onto their own visors. The copter's landing skids touched down, the rotor slowed, and the wind fell away. From somewhere, Panos Papadakis approached as a one-man welcoming committee, and then Gaby went to stand beside him. Other guests, drawn by the helicopter's arrival, also gathered nearby. Alix and Izzy remained on the edge of the crowd.

The passenger door of the pod swung open, and a dark-haired, youngish man with a sport coat slung over his shoulder hopped athletically out onto the deck, hand extended, already returning Panos's smile.

Behind Alix's sunglasses, her eyes widened.

You've got to be kidding, she thought.

15

The good-looking man who had dropped so effortlessly to the deck was—unmistakably, indubitably, inarguably . . . and inexplicably—Special Agent Ted Ellesworth of the Federal Bureau of Investigation's art squad. Alix was stunned not only into silence, but into total incomprehension. She had not the faintest clue to what was going on, so she simply stood quietly where she was and waited for him to call the shots.

"Well, now," Izzy said in a low, appreciative voice, "not bad. Hey, if his mother's a countess, does that make him a count?"

"It's his aunt, not his mother," said Alix, whose wits were beginning to reassemble, "and no, I don't think it does." She continued to watch as Panos, once again wreathed in oleaginous smiles, stepped forward. "Mr. de Beauvais, I welcome you greatly to my little boat. I am so glad you could come in place of your dear aunt, Countess Saskia. I hope she is not very hurt?"

"No, Aunt Saskia will be fine, but she didn't think it was wise to travel yet. She's grateful that you've allowed me to bid in her place."

"Not only bid, my dear man, my dear fellow, but enjoy yourself in every way as a most honored guest. And here is my beautiful wife, Gabriela, formerly Gabriela Candelas, who I am sure you heard of."

"Heard of and *heard*," Ted said to Gaby. "I was privileged see you in *Parsifal* at the Shubert in Boston a few years ago, Ms. Candelas. You were superb."

This had to be a tribute to Ted's research skills, not his love for opera. When they were in New Mexico, they had driven past the Santa Fe Opera amphitheater on their way back from Taos, and she had asked him if he liked opera. He'd said that, while he enjoyed the occasional Verdi or

Puccini production, there was no way anyone could drag him to another one by Wagner, not after he'd been taken with his high school class to a performance of *Tristan and Isolde*. He'd made her laugh when he'd told her that it was the most boring, exhausting experience he'd ever had. "They started it at five o'clock because it was so long, and when it went on and on, and I just couldn't stand it anymore I checked my watch to see how much more there could possibly be. And it was five twenty."

But Gaby was predictably charmed, and they exchanged a few more words. Then Panos began leading him around the semicircle of observers, making introductions. With Izzy, Alix was at the far end, so she had a little more time to put her thoughts together before she was face to face with Ted.

"Roland de Beauvais,"' was one of Ted's undercover aliases, the one he'd been using when she'd first met him in New Mexico. Somehow (the mind boggled) the FBI had transformed him into the nephew of this countess-client of Panos's and put him aboard in her place. Clearly, he was here to gather evidence on Panos's fractional-shares scheme; in short, to do—and do better—what she was supposed to be here for. So why did he need Alix? And why would he spring this on her as a surprise? Why had he not let her know he would be coming?

Panos and Ted had reached them. "And this charming lady," Panos was saying, "is our little art expert"—he made it sound like a private joke—"She—"

"Oh, Alix and I are old friends," Ted said, smiling at her.

Whatever she'd been expecting him to say, that wasn't it. Caught by surprise, with no idea what she was supposed to say, she smiled and adjusted her sunglasses.

"You do remember me, I hope, Alix—Rollie de Beauvais?"

"Yes. Sure. Of course. I'm happy to see you again, uh, Rollie. I didn't know you'd be here." *You crud, why didn't you tell me you were coming?*

"I didn't know it either," he said smoothly. "Not till yesterday. Well, I'm looking forward to getting to know you even better over the next few days, Alix."

He gave her a flirty smile, which did nothing to unconfuse her. Was he doing that so that nobody would think it odd if they were seen alone talking? Or was he simply flirting? If she had to bet, she'd put her money on the former. From what she knew of him, he didn't do too much that wasn't carefully thought out ahead of time, and he wasn't really the flirty type. Only, what *did* she know of him? All she had to go on were those four days in New Mexico, during which they'd spent a total of, what, maybe twelve hours in each other's company? And half of that time, he was being Rollie de Beauvais, not Ted Ellesworth.

"And this," Panos said, moving on to Izzy, "is—"

"And this," Ted interrupted, "unless I'm mistaken, is the famous Pocahontas. It's a *real* pleasure to meet you, Miss Clinke." And he held out his hand.

"Izzy, please," she said.

Alix, a little ticked off about that "*real* pleasure" business—what was he saying, that meeting Alix again wasn't a real pleasure?—was further annoyed by Izzy, who was practically simpering. If it was Ted who was asking her to sign her name on his forehead (or on any other part of his anatomy), Alix grumbled to herself, Izzy would leap at the chance.

· · ·

Ted was then whisked away by Panos, and Alix whisked herself away to her stateroom, where she hid out for the next few hours, until she was due in the music room and salon for her first "informal chat session." Izzy and Gaby, and maybe one or two of the others, had heard Ted say that he and Alix were "old friends," and she didn't want to try to field questions from them about how it was that she and Ted knew each other and just what kind of relationship they had and so on and so forth. She needed to talk to him first so that she didn't blow whatever story he'd cooked up. She was more annoyed than ever at him for not giving her any warning. For that matter, why wasn't he getting in touch with her right now to tell her what was going on? He had really put her in an uncomfortable spot. The man did have some attractive qualities, true, but he was a long way from perfect, and he could be *damn* irritating.

Grumbling about Ted did her good, but she spent most of the time reviewing her art resource materials so that she wouldn't make a complete ass of herself when it came time for the session. Midway through, she took a break, called in an order for a ham-and-cheese sandwich, and put "Pocahontas" into YouTube. Up came fifteen pages of videos, split about half and half between the Pocahontases of Walt Disney and Izzy Clinke. Watching one of Izzy's, she would have had a hard time believing that the sensuous, exotic, extravagant creature on the screen and the lanky, low-key, tongue-in-cheek Izzy were one and the same, if not for that unmistakable helmet of orange corkscrew curls. Gaby had done a good job of describing her, the hypnotically smooth, almost boneless movements, the emotionless, unchanging expression, and the strange, grating, chant-like singing. Hair excepted, she made Alix think of one of those Indian statues of a multiarmed goddess come to life. Her costume was some kind of Indian-Egyptian-Tahitian mishmash that left only the bare minimum (of Izzy) to the imagination. As Gaby had said, it was hard to stop watching her. One would think that if Izzy hated being hounded by the fans and the paparazzi as much as she'd implied, all she had to do was to go out in public in ordinary clothes, sunglasses, and a cover for her hair. No one would know her.

At three o'clock Alix headed for the music room. Only Mirko Koslecki, the Man With Six Countries, was there, standing in front of the collection's Renoir, one of his lush, fleshy nudes-in-the-bath. Alix walked boldly up to him and started right in doing some heavy-duty informal chatting.

"Hello, again, Mirko," she said brightly. "Beautiful, isn't it? Did you know that the woman is one of Renoir's favorite models, Suzanne Valadon? She modeled for Toulouse-Lautrec too, and Puvis de Chavannes. A fascinating person, born very poor—the daughter of a laundress—she became a circus acrobat as a child, until she fell off a trapeze and had to take to modeling. Believe it or not, she actually became a pretty decent painter herself. She was supposed to have had an affair with Renoir, but nobody really knows. Never married, but she did have a baby at eighteen, and she taught him to paint too. A lot of people believe Renoir was the father."

She paused in the interest of narrative tension, but also because she needed to take a breath. "And would you like to guess the name of that baby boy who may well have been the natural son of Pierre August Renoir?" she asked triumphantly. "None other than—"

"Maurice Utrillo," Mirko mumbled without ever once having looked at her, then pulled down his head and scuttled off on his tiny feet to the furthest corner of the room to look at a picture by Seurat.

Well, that went well. Obviously, Alix had pumped herself up and come on a wee bit too strong there. And just as obviously she'd been overly cavalier in taking it for granted that these people didn't know very much. *Okay, lesson learned, let's move on.* Toward the salon she strode. Mirko, fearing she was coming in pursuit of him, quickly crossed the room again, to a Sisley beach scene. Alix sighed. Had she done *anything* right since putting foot on the *Artemis*?

There were two people in the salon: Emil Varga—the one whom she'd overheard talking to Edward earlier, scoffing at her "credentials"—and a man she hadn't seen before. They weren't looking at the paintings but standing in the middle of the room having a spirited discussion.

Varga spotted her as she came in. "You're Alix London, aren't you? Come and join us, there's something we'd like your opinion on. We were just talking about you."

"Oh?" Alix said with a smile. *I can just imagine.* He was a bigger man than she'd realized, with wider hips and shoulders, and standing up he had a bearlike, lumbering quality to him.

"My name is Dr. Emil Varga, Alix."

That's two more strikes against you, chum. What kind of self-aggrandizing jerk introduces himself in a social situation as "doctor"? Besides which, technically speaking, "doctor" isn't your name, it's a title. You'd think a guy with doctorates from Harvard and Oxford would know that. Well, at least he didn't refer to himself as "Doctor Doctor."

Second, and more egregious in her opinion, if he was going to refer to himself as "doctor," the least he could do would be to address her as "miss." *This is going to be a hard guy to like.*

"A pleasure to meet you," she said, "Emil."

A single small tic below his left eye and a brief compression of the lips indicated that she'd hit her mark. She wasn't sure how happy she was about that. Antagonizing the guests was a totally dumb thing to do and yet she couldn't stop doing it. She was there, at least until further notice, to gather information, and that wasn't the way to encourage it. On the other hand, it did feel good to skewer the pretentious SOB.

But really, she'd have to stop indulging in these small-minded jabs. She could save them for Ted when she got the chance.

"And this is my good friend, *il professore* Lorenzo Bolzano of Firenze, Italia," Varga said.

"*Molto lieto, professore,*" said Alix.

"Lorenzo, please! And it is kind of you to speak in my language, but I enjoy speaking English very much. I am glad to see that you were not seriously hurt last night, Alix."

She was trying to figure out what it was that was so "indescribable" about him. A bit odd looking, that was true, but pretty describable as far as she could see: bald, beaky, and hollow chested, with moist, dim-sighted black eyes peering amiably out from behind wire-rimmed glasses that sat slightly awry on his pinched nose. His monk-like ruffle of gray hair was ridiculously long, so that it hung limply down all the way to his collar like the fringe on a cowgirl skirt. The accent was thick but his English was fluent and correct.

"Actually, Alix," Emil said, "we were talking about last night, about your, uh, interesting and—no offense, arguable—conclusion that the Manet is a forgery."

127

So Izzy had been right, she thought. Panos could forget about keeping any secrets on the *Artemis*. "Actually," she said, "I'd hardly call it a 'conclusion,' and I don't think I used the word 'forgery,' or at least I hope I didn't. That's a term I'm very careful with. Forgery is a slippery, woolly kind of concept that—"

"Exactly, exactly!" cried Lorenzo abruptly, his arms jerking about. "My point exactly, Emil! You see? What Alix is saying is precisely what I was telling you: that the application of so-called 'universal' objectivist definitions—this painting is authentic, that painting is not authentic—is absurd on the face of it, and I am speaking not merely of the contradictions and implausibilities inherent in the dichotomies of Aristotelian logic. No, in our post-modern world, there *is* no rational distinction between 'authentic' and 'inauthentic' art."

"Well, no, that's not exactly what I meant," Alix said. "What I was trying to say was that, even if you couldn't call it a genuine Manet, that didn't necessarily mean it would have to be a forgery. It could have been worked on by more than one hand, or badly restored at some point, or be a study, or a student exercise, or simply a copy—"

Emil pounced. "In other words, a forgery."

Well, yes, really, that was what she thought when you came down to it, but she didn't want to churn the waters any more than she already had. "No, I wouldn't say—"

Lorenzo was still too energized by his own off-the-wall reasoning to stay quiet any longer. "Alix, I wonder if you've read my paper, 'Is Art Real?'"

"No-o, I don't think so . . ."

"Ah. Perhaps 'Reality as Metaphor'?"

"I'm afraid not."

His enthusiasm flagged a little. "You don't read the *Journal of Subjectivistic Art Commentary*?"

Not only didn't Alix read it, she'd never heard of it. And if she had, it didn't sound as if it would top her list of reading priorities. *Reality as*

Metaphor? "Oh, I've seen it, of course," she lied, "and I've enjoyed some of the papers, but you know there are so many journals to subscribe to . . ."

"I'm a contributing editor. I'll arrange a subscription for you today. It's something you must have. Its overarching premise, you see, takes its theme from the epistemological foundations of *pittura metafisica*, especially as laid down by Carrá; that is, that the exterior, so-called 'real' world can only be imperfectly known through our senses, whereas the inner reality— the significations that we ourselves impose upon our disorderly, unknowable world—while perhaps equally mistaken, are necessarily more cogent, more coherent, more *real* than the 'real world' itself, ah-ha-ha. What would you say to that?"

Alix just looked at him. *What would anyone say to that?*

But Lorenzo wasn't really expecting an answer. "In other words, in reality—ah-ha-ha—'forgery' has no meaning, because 'authentic' likewise is meaningless. *All* of our old constants—time, space, reality itself—are now understood to be no more than cultural constructs that the human mind creates in its desperate need to invent order where no order exists— where *nothing* exists. As Heidegger so memorably puts it in *Was ist Metaphysik?*, 'What does the Nothing do? The Nothing *nothings*.' Of course, Carnap, as an analytical antimetaphysician, criticizes this as a pseudo-statement, but I would posit that we can be sure . . ."

What Gaby and Izzy had meant by *indescribable* was getting clearer. They were also right about his being hard not to like despite his quirky, barely penetrable "logic." In fact, it was largely his good-humored, effervescent goofiness that made him likable. And entertaining.

Not to Emil, though, but then no doubt Emil had had a lot more exposure to Lorenzo's wacky locutions than Alix had. "Could we cease and desist with the metaphysics, please?

"Let me put my question as simply as I can. Miss London, can you tell us what it is about the Manet that makes you entertain the possibility that it might be a f—I beg your pardon, Lorenzo—that it might not *be* a Manet?"

Suddenly, Alex was tired. She did think it wasn't a genuine Manet—and very likely a forgery in the generally understood meaning of the word (although she'd have to remember never to say that to Lorenzo)—but she still didn't know why she thought so. That made it hard to argue her point. That was why, when she was in her full senses, she kept such intimations to herself until she had something more than a gut feeling to go on.

"Emil—" she began uncertainly.

But he saved her. "Aside from the all-around brilliance of the work, which I should have thought would speak for itself, there are innumerable Manet hallmarks that, in my opinion, cannot be successfully imitated. I'm surprised that you would imagine that those warm, brown shadows, the uniquely buttery green grass of the background, the curving, flowing strokes that outline the . . ."

She was no longer paying attention. Unknown to Emil, his words had finally freed up the logjam and she was too excited to listen.

She knew what was wrong with the painting.

16

Dear Alix London,

Welcome aboard the Artemis. *This booklet is your personal copy and contains practical information about the vessel and your cruise. Mr. and Mrs. Papadakis and the staff of the* Artemis *are at your service and wish you a happy and unforgettable voyage.*

The eight pages of the leather-bound guest booklet offered deck plans, a telephone directory, meal times and cocktail hours, swimming pool rules, safety rules *(Please do not wear stiletto heels on the wooden decks or when the yacht is underway. Please do not sit on the railings at any time.)*, travelogue-type guides to their destinations, and finally, the page she was hunting for, the schedule. She already knew that they would be in Crete that evening, but now she learned that the launch would be motoring to Heraklion harbor for an on-shore excursion at about five thirty, after the *Artemis*, which was too big for the marina, had anchored a few miles out.

That was excellent, just what she was hoping: only a little over an hour to go until she could call someone she now needed to talk to even more urgently than to Ted. The guidelines she'd been given by the FBI said that any potentially sensitive telephone calls were to be made from dry land, and this would give her the chance. What she needed was the counsel of a first-rate, hands-on, expert forger. Alone among respectable art consultants Alix was fortunate (?) enough to have one right in the family, and she intended to telephone him the first chance she got.

She sat back in her chair, kicked off her sandals, put her feet up on a footstool, placed the laptop on her lap, and settled down to think through her conclusions about the Manet one more time and to use the Internet to do a little cyberchecking. The more she thought and the more she checked, the more her certainty increased. *Le Déjeuner au Bord du Lac* was a forgery, and nothing Carrá might or might not have said about the epistemological foundations of *pittura metafisica* was going to change her mind about it.

. . .

At 5:15, as the yacht was letting out its anchor, there was a meeting in the *petit salon*, the smallest of the four shipboard salons, at which Artemis went over the evening's plans for those going ashore. They would be met at the dock by limousines that would take them on the four-mile drive to Knossos, the fabulous—and fabulously reconstructed—Minoan palace of King Minos himself, of Minotaur fame. As a courtesy to Mr. Papadakis, the Greek government had arranged for the site to be closed to the public three hours early so that the *Artemis* party might have the use of it for their private function.

Alix was astonished. Knossos, she knew, was the second-most-visited site in Greece, outranked only by the Acropolis in Athens. To think that it would be shut down for the personal use of Panos Papadakis was amazing. Even assuming that he had paid for the privilege, surely it couldn't have been enough to make up for the thousands of admissions that would otherwise have been paid. And what about the people who would have paid them? What about their plans? People—families—who had planned for years and had come to Crete from hundreds or thousands of miles away for that purpose alone?

She glanced at the other guests—Gaby, Mirko, Emil, Lorenzo, and Izzy—and not one of them showed the least surprise or concern. Ted was there too, looking equally blasé, but that was to be expected. It struck her with more force than it had before that these people—not Ted, but the others—lived in a world of entitlement that made her own rich and influential ex-in-laws seem like skid row bums.

Once they arrived at the site, Artemis continued, they would be greeted by one of the ship's stewardesses and escorted to the bar that had been set up for them on the ancient flagstone walk at the foot of the Propylaeum—the palace's monumental north entrance—below the raised, pillared stone platform with the famous charging-bull fresco, one of Knossos's signature sights. They would have approximately two hours to wander at their pleasure. When it grew dark, security lights would be turned on. The complimentary services of a professional guide would be available to those who wished them. Boxed picnic dinners had been prepared that could be eaten at a table near the bar or taken anywhere on the site that they liked. Most of the barriers erected to limit public access to various areas had been taken down for their convenience, although a few of the most endangered objects and frescos were now protected with permanent iron bars that could not be removed—for which Artemis apologized on behalf of Panos and of the government.

Alix just shook her head.

Emil was shaking his head too, but for a different reason. "'Archaeologically important,'" he said sarcastically. "The whole thing's a fantasy, one big Knossosland. It's all straight out of the mind of, what's his name, the archaeologist who worked on it back in the 1890s—"

"I believe it was the early 1900s, mostly," Mirko corrected mildly. "Sir Arthur Evans." Alix noticed that he wasn't much for eye contact, seeming to look everywhere but at the person he was addressing.

"Yes, Evans, he made it all up, it's an illusion, it bears little relation to reality."

Such conversation was like catnip to Lorenzo, who bounced energetically in. "But as Einstein himself informs us, reality itself is an illusion. How are we to tell one from the other, since all that we think we 'know' of the 'real' world comes to us from our brains, which are after all encased in utter blackness, and get all of their so-called information from a few openings in our skulls that convert sensory impulses from—"

"Oh, come on, Lorenzo," Emil said, "I know what's real when I see it, and you do too."

Ted, obviously working to make himself agreeable, joined in. "I'm no philosopher, but I go along with the Marxian point of view—Groucho's, that is: 'I'm not crazy about reality, but it's still the only place to get a decent meal.'"

That brought a round of laughter, and Izzy added, "Well, I know what reality is. 'Reality is that which, when you stop believing it, doesn't go away.' Woody Allen."

"It was the science-fiction writer Philip K. Dick, actually," Mirko said, and when the others laughed, he seemed startled but eventually he smiled a little as well, not at any one person, of course. Alix was impressed. Loner, recluse, whatever he was, he seemed to have quite a fund of knowledge.

Emil was the only one who hadn't laughed. "Yes, it's all very funny, but I am simply saying—"

"We know what you're saying," Edward Reed said crisply. "Everyone here has been to Knossos before, I believe, and we are all perfectly aware that Sir Arthur's reconstruction, while based on the available research of the time, is somewhat speculative."

Emil huffed a bit and shrank into his collar. "My only point—"

Edward looked at Artemis. "Perhaps we could move on?"

"Oh, I believe I've finished," said the unruffled chief stewardess. "We can start on our way now."

When they got to the launch, in which Donny was waiting at the wheel, Alix thought it wisest to keep her distance from Ted and settled on the bench across from him. The way the seating then worked out, Mirko was talking to Lorenzo as the launch got underway, Emil to Gaby, and Ted to Izzy, who was wearing oversized Lolita sunglasses and did indeed have her hair tightly wrapped in a bandana. As a result Alix wound up with no one to talk to, and turned, her elbow on the gunwale, to take in the view.

Although Crete had been on the itinerary of the trip she'd taken as a teenager on her Uncle Julian's yacht and she had clear memories of Knossos, she had none at all of their approaching this same harbor, although they must have done so. Her interest had probably been focused on the bronzed, rippling muscles of Sergio's back and shoulders as he went about the deck doing the things deck hands do to prepare for docking. Looking out toward the city now, she found that the guide in the guest booklet, which she'd thought over-romanticized, had done a good job of capturing what it was like to arrive from the sea.

As it had said, from a few miles out, a tall, broad mountain loomed up as a photogenic backdrop to the city: Mount Juktas, according to the guide, and, according to legend, the burial place of Zeus. A more recent legend—Alix thought it just might have something to do with efforts to boost tourism—suggested that the mountain itself *was* the petrified god, and his upturned face could be seen in profile at the top. (If true, she thought now, it would mean that the supreme god of the Greeks looked pretty much like Bob Hope, ski-jump nose and all.) Whatever; it was green and craggy and picturesque.

Coming nearer, the thick, serpentine Venetian walls that still surrounded the oldest part of Heraklion loomed large, as the guide said they would, and gleamed like hammered copper in the slanting, late-afternoon sunlight. And after the sea wall was rounded and the old harbor entered, there was the great monolithic fortress of Rocca al Mare, right on schedule, also erected by the Venetians to defend the city when it was theirs to defend. Unfortunately for Heraklion, that more or less completed the list of must-see sights. Beyond that, the sprawling, bustling city had little besides its Archaeological Museum to offer tourists. Thus, the group from the *Artemis* would be following a path common to the island's visitors in heading directly out to Knossos, from which most of the objects in the museum had come.

Once Donny had turned off the engine, done some showy, cowboy-style twirls of the mooring line and lassoed one of the posts, Alix saw the anticipated pair of limousines a few yards off at curbside, one behind the other, their engines slowly idling. Glossy, black, and roomy, they looked as if they should have been flaunting a diplomatic flag on each fender. She thought they were probably refurbished London taxis of the older, more elegant variety—hackney carriages, as they were called.

But there was also something unanticipated, a gaggle of long-haired, grungy young guys converging on the launch from either side, five of them altogether. Alix might have taken them for touts for taxis or cheap hotels, except for the fearsome array of intricate-lensed cameras dangling from necks and shoulders.

"Paparazzi, God damn them to hell," Izzy said bitterly. "I *hate* them. How'd they even know I'd be here? I'm gonna have to make a dash for it, guys. Let me go first, okay?"

"But will they recognize you, Izzy?" Alix asked. "I mean with the bandana and everything?"

"Paparazzi? Are you kidding? They'd recognize me if I was wearing a gorilla suit. They'd love it even more if I didn't have any makeup on and I was wearing baggy shorts and I'd put on fifteen pounds and my hair was a mess. Lucky for me I decided to clean up a little."

"Hey, Poke," one of the photographers called amiably, "so how's it going?"

A couple of them took her picture, but there was something oddly listless about it, Alix thought.

"Here I go," Izzy said as the launch bobbed gently against the dock's rubber-tire bumper. Teeth clenched and head down, up and over the gunwale she went, making a beeline for one of the limos, apparently intending to bull her way through the clustered bodies. But to Alix's surprise—to everybody's surprise—she didn't have to. It was like watching the Red Sea parting, some of them going left, others to the right, giving her an unobstructed path to the car.

One of them did turn to follow her with his camera but spun quickly back when another one blurted, "There he is, that's him—the little guy!"

Alix, who had been watching Izzy's progress, now saw that Mirko was making his own hunched, frightened dash for sanctuary, but the five photographers surrounded him, some of them running backwards, engulfing him like hungry lampreys homing in on a juicy tuna fish.

"Hey, Mirko, look over here, will ya?"

"Hey, Mirko, come on, man, give us a break, one lousy smile!"

"Mirko, you gonna buy that boat out there from Papadakis?"

"Hey, Mirko, is it true you're buying Ecuador?"

One of them was yelling his questions in French, but they were clearly at about the same level of discourse as the ones in English.

"Once upon a time," Gaby said softly, as Mirko ducked safely into the limo without ever having said anything, "they would have been all over me too." She must have heard the maudlin overlay in her voice, because she immediately trilled a laugh. "Thank goodness I don't have to go through that anymore."

The remaining passengers, Alix, Ted, Gaby, Lorenzo, and Emil, climbed out more or less as a group and made their way to the limos, ignored by the photographers, a couple of whom were still fruitlessly beseeching Mirko through the smoked windows of the limousine, while others had hunkered down on the sidewalk, phoning or e-mailing their shots to their newspapers or magazines or agents.

When they got to the vehicles, Emil, Gaby, and Ted climbed into the one with Mirko, while Alix and Lorenzo joined Izzy, Lorenzo sitting beside Izzy in the back seat, and Alix facing them in one of the bucket seats behind the driver.

"Well, that sucked," Izzy said as the driver closed the side door and got back behind the wheel. "Did you see that? All those years of being dogged by those jerks, and now I get upstaged by Mr. Reclusive himself. There's only one explanation. My career's really in the toilet."

"Not so, Izzy," Lorenzo said. "It's simply a question of supply and demand, in the tabloid world as much as anywhere else. The rarer the commodity, the greater the value. Our friend Mirko has managed to be famous and yet has largely avoided the intrusive scrutiny of the camera's eye. Whereas you, on the other hand, have become—what shall I call it—?"

"Call it old hat."

"—Familiar and beloved," Lorenzo countered, "like an old and well-loved friend. Your many fans can find pictures of you everywhere, but how many people know what Mirko Koslecki looks like? Ergo, to the muckrakers responsible for keeping filled the ravenous maw of the gossip machines, a photo of Mirko is worth more than a photo of you or Brad Pitt or the president of the United States."

What do you know, Alix thought, *Lorenzo could actually be not only coherent, but cogent as well.*

"I appreciate the company you're putting me in, Lorenzo," Izzy said, "and, yeah, sure, you're right about pictures of Mirko being a lot harder to find than pictures of yours truly. But . . ." She paused for a reflective smile. "It's funny, but, you know, when I say—and I know you've both heard me say it—that I really resent the intrusions into what I laughably call my private life, I'm telling the truth. I hate them, I really do, especially the paparazzi, cursed be their DNA."

"I don't blame you," Alix said. "I'd hate that kind of attention too."

"Sure, only if I really mean it, how come I'm sitting here right now, down in the dumps because I *didn't* get intruded on?" She shook her head. "It's pathetic. Story of my life: First third, work like hell to get to be a famous celebrity. Second third, go around wearing sunglasses and a scarf so no one recognizes you as a famous celebrity. Third, get pissed off when they don't. Go figure."

Lorenzo had an answer for her. "Wouldn't you agree, dear Izzy, that it very likely stems from the necessarily dysfunctional antipathy between codependency and rivalry that surely must exist between the Izzy-you and the Pocahontas-you, especially taking into consideration their inevitable duality of purpose?"

There, Alix thought, *that was more like it. Lorenzo was sounding like Lorenzo again. Whatever the subject, the man seemed to be fluent in incomprehensibility.*

"Absolutely, Lorenzo," Izzy said. "How could anyone argue with that?"

17

The rest of the short drive passed quickly, and as soon as all were escorted to where the tables had been set up below the Propylaeum and everybody headed for the bar, Alix found it easy to peel off by herself. She went up a flight of stone steps to the Central Court, a wide courtyard that had once been the ceremonial center of the palace. The last time she'd been here she and her relatives had waited in line with a few hundred others for half an hour in order to get a peek at the throne room that was just off it, and then it had to be seen from the outside, because entry into the room itself had been closed to the public. Now she had the entire courtyard to herself, and the throne room too, if she cared to look in on the simple stone seat that, according to Arthur Evans, was the throne of King Minos—or to sit on it, for that matter.

That was exactly what she decided to do, although it took a little arguing with herself. In her heart, Alix disapproved of the government's opening these normally barred areas of the site, partly because it was such blatant toadying to the superclass, but mostly because they had been closed to entry for good reasons. Like the Parthenon (also off-limits to the public) Knossos was irreplaceable, historically and artistically unique, and its treasures couldn't take the depredations of thousands of tourists tramping through every day.

That was what she felt in her heart. But in her *heart of hearts*, she already knew she was going to take advantage of this once-in-a-lifetime chance to actually place herself upon the legendary, starkly unadorned alabaster seat of the storied king of the Minoans, the most ancient royal throne in all of Europe. *Well, who wouldn't?* Especially because there was the shameful, added little fillip of knowing that almost nobody else in the world could. She smiled, thinking that Lorenzo would be ready with an explanation. He would tell her that her Alix-the-art-lover-you had been warring with her Alix-the-gawking-tourist-you, and the tourist-you had won out. And now that she thought about it, that seemed right to her, so either she was getting nuttier or Lorenzo was starting to make sense.

So in she went and plopped herself royally down. On the frescoed wall behind her, on either side, were the two stately frescoed griffins that eternally guarded the chair of state, their lion bodies relaxed and elegant, their eagle heads fiercely alert. For a minute or two she simply soaked it in, then got out her phone. At Jamie's suggestion, she had configured it to its highest security setting. Unlocking it meant letting it approve both her face and her voice, so first she had to hold it in front of her at eye level until it decided that she really did look like the person she claimed to be, after which she was required to say a six-syllable word in a normal speaking voice. Examples had been provided, but she'd chosen one of her own. The word she'd come up with, God knows why, was *kleptomaniacal*, which the phone now did not recognize as coming from her, so she had to try it again and then again, slowly and then more slowly and clearly, feeling more ridiculous every time. Even the griffins seemed to be snickering.

But at last she was given grudging approval to use her own phone. There were five messages for her, but they could hold. She tapped the quick-dial line for Geoff and waited for the call to go through, hoping for the best. Surely this was the first cellular phone call that had ever been placed from the royal throne. But it worked just fine. Geoff picked up on the second ring, sounding as clear as if he were just outside.

"Ah, good *morning*, my dear, I was wondering when I might hear from you. How is the cruise progressing? How are you?"

"The cruise is fine, and so am I." *Only been knocked on the head once so far, and I've been on it for over twenty-four hours now.*

"And where exactly are you at the moment?"

"Exactly? I'm sitting on King Minos's throne."

"Really? What a coincidence. I myself am in the Crimson Drawing Room at Windsor Castle, where, at the request of the Queen, I was having a heart-to-heart chat with young Prince Harry. Trying to straighten the lad out, don't you know."

Alix grinned. Plenty of time to elaborate when she got back. "Geoff, I only have a little time, and there's something I need to talk to you about. There's a Manet in the collection that I have some serious reservations about. I'm pretty sure—*very* sure—the thing's a fake, but a really excellent one."

"Do you now?" She heard the scraping of a chair on Venezia's concrete floor. He was sitting down, his interest piqued. "Tell."

"Well, it's a picture of what appears to be a family, three people—nice, middle-class Parisians, judging from their dress—having a picnic on the grass beside a lake—"

"Sounds very Manet."

"Yes. Now, what if I told you that it was painted in 1861—"

"Fairly early. Two years before the other picnic on the grass, the one that dared not speak its name."

"Right. And what if I told you that the entire scene—the people in the foreground, the boat, the trees and grass in the background—are all beautifully done; warm and oil rich, lots of deep browns, a softly but convincingly rendered sense of depth. Very much like his *Argenteuil* paintings . . ."

She waited, expecting him to react, but he said nothing for a few seconds, then cleared his throat. "Apparently I am supposed to say something of value at this point, but I'm afraid I have to disappoint you, Alix. I don't really claim to be much of an expert on Manet. He's one of the artists whose paintings I've never, ah, restored—"

"One of the *few* artists you've never 'restored,'" she said out of the side of her mouth, away from the phone.

"I heard that!" Geoff said huffily, but she couldn't miss the chuckle behind it. Her one-of-a kind father wasn't merely unrepentant concerning his past misdeeds; he positively basked in them. Any reference to his prowess as a forger was always met with pleasure. "But listen, child, let me get Tiny in on this. When it comes to Manet, he's the man for the job. Tiny," he called, the sound muffled—he probably had the phone against his chest—"pick up, will you? It's Alix."

"Hey, Alix," she heard a second later, deep and slow and affectionate. "Everything all right?"

"Everything's fine, Tiny," Geoff replied for her. "She wants to ask you about a Manet. She thinks it's a forgery."

"Well, I think it *might* be a forgery," said Alix. Confronted with these two certified and venerable experts, she was suffering a sudden loss of confidence.

"Tell him what you were telling me, Alix."

Alix did, in even more detail. "The whole scene is exquisitely done," she finished. "Deep and rich, the colors are heavy and dense, a lot like his—"

"What do you think, Tiny?" Geoff interceded.

"First guess? I'd say the label's wrong. Doesn't sound like 1861 to me."

Alix's spirits rose. Tiny's thinking was in line with hers. "Not to me either," she said, "but it shows up in Venturi's 1967 Manet catalogue raisonné, and it's dated 1861 in there. It also says that he exhibited it in that year's Paris salon, so we know for sure that it couldn't have been any later than that."

"Yeah, but how sure are we that the painting you been looking at and the one in the catalog are the same one?"

"I'm not. I *don't* think they're the same. That's what I'm calling about. Unfortunately, the picture of it in Venturi—and I'm assuming that's the real one—is just postcard size and it's in black and white, so I can't really compare the details, and I couldn't find any other pictures of it on the Web. The measurements and all the rest in Venturi do match, but I still think it's a forgery. Extraordinarily well-done . . . just about faultless, in fact, when it comes to technique . . . but a forgery all the same."

"Yup, I think you're right, kiddo," Tiny said bluntly.

"*What?*" Geoff exclaimed. "Did I miss something here? You haven't even seen it, Tiny! Why is it a forgery?"

"You don't know?" Tiny said.

"No, I don't know," Geoff said, getting a little grumpy. When it came to art, it wasn't very often that he got one-upped, but then of course he'd already admitted that he couldn't claim expertise on Édouard Manet.

"The old guy's losing it," Tiny said happily. "Explain it to him, Alix."

"I am not—" Geoff began, but he never could stay miffed for long, and he stopped in midsentence. His voice took on a creaky whine. "Yes, child, explain it to your poor old da. I'll . . . I'll do my best to follow, if I possibly can."

"It's the background that's the giveaway, Geoff. It's all wrong."

"The background? Is my hearing going too? Did I not hear you say only a moment ago that it was quite Manet-like? Dense, and rich, and all that, very similar to his *Argenteuil* series?"

"I did," Alix said.

"She did," Tiny said, clearly relishing this rare opportunity to tell Geoffrey London something he didn't know.

"So . . . ?"

"So when did he do the *Argenteuil* paintings?" Tiny asked, unable to stay out of it.

"When he was in Argenteuil, would be my guess," Geoff said archly.

"Which was?"

"In the 1870s, I believe."

"And when did—?"

"And when are you going to stop asking me questions and start giving me answers? *Why* is the damn thing a forgery?"

"Well, what did—?"

But Geoff was getting impatient again and Alix thought she'd better take charge once more and get to the point, although, like Tiny, she too was having fun. "Geoff, *Déjeuner au Bord du Lac* was painted in 1861. It wasn't until 1868 that Berthe Morisot convinced Manet to actually go outside and try some plein-air painting. In 1861, he was still strictly a studio painter; he worked inside, and his pictures show it. His foregrounds—his subjects—are fine: rich, and dense, and thickly painted because he was working from live models, but his backgrounds look flat and fake—because they are. They're more thinly painted, more roughly worked. They look like canvas backdrops, or tapestries, not real, three-dimensional, outdoor scenes."

"That's so," Geoff allowed. "*Le Déjeuner sur l'Herbe* is like that, and that was 1863."

"Right."

"So . . . what the two of you are telling me"—he was speaking slowly, thoughtfully—"is that the background of *your* picture, Alix, your *Déjeuner*, is *too* well done, too real, to be by the Manet of 1861. Whoever copied it *improved* on it—by painting the background in the more finished style that Manet himself didn't arrive at until years later. Is that about it?"

That was it, both Tiny and Alix agreed.

"That's very clever," Geoff said, and Alix felt that childish swell of pride that no son or daughter ever got old enough to outgrow.

"Thank you, Geoff. I knew there was something wrong, but it sure took me a while to figure out what it was. Listen, basically, I'm calling because I wanted to ask you a question—the two of you, really—"

"It's interesting," Geoff said, his tone suggesting that he was off in his own mind. "I can think of only one man in this world who has both the talent and the skills to make a 'faultless' copy of the work of a great master—*and* who has an ego big enough to actually think he can *improve* on it."

Oh, really? Alix thought. *That's funny, I can think of two.*

"Weisskopf," Tiny declared.

"Exactly."

"Who's Weisskopf?" Alix asked.

"He's—" Tiny began.

"He's an old friend," Geoff said. "Well, more or less. Let me get in touch with him and see what I can learn— "

"In *touch* with him?" Alix's voice shot up a notch. "Geoff, doesn't your parole prohibit you from consorting with felons?"

"*A*," Geoff said icily, "I am not *on* parole, and the conditions of my *release* make no such stipulation; if they did, I couldn't associate with Tiny here, could I?"

"Or Frisby either," said Tiny. "Or—"

"*B*, Christoph Weisskopf is not a felon. A fine fellow, he may have been arrested, oh, once or twice, but to my knowledge, he has never been convicted. And *C*, I can't say I care for the sound of that word, 'consort.'"

"Sorry, Dad, I apologize. But what could he tell you anyway? He's not going to admit he forged it, is he?"

"Oh, he forged it, all right."

"You bet," Tiny contributed.

"The thing is, though," Geoff said, "he's a bit on the secretive side—"

"Really? A forger? My, what a surprise."

She heard Geoff sigh. "But, employing my celebrated tact and subtlety, I might be able to dig something out for you. I'll give you a call and we can proceed from there."

"Oh, listen, though. Instead of calling, how about e-mailing me? It'd be safer."

The pregnant pause told her she'd made a mistake, as indeed she had. "Safer? Why would it be *unsafe* to call you? Alix, what have you gotten yourself—"

She resorted to her usual strategy when she got herself in a bind: babbling. "Oh, I don't mean 'safe' as in 'safe,' but as in 'I'm more likely to get it.' You know how hard it is to get cell service in Europe. And if you're in a boat in the middle of the ocean, well then—"

Tiny unintentionally came to her rescue. "Alix, you said you had a question for us, no?"

"I do, yes. The thing is, this painting has some pretty good backup. Apparently, it's got at least two credible letters of authentication—"

That brought bouts of laughter from both of them, deep, genuine guffaws of amusement, and Alix understood why. Boiled down to its essentials, a letter of authentication was an evaluation from an art scholar—or someone reputed to be an art scholar, or someone who claimed to be an art scholar, or someone who someone said was an art scholar—and was based on that person's judgment as to technique, materials, context, subject matter, style, and skill. Their batting average, as far as getting it right went, was probably somewhere around .500: great if you're a baseball player, not so great in this business. In other words, they often got it wrong, as the two men on the other end of the line would be only too happy to prove to her, based on their own extensive experience.

"Okay, forget that," she said, "but what about this—the *Laboratoire Forensique Pour l'Art* has run it through their tests and they say it's the real thing too. Their seal of approval is stamped right on the back."

"That's all very well, but you must remember—" Geoff began.

"I know," Alix said. "You don't have to tell me. Forensic tests can definitely spot clear-cut fakes. Wrong paint for the time and so on. Or they can say that something—this Manet, for example—checks out; the pigments were indeed the ones used by Manet and his circle, and the backing and the canvas are from the right time and place, and even that the brush strokes are laid on in the way that Manet laid them on. But what they *can't* say with certainty is that it was Manet himself who painted it—only that they could find no evidence that it *wasn't* Manet."

"Exactly," Geoff said.

"Yes, but the thing is, they found no such evidence. That means that they determined that the materials and techniques *are* consistent with Manet's, and that it was painted over a hundred years ago. That's my problem, Geoff. I *know* it's a fake, a copy of the real thing, but the lab says it was definitely done in the nineteenth century, with the right materials for the time and place. How can that be?"

"Could have been a student copy," Tiny suggested. "Or hey, how about an early version that Manet himself made, a study for the final painting?"

"No," Geoff said. "We've established that it's *more* finished than the final painting. Obviously, you wouldn't find that in a study. So scratch that. We're dealing with a later copy here."

Not so obviously, thought Alix, to whom this helpful perception hadn't occurred. Tiny was wrong; the old guy was definitely not losing it.

"Well, then, how do you explain it, Geoff? Assuming I'm right, how could the lab get it so wrong?"

"Well, I need to think about that. This *Laboratoire Forensique Pour l'Art*—their tests are the most exhaustive in the business. Thank goodness they never had a go at anything I did," he said with a smile in his voice. "They really are very, very good."

"I know, but I'm very good too," Alix said in a rare fit of braggadocio, "so I repeat: How did *they* manage to get it wrong?"

Geoff laughed. "My goodness, no one can accuse you of false modesty, can they?"

"Yeah, I wonder who I got that from."

"Look, dear, the truth is, I just might have an inkling of how it could have happened. It's a bit outlandish, but if anybody could bring it off, Weisskopf would be the man. Let me look into it for you."

She had heard people talking— Gaby and Emil—in the courtyard outside and thought she'd better finish. "I have to run now—"

"King Minos must want his throne back," Geoff said. "Give him my warmest regards. Goodbye, then, child. Lovely to talk to you, as always."

"Same here. Let's stay in touch. Thank you, Geoff . . . and thank you, Tiny."

"*Prego, mia bambola. Ciao.*"

18

The moment she stepped back out into the Central Court—even before she was entirely through the entryway—she winced with embarrassment, regretting that she hadn't thought to cough or shuffle her feet to let them know she was coming. Gaby and Emil were sitting side by side on a low stone wall, part of the foundation of a building that was no longer there, and it wasn't that she actually caught them doing anything that either she or they had to be embarrassed about, but the sudden, startled way they sprang apart at her appearance made it obvious that she'd just barely missed it.

The movement took perhaps half a second and didn't cover much space, but it left no doubt in Alix's mind that Gaby Papadakis and Emil Varga were lovers.

Yuck. With Panos for a husband, she really couldn't fault Gaby for looking for extracurricular companionship—but *Emil*? Carping, shambling, nit-picking Emil? Alix was disappointed. She would have thought the woman had better prospects than that. And better taste.

"Hi, there," she said brightly. "Didn't know anybody was out here."

"Oh, is that Alix? Hi, there!" Gaby said equally brightly, pretending that she didn't know Alix was pretending. She was flustered, though. Her hands fluttered at her waist and the neckline of her shirt, checking to see how disarranged she might be.

"Hello, Alix," Emil said rather boldly. He might not have liked being interrupted, but he didn't in the least mind Alix's knowing he and Gaby had something going.

Eyes front, Alix kept moving across the courtyard. "See you later, people. I haven't checked out the buffet yet and I'm starving."

. . .

Alix was telling the truth when she said she was hungry, and she went straight back to the buffet. She was still thinking about Gaby and Emil and the way they'd leapt apart when they'd become aware of her. Could she have jumped to a false conclusion? Well, of course she could have, but with people, as it was with art, if her intellect and her stomach disagreed, she generally put her money on her stomach. Too, she remembered now that she'd sensed a history between Gaby and Mirko as well. Maybe becoming Mrs. Papadakis hadn't put her old opera-star lifestyle behind her after all.

Interesting to think about, but right now it was the buffet that was on her mind. Three small, linen-topped picnic tables had been set up in the area. One stewardess stood behind the buffet table to assist, and a second stood by, available to serve those who chose to have their dinners there. Panos and Edward, who must have arrived after the others, had their heads together in conversation at one, and Izzy and Lorenzo were dining at the other. That is, Izzy was dining; Lorenzo, with a knife waving alarmingly around in one hand and a fork in the other, was excitedly declaiming away. Alix heard only a few snatches— ". . . Even Frege's propositional functions cannot . . . ," ". . . Yes, but only if one considers the performative function of language as separate from . . . ," "I don't have to tell you what Wittgenstein would say about that, ah-ha-ha"—but they were more than enough to dissuade her from joining them. The third table was occupied by Mirko, who had unsurprisingly arranged himself so that he was as far from the others as possible and facing away from them. Alix wasn't about to intrude on his privacy.

It was Ted she was hoping to find, of course, and there he was, near the buffet table, looking as if he were thinking about joining Panos and

149

Edward for a little undercover legwork, but was perhaps doubtful about seeming too pushy too soon. When he spotted Alix, he smiled and waved her over. He looked pleased to see her, but with Ted in undercover mode, you never knew if it was all part of the act or not.

"Hey, Alix."

"Oh, hi . . . Rollie." She couldn't believe it; she'd come within a millisecond of calling him "Ted." She'd practically had to bite her tongue to stop herself. One more indication that maybe, just maybe, she wasn't quite as ready for this kind of work as she thought she was. Well, she'd make sure that didn't happen again.

"Alix, what do you say we grab a couple of dinners and find some place where we can sit down and do some catching up?"

"Sure, Rollie." Smoother that time. "Love to."

The smiling stewardess behind the buffet table (Did they ever stop smiling?) provided them each with a handsome, over-the-shoulder canvas satchel trimmed with leather and embroidered with a tiny *Artemis* logo in the usual Prussian blue. "If you could bring back whatever is left, it would be appreciated. Or, if you prefer, simply let me know where to find it. The satchels themselves are yours to keep, of course. They're specially made for us by Balenciaga."

Alix laughed, and when Ted looked quizzically at her, she shook her head. "Nothing." The thought that had popped into her mind was *How nice for Mirko, the Homeless Billionaire. Now he won't have to use a paper bag anymore.*

With their satchels they wandered away from the others, with Alix steering them clear of the Central Court.

"Ted—"

"Rollie," he corrected with a smile of patient endurance.

But Alix was in no mood to be endured. *"Rollie,"* she said crossly, "don't you think you could have warned me you were coming? I mean, really, if this is the way—"

"Warn you? I tried to call you three times yesterday and Jamie tried twice."

Oops. "Oh, those were from you?" she said lamely.

"You might want to try checking your messages every now and then."

"Okay, my fault, sorry about that. I'd do it more often if I didn't feel like such a moron sitting there repeating *kleptomaniacal* to a telephone until it decides I'm telling the truth when I say it's me."

Ted laughed. "Maybe you need another word."

They walked companionably for a few minutes through brightly colored reconstructions and evocative ruins. It wasn't quite dark yet, but the soft, amber security lights had been turned on, so there was a lovely, warm luminosity to everything. The old stones themselves had a velvety sheen.

"Rollie, should we really be talking like this, off by ourselves? Won't it make the others wonder?"

"About what? A rich, young bachelor gadabout like me glomming on to the only really good-looking, sexy woman aboard? They'd wonder a lot more if I didn't."

"Hm, did I hear something like a compliment in there?"

"Completely inadvertent," Ted said, laughing. "Not that it isn't true, of course." The laugh settled down into what she thought was a genuinely warm smile. Even those usually steely blue eyes softened. "I'm glad to see you, Alix. I was glad when the chance came up."'

"I'm glad too. In fact, when I . . ." She was starting to babble, and she cut herself off. *What was it with this guy?* She couldn't remember the last time anybody had a knack like his for throwing her off her stride. "It's very nice to see you too," she finished politely.

"Hey, what do you say we have our dinner in there?" Ted was looking into the open-sided room on their left, with another of Knossos's more famous frescoes on one wall.

"The Queen's Megaron," Alix said.

"Is that what it's called? That dolphin fresco on the wall, I remember seeing a picture of it in a book when I was a kid. It was like a new world opened for me. The thought that these people from so long ago—almost four thousand years, isn't it?—could have art up on their walls that was so . . . so playful, so pretty, hadn't ever really registered before. I thought of Bronze Age people as, you know . . ."

What was this? Was he a little flustered too? He was certainly babbling. Food for thought there. "Sure," she said, "I love the dolphin fresco too. It's not real though, you know."

"I know. All these frescoes are replicas. The originals are in the Heraklion Museum, aren't they?"

They navigated around a giant clay storage jug, climbed over a low, slab-like plinth that served as the base for several of the Minoan culture's distinctive, red, downward-tapering columns—originally wood but replaced by Evans with concrete—and sat themselves down on the lip of the plinth, in an open embrasure that permitted a clear and easy view out to the sides, up and down the pathway that led to it.

"Yes, they are replicas," she said, "but what I meant was that not even the original fresco is really original. Or real. There's no such thing as a 'real' dolphin wall fresco. It doesn't exist. It never did."

He frowned at her. "You've been spending time with Lorenzo, haven't you?"

That made her laugh. "Actually, I have, but what I'm talking about is that Evans got it wrong. The dolphin fragments that were found in the ruins had originally been in the Treasury, not this room at all, and they came from a floor painting, not a wall painting."

"Is that so?" he said with a smile. "I'm impressed. Here I thought *I* had a lot of useless information. So tell me, is there anything 'real' around here?"

"Yes, right next door, the Queen's Toilet, an honest-to-God flushing toilet, possibly the oldest one in the world. If you'd prefer—"

"Thanks, but I'd rather eat in here, if it's all the same to you."

"I agree, Rollie—look, can I call you Ted in here, since nobody's around?"

"Can you do that—call me by one name sometimes and another name at other times, without slipping up?"

"Sure, no problem."

"Because not everybody has an easy time with that—which is understandable." He was giving her a chance to change her mind.

"It will *not* be a problem," she said firmly, as much to herself as to him. "And while we're talking about good old Rollie, where's that awful 'Bahston' accent he had in Santa Fe?"

"Hey, that hurts. I was proud of that accent, but I don't need it here. Look, the only reason I'm Rollie de Beauvais at all this time is that I already had all the paperwork ready and waiting—driver's license, Social Security card, business cards, even a birth certificate if I ever need one. Everything checks out. And it doesn't hurt that 'de Beauvais' fits for the nephew of a Belgian countess."

"And *is* there a Belgian countess in reality?"

"Oh, sure, and she was really meaning to be on the cruise. That much is true, but—"

"But she doesn't really have a wrenched knee."

"No, she doesn't. But she does have some suspicions about these investments Papadakis has supposedly been making for her, and she's had them for a while now. I've spoken with her about them several times, and just a couple of days ago, when we were talking, I came up with the idea. She loved it, and here I am."

"Okay, I understand all that, but how—"

He held up his hand. "At some point, do I get to ask some questions too?"

She smiled. "Ask away; the floor is yours."

"All right, question one. What do you say we have something to eat?"

"I'll second that." She opened her satchel, which held what looked like enough for three people, and that suited her fine. She started with a transparent carton that had hummus in one compartment and sticks of radish, celery, and cucumber in the other, and quickly got to work on it. Ted did the same.

"Two," he said, "how about filling me in on what's been happening so far?"

"Whew, where do I start? I assume you've already heard a little about my, ah, misadventures?"

"No, I've heard a lot about your, ah, misadventures. You seem to have made yourself the number-one topic of conversation. Not that I'm being critical, you understand," he said, munching away, "but generally speaking, we in the spook business don't consider that the best way to start off an operation."

"Oh, well, excuse me. I sincerely apologize for getting whacked on the head."

"I'll let it go this time, but see that it doesn't happen again."

"Trust me, I'll do my best."

He stopped chewing. "Alix . . . you are okay, aren't you? I understand you refused to see a doctor."

"I didn't need a doctor. Honestly, I'm fine, thanks. It's still a little tender where I got hit, but that's all."

"Good." He poked around in his satchel. "You think there might be some wine or something like that in here? Ahh . . ." He pulled out a half bottle and let out a sigh as he read the label. "Bollinger Special Cuvée Brut. Damn, more champagne. I was hoping for some simple, plain white wine, Chablis or something."

"Aw, I feel for you. Life can be hard sometimes."

"Well, I guess I can stand it if I have to. Want me to pour you some too?"

"Please." She laid some more cartons out on the plinth beside her. "This is wonderful, a feast." There were oily black olives, Greek salad, string beans with almonds, and cold salmon with capers and what looked and smelled like fresh dill sour cream dressing. Rolled inside a thick napkin were sturdy, full-size metal utensils and tiny silver salt-and-pepper shakers. The plastic glasses were stemmed champagne flutes.

Ted got the cork out with a soft *pop* and poured both their glasses from it, topping them off as the fizz settled. "Alix, what's your take on what's going on?" he asked, handing her a glass. He raised his to hers and they nonchalantly clicked glasses.

"I don't have one. All I have are questions." Between bites of salmon, she went over the confused and confusing thoughts that had racketed around her head when she'd awakened that morning: Who had slashed the painting? Why? Did it have something to do with her raising doubts about it, or was that simply coincidence?

Ted came up with no better answers than she had. At one point near the end he laughed, and she raised an inquiring eyebrow.

"Oh, it's nothing," he said, "I was just thinking that I left DC yesterday on an assignment concerning a pyramid scheme involving fractional-share investments. Interesting in its own way if you like that kind of thing, but really pretty straightforward, even pedestrian. And when I get here I find out that you hadn't been onboard for five minutes before you'd totally stirred things up—"

"Ted—"

"You managed to get yourself assaulted and damn near killed—"

"Ted—"

"You've gotten everybody all shook up with the accusation—an unsubstantiated accusation, I gather—that the most valuable and coveted painting on the ship is a fake—"

"Ted—"

"And that same painting has since been slashed by some villain, identity unknown—"

"Ted—"

"And all of this was accomplished within half an hour of your setting foot on the *Artemis*. Amazing, really." He was laughing again. "I can see that working with you might have its problems, but being dull is never going to be one of them."

"*Ted, dammit—*"

"Yes?"

But she'd forgotten what she was trying to say, so she jumped to the attack. "It was not an *accusation* about the Manet. I haven't accused anybody of anything, have I? It was an observation, an educated deduction. And it was certainly not unsubstantiated. It *is* a fake. And yes, I know about the letters of authenticity and the lab tests and all that. How it got by the lab . . . okay, I can't explain that. But I do know it's a fake, a copy."

"I must have missed something. What's your substantiation again?"

She went through her rationale with him, judiciously leaving out the fact that she'd consulted with Tiny and Geoff. Ted, she knew, had some lingering doubts about Geoff's moral fiber and credibility. Not that Alix didn't have them as well, but there was a big difference. Ted had gotten to know him as a member of the team that had worked so hard and successfully to get him put away for his several crimes; Alix had known him as his well-loved child.

"'The background's too *good*'?" he repeated doubtfully. "That's your proof?"

"You don't think I'm right?"

"Well, maybe when we get back to the yacht, you could show me—"

"I can't show you. Panos has locked it away in some special storage place and nobody can get near it."

"I see." He frowned down at his glass.

"You *don't* think I'm right, do you?"

"Alix, you made a believer out of me in Santa Fe, so when you say something like that, yes, I do think you're right—well, *probably* right. But you have to admit it's not what anyone would call incontrovertible proof." He held up the second small bottle, taken from her satchel, and when she nodded he twisted off the cork and refilled their glasses.

"Ted, I'm just telling you what I saw and what I concluded from it. I'm convinced I'm right, but I don't know how I'm supposed to prove it, especially since the lab decided there was nothing suspicious about it, and I can't get another look at it anyway."

"Huh. I might have an idea about that, though. The fact—if it's a fact—that it's a *copy* of an existing, known painting, rather than some kind of 'in-the-style-of' pastiche, might make it possible to . . ." He stopped and sipped thoughtfully for a couple of beats. "You know, I'm not familiar with the painting myself. You did say it's pretty well known?"

"No, I wouldn't say 'well known.' It's never been on permanent exhibition in a museum, as far as I know, but it's in Venturi's catalogue raisonné, and it's got a provenance going all the way back to the 1861 Paris salon show. Why, what difference does it make?"

Instead of answering he opened his phone and pressed a key. "Jamie? Hi. Listen—yes, the flights were a piece of cake and everything's fine here. Listen, I need you to see what you can get in the way of digital photos—the highest resolution you can find—of a Manet painting. *Le Déjeuner au Bord du Lac.*" He repeated the name more slowly. "Painted in . . ." He looked at Alix.

"Eighteen-sixty-one, same year as the salon."

"Eighteen-sixty-one," he said into the phone, and then again to Alix: "Do you have any idea how long Panos has owned it?"

"No. Yes. I heard him say he bought it fifteen years ago."

Ted returned to Jamie. "Make sure you get something from before 1997, which shouldn't be any problem, but then, if you can possibly find any that've been taken since then—he may have lent it to a gallery or a museum for a showing or something—I want those too. Got it? Hey, what kind of question is that? When I *always* need it by, of course. Right away. E-mail it to me when you have something, okay? Thanks. Yes, I'll tell her. Bye now."

"She says hi," he said.

"Thanks." Alix had had all the salmon she wanted and was now using her fork to dig into a sinfully sweet and gooey square of baklava, studded with slivered almonds and glistening with honey. "What was that call about? What's getting a photo supposed to do?"

"Nothing, probably, but give me a chance to see if anything comes of it, and I'll let you know. Jamie's good; I should know something tomorrow."

It had gotten dark as they'd talked, and they gathered up their plates and cutlery to take back to the buffet area (the satchels had been provided with removable inner linings so they weren't stained by the leftovers). Ted stood up and extended a hand to pull her up too. "I guess I'd better get back and do some mingling. Oh, and may I make a suggestion? I realize all this forgery stuff is highly absorbing and exciting, but if you find yourself with some free time, and you're getting bored, maybe you might also keep alert for anything that might come up about what you've been sent here for—those fractional investments?"

"Those what?"

"Those——" he began, but broke out laughing when he realized she was kidding.

"I will, Ted," she said. "I promise. But . . ." She paused. "You're here now. You're a professional. I hardly know what I'm doing. You can talk to Panos about his investment system right out in the open, which I obviously can't. So is there still really anything useful for me to do on that count?"

"Well, that is a point." He paused. "You're right. What the hell, why don't you just kick back and enjoy the ride?"

"No, I'm not comfortable with that. Look, I think there are still things I can bring to the table. Unless you don't want me to, I'd like to keep working on this Manet thing and see what develops. For all we know, it'll lead us somewhere on the investments."

"Could be," Ted conceded. "Wouldn't exactly bowl me over if it's all connected." He nodded to himself. "Okay, do that. But discreetly, right? It would seriously tick me off if you really got your head broken."

19

When they got back to the buffet area Panos and Edward were still talking and Ted got himself some coffee and went to sit with them. Alix, not yet fully herself and starting to feel it, was the first to leave. She had the limo to herself on the way back to the harbor, where Donny was smoking a cigarette, waiting with the launch.

He perked up when he saw her. The cigarette was flipped into the water. "You want to go back?"

"Yes, please."

"Nobody else here yet. We could go get cup of coffee, glass of wine, nice little café right there."

Tempting as the idea was of having a one-on-one chat with the *Artemis*'s one-man information machine over a glass or two of milky, tongue-loosening ouzo, she wasn't about to go off to a dark little hole-in-the-wall bar at night in a seedy port area she didn't know with a scuzzball like him.

"No, thank you," she said demurely, "I'd just like to get back to the boat."

Dark as it was, she could see that he was pouting away as he started up the engine, but she was fairly sure she knew her man, and it wouldn't be long before he came back with another offer, perhaps a better one. Something in the daylight, for instance.

He continued to mope on the short trip back to the boat, however, and she'd begun to wonder if she'd blown her chance at him, but as they neared the bay door to let her off, he said offhandedly, without turning from the wheel, "You know, tomorrow morning, I got to go pick up some fresh fish and stuff at this market up the coast—ten, fifteen kilometers. I figure I take the *Hermes*. You know, you got to take them fast boats for a spin every now and then." His shoulders went up and down in a couldn't-care-less shrug. "I guess if you want to come I could take you too."

"That might be fun, Donny," she said, shooting for something friendly, but without coming on too strong, which even Donny would perceive as counterfeit. "When would that be?"

"Oh, I don't know. Got to be early, because we get going again at two o'clock and I got a lot to do. Maybe . . . seven o'clock?"

"I think I could make that. I'm usually up early. If I do, where should I be?"

"I think best you be by swim platform, you know it?"

"You mean here, by the bay door?"

"No, not here. The swim platform. Deck three, the main deck, aft. You know, back of the swimming pool. You be there, okay? Hey—if we got time, maybe we have that picnic? I could bring what to eat."

"Could be," she said, putting a becomingly hesitant but promising smile in her voice. "We'll see."

"Just talk about stuff, that's all. You know?"

You got that right, she thought.

.   .   .

At 6:40 a.m. the next day, Alix went looking for the swim platform. In back of the swimming pool, Donny had said, although she couldn't imagine how you could possibly have a swim platform on the yacht's main deck, fifteen feet above the water line (a diving platform, maybe, but a swim platform?). The ship was still anchored, the morning gorgeous, the smooth, gently heaving Aegean still pink-tinged from the dawn and the Cretan mountains shadowed in tints of rose and gold. Assuming she was the only one of the guests who'd be up at this hour, she was startled to hear a voice coming from a canvas sling chair beside the pool.

"Alix, good morning!"

"Gaby? You're up early."

"Since three." She patted the arm of the chair next to her. "Come join me if you have a little time. I could stand some company." If she was embarrassed about having been seen smooching with Emil the night before, she gave no sign. If anybody was embarrassed, it was Alix, but if Gaby was willing to forget about it, Alix was glad to go along.

"Fifteen minutes or so—sure, I'd like that." She saw now that there was a little table beside Gaby with a pitcher and a cup and saucer on it. "Especially if you can order me some coffee too. It smells like heaven."

"Only the very best," Gaby said. "Of course. Nothing but one hundred percent Kona."

Alix eased herself into the sling chair—fell into it was more like it; how to do it gracefully was something she'd never gotten the hang of—while Gaby got on the phone. "Another pot, please. And a cup."

"Up since three?" Alix said. "Are you not a good sleeper, then?"

"You know, when you're in opera, there's always a party—*always*—or a reception, or a huge dinner, at least for the featured performers, and since you're starving and your adrenaline is still pumping away, you always eat way, way more than you should, and you have about five drinks too many, and midnight or one o'clock is just the wrong time for stuffing your face, especially when you're in Vienna, but your biological clock is still on Sydney time or wherever the hell your last stop was. It throws off your sleep rhythms, and, as I'm learning, you never get them back. It's like—I don't know, I feel like I've forgotten *how* to sleep sometimes. My brain just refuses to shut down when it's supposed to."

"Isn't there something you can take for it?"

A stewardess came with Alix's coffee and a couple of the luscious croissants, poured Alix a cup, and, at Gaby's nod, poured a little more for her as well and left with a little bow, without having spoken.

"Oh, sure. God bless ketamine."

"Pardon?"

"My fairy dust. Nothing else works for me. It's mainly an animal anes-thetic, if you can believe it, but there's nothing like it for turning off your mind and giving you a good night's sleep. I'd take it seven nights a week, if I could, but I don't want to get addicted—I did to a couple of other sleeping pills, and breaking the habit practically killed me—so I limit myself to three nights a week. Unfortunately, last night wasn't one of them, and I really could have used a little after what . . . well, Panos was . . . was . . ." She shook her head and lifted her coffee to her lips with both hands.

Alix had the impression that Gaby was trying to decide whether she wanted to say something more or if she'd already revealed more than she should have. Alix drank some of her own coffee and waited. She'd already had waffles and fresh strawberries for breakfast in her stateroom, but the aroma of the warm croissants was too much to resist, and she tore off a melt-in-your-mouth morsel and chomped it down, by which time Gaby had made her decision.

"Panos was on the warpath last night," she more or less blurted out, speaking low but fast, as if she just couldn't hold it in any more, "which is not a pretty sight."

"I know. If you remember, I just happened to be there when he saw the Manet."

"This was just as bad."

"What happened? What was it about?"

"He saw my charges from the shopping I did in Mykonos on Tuesday, and he hit the ceiling. Usually, our accountant sort of buries that kind of thing, but this time there wasn't—"

"Gaby, do you mean you have to hide your purchases from your husband?"

"That's exactly what I mean."

"But he's enormously wealthy, isn't he? I mean, this yacht and everything . . ."

"Oh, he's as rich as Croesus, but he's also as cheap as . . . I don't know, Silas Marner?"

"Yes, but how much could you charge in Mykonos in one day? It's not as if you could spend ten thousand dollars . . ." The look on Gaby's face made her hesitate. " . . . Could you?"

"Twenty-one thousand, actually. Euros, not dollars." An impish smile flitted across her face. "All right, I was naughty, I admit it."

"Twenty-one thousand euros in *Mykonos*? Good heavens, what did you buy, a house?"

"No, don't be silly, nothing big. A few accessories, that's all. Some bags, shoes, a nice summer coat-and-hat set . . . no, it was a couple of summer coats, I don't really remember. I sent Artemis in afterward to pick up the packages. I think she said there were eighteen altogether. She had to hire a car."

Alix couldn't think of anything to say. She was remembering Gaby's earlier remark about possessions—things—being meaningless to her. She took a quick look at the deck beside Gaby's chair, and sure enough, there was another unmistakably expensive designer bag casually flopped on its side: not the burgundy one she'd seen the day before, but a black leather one with lots of buckles. At three or four or five thousand euros a pop, she realized, they wouldn't take long to add up to twenty-one thousand euros.

Gaby followed her gaze. She reached over and awkwardly put a hand on Alix's forearm, then quickly removed it. "I know; I do have a lot of things. I do shop a lot. And what I said yesterday was the truth: They don't mean anything to me, not really. But please try and understand—shopping is *all* I have. I gave up my career, my beautiful career, when I married Panos. What else do I have? I don't really know how to do anything but sing, and I can't do that anymore, and I can't even do any teaching or coaching, which is what most of us old prima donnas wind up doing. The thing is, we're always on the move, from one house to another, or off on another damn cruise. And I always have to go with him, so he can show me off." Her fingers wandered to the loose flesh below what had not so long

163

ago been a firm and lovely chin. "Although who knows how much longer that's going to last." She jerked her head. "God, listen to me whine. Pathetic. It's just lack of sleep, Alix. Makes me goofy, pay no attention." She stretched out in the chair with a sigh and put a hand over her eyes.

Alix's attitude toward Gaby softened. Sure, Gaby had willingly signed on for the life she now had. Yes, it was nobody's doing but her own. Yes, 99.9 percent of the women in the world would trade places with her in a heartbeat. And still . . .

It was an old story. Gaby had wanted money and security, Panos had wanted arm candy and a whiff of culture, and they'd each gotten their wish. That had been ten years ago. Now Gaby was getting old for a trophy wife, and surely she had to know that he could easily discard her for a new young and beautiful wife who was interested in the same deal that Gaby—who was herself wife number three—had gotten. If Alix's guess was right, Panos had had an ironclad prenuptial agreement drawn up that would let him do just that and do it cheaply. Her heart went out to the aging opera star. *If Emil (and Mirko?) offered some comfort and happiness,* she thought, *then go for it, girl.*

"Gaby—"

"But what are *you* doing up at this time of day?" Gaby asked with a bright, brittle smile. "For most of the others, this is the middle of the night. Are you a lousy sleeper too? Want to try the ketamine? It's a lifesaver." She began to reach for her bag. "I always have some—"

"Oh, no thanks, I sleep fine, knock on wood. Donny's going off for supplies in a few minutes, though, in the *Hermes,* and he offered me a ride, so I—"

Gaby surprised her with a harsh laugh. "I wouldn't count on that, honey. I doubt if Donny will be doing anything like that this morning."

"Why not?"

"Well, I did talk to Panos about him. It wasn't just what Izzy said. There have been other . . . complaints from guests, especially from women. The boy has become truly insufferable. But I still didn't expect Panos to react the way he did. I guess he was still steaming over those credit card bills and looking for someplace to get it off his chest because he charged off looking for Donny like a bull hunting for a china shop—hey, I think I just invented a metaphor."

Telling the story had perked her up, and she looked down at the remaining croissant on Alix's plate. "If you're not planning on eating that . . . ?"

Alix shoved the plate in her direction. "Please. I shouldn't have had the first one. I already had breakfast."

Gaby took a bite, chewed it slowly and appreciatively, and continued. Panos had returned ten minutes later, still angry but with a satisfied look on his face. He'd finally given Donny his walking papers, he told her, and the hell with whatever Donny's ogre of a mother, who was Panos's domineering, Medusa-like Aunt Polyphema, happened to think about it. When they arrived in Corfu tomorrow morning, Donny would be put off the ship and forbidden ever to come anywhere near it again. Out of the goodness of his heart ("I'm quoting," Gaby said), Panos would give him two hundred euros to get back home to Karavostassis.

"Well, I guess it's all for the best," Alix said. "I'm sorry to miss that ride in the *Hermes*, though."

"Why do you have to miss the ride? Somebody's going to be going. You can go with whoever it is. If they're taking the speedboat, it'll be Yiorgos. He's the only other one who drives it."

Alix brightened. "The security guy? Do you think he'd take me?" The stalwart Yiorgos Christos, she was pretty sure, wasn't going to be the fountainhead of information that Donny might have been, but that didn't mean she had to pass up the ride. Besides, she'd been more or less relieved of information-gathering duty by Ted, hadn't she?

Gaby laughed and got out her cell phone. "Yiorgos, you're going out for supplies this morning? In the *Hermes*? Alix London would like to ride with you. That's all right, isn't it? Yes, I'll do that." She put the phone away. "He's in the process of getting the boat now. Better go and wait for him on the swim platform. And Alix?" she said as Alix fought her way out of the sling chair, "don't take everything I said too seriously. I just need to vent from time to time, and you happened to be here for one of my better venting sessions. I've got a pretty good life, and I know it. The truth is, I'm really a pretty happy person."

Alix didn't believe it for a minute. "Gaby," she said on a sudden urge, "did you know my father spent eight years in prison?"

"Yes, I did," she said with a smile. "We have a lot in common, don't we? There's nothing that can beat that look on someone's face, is there, when they hear your name, and their eyes squish up, and you see the little wheels going around in their head, *chunka chunka*, and they're thinking, 'Don't tell me she's the daughter of that . . .'" She finished with that warm, liquid laugh of hers.

Alix smiled in response. Two of a kind, all right. "Well, at least they never think you're boring," she said lightly. "I'd better get going, Gaby. See you later."

.   .   .

When she got to the stern, Alix saw how it was that the swim platform could possibly be on the main deck, which was so far above the water. The stern of the *Artemis* was another of its design features that had been revolutionary when it was built, but was now commonplace on luxury yachts. The rear of the third deck, the open main deck, didn't end sharply at a more or less vertical transom, but descended at a long, shallow angle, with curving, symmetrical steps on either side, down to an eight-foot-wide shelf on the second deck—the water-level deck—that ran the width of the ship. There were a few padded wicker deck chairs and a couple of cocktail tables on it lined up facing rearward, toward the sea. From the shelf projected a foldaway diving board in the center and two removable pool ladders at the sides for climbing back out of the water.

Alix regretted that she hadn't gotten up even earlier for a solitary sunrise dip. If there was another chance for one she'd take it. The best she could do at the moment was to sit on the edge and dangle her rubber-sandaled feet for a quick dip in the cool, velvety sea. Delicious, but she'd barely gotten her toes wet when the *Hermes* came sliding around the starboard side, its gentle *putt-putt-putt-putt* sounding more like a neighbor's idling lawn mower than a fearsomely powerful cigarette boat. And, in fact, it didn't look like her idea of a cigarette boat: Where was the spear-point bow, the gleaming, bullet-shaped hull? This little stub-nosed craft seemed more like the kind of weekender you saw by the dozens at any marina, and at first she was disappointed.

But the more of it that came into view, the more impressed she was. She realized now that she'd never seen anything like it. It was both lower slung and more massive than she'd thought at first, and its bulk gave it an aura of power that the skinnier cigarette boats didn't have; at the same time, there was something about it that made her think of some sinewy beast—a leopard, a cheetah—relaxed for the moment but full of impending menace and latent speed. It was like some improbable prop for a sci-fi movie. Indeed, it was the kind of machine in which you might expect to find James Bond at the wheel.

Instead, of course, it was Yiorgos, looking more than ever like Özbek, the Turkish Giant, in a bursting white T-shirt that outlined every swelling muscle like a diagram in an anatomy book. He was an amiable, welcoming giant, though, reaching out one bulging-biceped arm to help her hop aboard. He gestured her into the front passenger seat and slowly started up. There were other yachts, small and large, anchored nearby, so the lazy *putt-putt*-ing continued as he wove through them. The windshield had been folded down, so the movement created a pleasant breeze on her face. She ran her hand along the smooth ebony of the instrument console and over the convex faces of the dials.

"This looks so familiar. . . ."

"You have been in such a boat before?" Yiorgos asked.

"No, or at least I don't think so. I must have seen a picture of it."

"Ever drive a Lancia?"

"The car, you mean? Yes, a Lancia Delta S4. Why?"

Yiorgos threw back his head and laughed, the deep, rolling *har, har, har* that would have been expected from him. "You don't mean the S4, I think. I think maybe you mean the nice little Delta hatchback. The Delta S4 is a famous racing car, *har, har, har.*"

"That's the one I mean," Alix said, and then, just for the fun of rubbing it in, "the 1800-cubic-centimeter, 560-horsepower, turbocharged model that won at San Remo, Monte Carlo, Lombard—"

Yiorgos's mouth was open. His eyebrows had lifted halfway to his hairline, and it took him a moment to find words. "You are kidding me. You are . . . you are a *race car driver*?"

"No," she said, laughing, "but I did drive an S4. More than once. On the Amalfi Coast."

It had been when she was in Italy studying with Fabrizio Santullo, she explained. Santullo, a stern critic and a demanding, no-excuses teacher in the workshop, had been a kindly man once he got out of it, and after a while he had fallen into the habit of inviting her to his summer house in Ravello for the weekend. His son Gian-Carlo had raced as an amateur for a few years and had been pleased when she'd expressed interest in the amazing collection of six racing cars that he maintained. He had given her a few lessons in several of them, including the Lancia S4 and the even more spectacular Lamborghini Gallardo LP 560. She had spent many wonderful hours cruising down the glorious Amalfi coastline just after sunup, before the traffic began to build.

Yiorgos gave her a lustrous smile. "Ah, so romantic: the Amalfi Coast at dawn, the Lamborghinis, the Lancias, the handsome Gian-Carlo."

Alix smiled thinking of the balding, rotund, five-foot-five, forty-nine-year-old, contentedly married father of five they were talking about. "Oh, yes, very romantic," she said. "But why are we talking about this? Why did you ask?"

"Because *this* is a Lancia," he said, patting the console. "That is why the controls, the . . . ." He couldn't come up with the word for *dials*, so he made a spinning motion with his finger. " . . . Why they look to you familiar."

"Lancia makes boats? I thought they only made cars."

"Only this one, and only for two years they made it. A wonderful boat, it can skim over the water like a jet plane, but it was too much money for people to buy."

They had reached open water now, but rather than speed up, Yiorgos slowed to a full stop, so they remained there, bobbing and gently *putt-putt*ing. "Would you like to have the wheel?"

"*Really?*"

"If you can drive the S4, you can drive this. It is the same thing, almost."

"I'd love to—thank you!"

They switched seats. Excitedly, Alix scanned the panel. "I don't know what some of the dials mean."

"I will watch the dials."

She put her hand on the double-levered throttle. "And this is new to me. This is the same as a gear shift lever?"

"Sure. You want to go forward, you push forward this part, that's all."

"And what else do I do?"

He shrugged. "Nothing else. You turn the wheel like a car to go where you want to go."

"And where do we want to go?"

"Straight ahead, up the coast. Don't worry, I tell you when we get there."

"Push the throttle forward . . . ," she murmured to herself, excited but also a little nervous.

Yiorgos made an encouraging go-ahead gesture. "That's all. Push, push."

She pushed.

*VrroooOOOO*AAAHHHMMM*!*

Off flew her visor. Back jerked her head. For a split second her hair was snapping at her eyes, and then it was streaming out behind her. She was sure she could feel her cheeks rippling, the way they do in those videos of astronauts hitting six Gs in the training centrifuge. The ride was smooth for a few seconds, but then began bumping wildly, bouncing her in her seat. The bow rose in front of her, higher than she thought possible without upending the boat. She had to peer around the side to see where she was going. All of this in a space of five seconds. She pulled back on the throttle. The boat slowed. The bow flopped back down into the water with a *splat*.

"Wow," she said, and she knew she was bug-eyed. "Yikes. Oh my God, that is really something."

Yiorgos was laughing. "Maybe not push so hard next time."

"You know, I think you might be right," she said, *easing* the lever forward. This time the buildup was lengthier, but in sixty seconds they were back up at the same earsplitting, kidney-jolting, utterly thrilling speed. Alix simply gave herself up to the sheer joy of it, taking the marvelous craft in grand, sweeping curves so great and exact that she could see their own wake running parallel alongside the boat but going the other way. Lost in sensation, she was unaware of Yiorgos's trying to get her attention until he tapped her on the shoulder. She'd been laughing without realizing it, but the look on his face put an end to that. She eased back on the throttle.

"What is it?" she asked when the racketing had died down enough for her to be heard. "What's the matter?"

He put a finger to his lips and she saw that he had his cell phone pressed to his ear. He said a few curt words in Greek, listened for a while, added another brief phrase or two, closed the phone and then opened it a moment later, hit another button, and placed it to his ear again.

"What is it, Yiorgos? Is something wrong?"

He made another shushing gesture and indicated that she should set the boat to idling again. While it *putt-putt*-ed away, he spoke into the phone at some length. His clipped, authoritative sentences didn't sound to her as if they were part of a two-way conversation. He was issuing orders.

When he was done, he pocketed the phone. "I drive now."

Once they had exchanged seats and he'd gotten the boat up to a moderate speed, he spoke. "They find Dionysodaurus. Near Agia Pelagia. Other side of Heraklion, a few kilometers."

She didn't understand. "Donny isn't on the yacht? I mean, I know Mr. Papadakis fired him, but I thought he would be getting off in Corfu."

He glanced at her. "Who tells you this information?"

"Well, people are talking about it," she said, afraid of causing difficulties for Gaby.

He nodded. "This is true, yes, but Dionysodaurus, he didn't want to wait until Corfu."

Donny had not appeared at the early staff breakfast that morning, he told her, and when looked for he couldn't be found. On a hunch, Yiorgos had checked the "petty cash" box, 3000 euros kept for buying food and supplies at village shops and markets that didn't take credit cards. All of the paper money, approximately 2,700 euros, was gone. A more thorough search had made it clear that Donny was also gone.

"But the *Artemis* must be two miles from shore," Alix said. "How could he—oh, of course, he was a swimmer; he told me he'd been, what was it, the swimming champion of the Cyclades. He must have—"

"Of the Cyclades?" Yiorgos snorted. "He was second-place winner of his village, Karavostassis." He sighed. "Not good enough, it looks like."

It took a moment for her to grasp his meaning. "He's *dead*? They found him *dead*?"

They had indeed. When the *Philomena*, an ancient shrimp trawler out of the fishing village of Agia Pelagia, returning at dawn from a nighttime drag, had winched in a heavy, promisingly bulging net and loosened its pursed mouth to let the contents flow into the sluicing box, what slithered down seemed at first to be no more than the beautiful, shining, gray-brown rain of shrimp they'd expected. But as they hosed the creatures down into the refrigerated hold, they found something that no man among them had ever encountered before.

Among the thousands of crawling, ten-legged *Steiracrangon orientalis* was a single, two-legged representative of the phylum *Chordata*, subphylum *Vertebrata*, class *Mammalia*, order *Primates*, family *Hominidae*, genus *Homo*.

In a word, Donny, much the worse for wear after spending a few hours among the hungry crustaceans.

There was little doubt as to his identity. He had personal identification in his wallet, he was wearing a shirt with the logo *Artemis* woven into it—and in a plastic bag inside a travel pouch attached to his belt was a thick wad of euros, as yet uncounted.

Final confirmation came as Yiorgos finished his explanation. His cell phone buzzed gently, and when he opened it he took a long look. "They took a photograph," he said. "It is him for sure."

Alix put out her hand. "May I see?"

Yiorgos shook his head. "Not good to look at. The shrimp, the crabs . . ." He ended with a grimace.

"Do they know what happened to him? I mean, he just drowned? There wasn't any . . . ?"

"That is what we must find out. The Agia Pelagia police—it was they who called—they find no signs of foul play, no injuries but the . . . the nibbling of his flesh. They believe he drowns while trying to swim to Heraklion in the night, and the current takes him in that direction. The current here, it flows from east to west, so it may be so. We will see."

"You think it might not be?"

He shrugged. "Dionysodaurus, for him it was easy to make enemies. And these local policemen, they are not trained to look into such things. Already I have notified the Hellenic Police, the national police, to take charge. They will be here in an hour. Until then, I will take charge myself."

"But I thought you weren't with them anymore."

"No, I am a lieutenant colonel. Only for a month I take leave to help because my wife, she asks to make a family favor. You see, she is the cousin of the husband of Panos's Aunt Eleni's nephew's wife's brother Kostas. Panos, you see, he fires his old security chief, his own cousin, for various . . .

well, it makes no difference. I am here for one month, no more. If he picks a new chief before one month, I am through. The sooner the better," he muttered as an afterthought. "There, that is Agia Pelagia."

They were approaching a terraced village rising from a small, blue-green bay. There was a sandy beach onto which four midsize fishing vessels had been pulled up. Around one of them a crowd milled, a couple of uniformed policemen among them.

"The *Philomena*, I think," Yiorgos said, turning the *Hermes* toward it.

"What do you want me to do?" Alix asked. "Can I help?"

"No," he said bluntly. "A police car will drive you back to the marina in Heraklion. The launch from the yacht will come for you. It has been arranged."

She very nearly objected, much preferring to be there for whatever was going to happen. On the other hand, whatever was going to happen was going to happen in Greek, so she wouldn't have gotten much out of it anyway. "Thank you," she said submissively.

20

Ted had spent the early part of the morning exploring the yacht and had come upon Lorenzo Bolzano, Emil Varga, and Mirko Koslecki, the Man Without a Country, relaxing in a grouping of armchairs in the *Al Fresco* lounge, an informal, open-air room on the forward part of the main deck, which was overhung by the half-length bridge deck and thus shielded from the sun. He wasn't surprised to find them there. All three were pallid men who looked as if they hadn't been caught out in the sun in years. The mysterious Mirko in particular gave off distinctly Dracula-like emanations.

They were being served coffee. Ted ordered some for himself and joined them without being invited, and a few minutes later along came Panos and Edward Reed, and they sat down too. Ted was pleased. The more of them he had to talk with, the better.

"Panos," he said at a break in the meandering small talk, "Aunt Saskia asked me to tell you how pleased she was with the returns on that Turner you sold recently, and the Pollock before that."

"Thank you, my friend Rollie." Panos smiled, Buddha-like, his hands folded on his belly, and turned to the others. "We got a good price on the Pollock, didn't we? Didn't I said we would?"

"Very nice," said Lorenzo. Mirko mumbled his agreement, but Emil shook his head ruefully. "I *knew* the Pollock would do well, but you, you old scoundrel, you wouldn't sell me a single share, would you?"

"Don't blame me, Emil. Too late, you waited for. Already, it was one hundred percent subscribed." He spread his hands in mocking apology. "I can't sell more than a hundred percent of something, can I?"

The hell you can't, Ted thought. "Panos, my aunt was wondering if you expect to have any other pieces available for similar investment in the near future."

The others showed interest as well, but for whatever reason, Panos wasn't biting. He clucked his disapproval. "Gentlemen, gentlemen, such talk. Fractional investments," he said contemptuously. "Why we are here? We are here for to relax among our own kind and to live with the great art that is on the walls for a few days. Let us hear no more about 'investments.' Pah."

"Not until the auction, at any rate," a smiling Edward amended.

That brought a great gust of laughter from Panos, who clapped Edward good-humoredly on the forearm. "Yes, for that we make an exception." He hauled himself to his feet. "Gentlemen, things to do," he said and went on his way toward the stern. "Enjoy yourselves. Anything you want, ask."

Ted got up and followed. "Panos, there's something else I want to talk to you about: the Manet."

Panos stopped and turned with a scowl of sharpened interest. "You know something?"

"No, what would I know? I haven't even seen it. But I'd like to."

Panos sagged a little. "It's wrecked. I put it away. I can't stand anymore to look at the damn thing." He began walking again.

Ted stayed where he was. "I was thinking I might make you an offer on it."

Panos had gone only a few steps. He stopped in his tracks and came back. Ted expected to be asked why he would want to buy a ruinously damaged painting, and he had a studiously prepared rationale ready and waiting, but he didn't need it; Panos got right down to brass tacks.

"How much?"

"Well, I don't know; I haven't seen it."

"The estimate was, it would go for ten million. At least ten million. A good chance for fifteen."

Ted smiled. "Well, it sure as hell isn't going to go for that now, is it? I was thinking maybe, oh, five million, if I like the looks of it. It'd save you a lot of worry and expense and time before you could even think of putting it up for sale. And you know what they say: a bird in the hand . . ."

Panos responded with a hoarse laugh. "Five million euros? Forget it."

"Five million *dollars*."

"You're insulting me."

"Maybe as much as seven or so. It depends. Let's have a look."

"You want it for Countess Saskia?"

"No, for myself. My aunt has nothing to do with this."

Panos peered at him. "What for do you want it? You ain't a collector."

"No, but I am a dealer . . . of sorts." He glanced around, as if to make sure nobody could overhear them, then leaned closer. "Panos, let me be frank. I have certain . . . clients . . . in Asia and the Middle East, who would love to own a Manet."

"A Manet with a big rip down the middle?"

"No, of course not. I'd have it repaired before offering it. I have a first-rate restorer, the best in the world, in my opinion, with whom I work from time to time."

"You do, huh? Who's that?"

Ted smiled. "Sorry. Confidential."

Panos made a sour face. "All right, so this client of yours—"

"Clients. I have several possibilities in mind."

"You do, huh?" Panos thought for a moment. "Okay, all right, come with me."

They took the forward stairwell up to the bridge deck, the top level, and to the Captain's Bar, a cozy little room that was startlingly different from most of the ship's Grecian or Classical décor. This place looked like an interior decorator's vision of an officers' club in colonial India, with porcelain tigers sitting at either end of a curving bar, the surface of which was softly glowing, back-lit agate. There were just four stools, their seats covered with what Ted suspected was elephant hide. Intricately carved, three-foot-long tusks stood in the corners. Behind the bar, in back of the shelf that held the bottles, where a mirror or a portrait of Queen Victoria might have been expected, was a wall of glass that looked directly into the pilot house, an airy, spick-and-span space with six big monitors lined up on the wide walnut console at the front. There was a keyboard and a mouse in front of each, but if there was a wheel or a control lever of any kind, Ted couldn't see it. There were three crewmen in the room, none of them doing anything much, and a gray-haired, neatly bearded man—the captain, judging from his aloof, military carriage and the gold stripes on the cuffs of his black uniform—who was standing in front of one of the screens, his hands clasped, statesmanlike, behind his back.

Ted and Panos's entrance caught his attention. He saluted and gave an order to one of the crewmen, who started for the opening in the glass wall that led to the bar, apparently to serve them. Panos waved him back and got behind the bar himself as Ted took a seat on a stool.

Panos banged both hands on the bar. "Let's have a drink, or is it too early for you?"

It was a little after nine a.m., a good eight hours too early for Ted—but of course it was never too early for Rollie de Beauvais, and over the years he had found that a little shared alcohol made negotiations like this easier and more productive. An extremely moderate drinker himself, he was in little danger of overdoing it. "I'll have a Scotch, neat."

Panos poured them each a couple of fingers of Macallan 21 Year Old Scotch—about three hundred dollars a bottle, if Ted remembered right. "*Skol*," Panos said and chugged it down.

Ted took a sip of what was without a doubt the best Scotch he'd ever tasted—peaty and smooth, almost syrupy, with just the smallest hint of smokiness—but he managed to look as if it was what he drank every day, just another Scotch. He waited for Panos to pick up the conversation.

"Tell me this, Mr. Rollie de Beauvais. Why I should sell it to you for you to sell it to someone else? Why not I just sell it myself? Cut out the middleman." He poured himself a little more Scotch and tossed it down his throat.

"Go ahead," Ted said, "suit yourself."

"If I wanted to, I could—"

Ted started to stand up, putting a little exasperation into the movement. "Enough already, Panos. Let's have a look at the damn thing, and then *maybe* we'll have something to talk about. If you're not interested, just say so."

"Hey, hey, hold your horses, what's the rush?" He put an ingratiating hand on Ted's shoulder, pushing him gently back down, then used a telephone on the bar to issue some quick instructions in Greek. "One minute, it'll be here." He began to top off Ted's glass, but Ted put his hand over it. Panos set the bottle back down without pouring any more for himself. "So," he said, "these *clients* of yours, of course you are planning to tell them about the damage?"

"I am not. I *am* planning to tell them it comes with a reliable provenance going right back to the year it was painted, with several authoritative letters of authentication, which you will give me, and with a clean bill of health from the *Laboratoire Forensique Pour l'Art,* of which I will also want a copy. All of that is true. However, I feel no obligation to inform them of every little scuff and scratch it may have suffered over the centuries."

"Scuff and scratch," Panos said, laughing. "That's some scratch. So tell me this. How much you expect to get for it?"

"That's the wrong question for you to be thinking about, Panos. The right question is, what would *you* get for it?"

"Yeah, but what makes you think—ah, look, here it is."

Édouard Manet's *Déjeuner au Bord du Lac*—or rather an expert copy of Édouard Manet's *Déjeuner au Bord du Lac,* according to Alix—now made its appearance atop a steel kitchen cart being wheeled in by one of the stewards.

Ted got up to look at it. He propped it at an angle against the cart's handle so that he could take it in more directly. He folded his arms. "Mm."

Panos muttered a single word to the steward, who turned and left.

"It's worse than I expected, Panos," Ted said, shaking his head.

"Oh, not so bad as that," Panos said, seeing a sale slipping away, "now that I see it again."

"Not so bad? That slash is a foot-and-a-half long, and it's jagged, more like it's been ripped than cut. That's harder to fix. This is not good, Panos. I don't know; I have to think about this." He stepped a few feet back from it, took out his phone, and held it up to the painting.

"Hey, what are you doing?"

"I need to take a few pictures."

Panos didn't like that. "What for?"

"So I can send them to my restorer and see what he says. For my purposes, the fact that it's been repaired has to be undetectable—well, undetectable to the naked eye. I want to see if he thinks it's possible."

"Sure, it's possible. Of course it's possible. That girl, Alix, she said so too."

"Mm," Ted said. He took five photos, mostly from up close. "I'll have to let you know; tomorrow, I hope."

"I might take seven," Panos said. "Depending on the conditions. But not a penny less."

. . .

By road, Agia Pelagia was only a few minutes from Heraklion, so the launch hadn't yet arrived when Alix was dropped off at the marina. She could see it a couple of miles out to sea, still being trundled out through one of the *Artemis*'s big bays. It would be a good five minutes before it arrived. She sat on a bench and opened her phone to check her e-mail, hoping for something from her father on Christoph Weisskopf, the painter he'd suspected of being the Manet forger. And there was something, an e-mail sent at 6 p.m. Seattle time last night.

> *My Dear Alix,*
>
> *I'm afraid I have some rather disturbing news about my old friend Weisskopf. I've attached a newspaper article that explains. I don't know what's going on here, or whether it has any connection to your Manet, but to speak frankly my dear, it frightens me. I fear you are sailing in dangerous waters, and I am not referring to the Aegean. I don't know what it is you've gotten yourself into, and I'm not at all sure that you do. I don't mean to be intrusive, and I know only too well the futility of expecting you to follow any advice that I might give you, but you must allow your old dad the privilege of being concerned. Please tread carefully. Keep a low profile, as they say on this side of the Pond. Call me often.*
>
> *Love . . . and safe travel,*
>
> *G*

Alix frowned. *What now?* She hit the paper clip *attachment* icon and up came a ten-week-old article from the *Brooklyn Daily Eagle:*

> ### Grand Ferry Victim Identified
>
> *The strangely dressed man found shot to death in Grand Ferry Park late Saturday night has been identified as Christoph Weisskopf, an artist who had resided on Williamsburg's South Sixth Street for about ten years. Mr. Weisskopf was dressed in seventeenth- or eighteenth-century garb when his body was discovered at a little after 11 PM. He had been shot three times from close range and had been dead about five hours.*
>
> *Neighbors explained that Mr. Weisskopf, who often painted historical scenes, sometimes dressed in costumes of the era to put himself in the proper mood.*
>
> *Police are investigating the matter. Anyone with personal knowledge of Mr. Weisskopf's activities or associates, or with information on persons or*

activities in Grand Ferry Park on the night of March 17 are urged to call the 90th Precinct at (718) 963-5311.

Her frown deepened. *Murdered? And now Donny was dead as well? Surely—*
She turned at the sound of a car door slamming behind her. Edward, Emil, and Gaby were climbing out of a limousine.

Edward smiled his greeting, Emil seemed to find something in the middle distance that completely absorbed his interest, and Gaby asked pleasantly: "Oh, did you go back to Knossos too this morning, Alix? I thought you were out with Yiorgos."

"I was, but something came up that he had to take care of, and he got a local policeman to drop me off here." They would learn soon enough about Donny's death, but she wasn't going to be the one to tell them. It was Ted she needed to talk to. "So was it a good tour?" she asked.

By this time the launch had arrived, driven by one of the crew, and the four of them clambered aboard.

"It was excellent," Edward said. "Our guide was a Princeton professor, here for a summer program."

"He *should* have been excellent," Gaby said, "considering what he was being paid."

"Oh, he was all right on Minoan culture," Emil opined, "but his knowledge of the Cretan Neolithic was, not to put too fine a point on it, pathetic." He smiled thinly. "But then, of course, that's Princeton for you."

Conversation died as the launch got underway, but after a minute Edward asked, "Alix, have you had a chance to look over the collection? I was wondering if you had any views you'd care to share." He held up his hand. "Unless you've found something 'funny' about the Gauguin or the Renoir. Or the Caillebotte. Or anything. That, I beg you to keep to yourself."

"No, nothing like that, but I've been meaning to ask you something. I couldn't find the Monet. Isn't there supposed to be a *Rouen Cathedral* somewhere? Is it in another room?"

"There had been one, yes, but we had to take it out before the cruise began. Didn't you see the updated catalog?"

"I guess not. I just remember the one catalog you sent out."

"No, there was a follow-up one. The laboratory in Lyons determined it to be inauthentic, and Panos promptly—and properly—agreed to remove it. Not happily, though, I might add."

"You have no idea," murmured Gaby. "'Fit to be tied' doesn't come close."

"Well, he had reason," Edward said with a touch of sternness. "He had a great deal of money invested in that painting." Smiling, he shook his head. "I was just thinking. When I told him about the laboratory report, it was the Manet he thought I was talking about, not the Monet. He never has kept them straight. And now he's lost both of them, almost as if he brought it on himself. The gods laugh."

They had pulled up to the *Artemis* now, and Artemis was there to help them aboard. "Welcome back, everyone. I hope you've had an interesting morning."

. . .

When she looked in the mirror in her stateroom she got a jolt. She hadn't combed her hair since that wild ride in the Lancia, and it looked as if she was wearing a bird's nest on her head. It took her twenty minutes to get the tangles out, and once tidied up, she called Ted on his cell phone. He answered from a beachfront café in Heraklion, where he, Panos, Edward, and Lorenzo had gone for a midmorning snack of thick Turkish coffee and rosewater-flavored Turkish delight.

"*Greek* coffee!" she heard Panos bellow with a laugh. "And *Greek* delight—*loukoumi*! You don't see me eating nothing Turkish."

"I need to talk to you, Ted. There have been some . . . unexpected developments. Things are a lot more complicated than I thought."

His tolerant, long-suffering sigh was audible. "Why am I not surprised? All right, the launch will have us back pretty soon. I'll call you. We'll find someplace quiet on the yacht. No, on second thought, why don't you catch the launch over here? I'll wait for you. We can have lunch in town."

21

"How about a pizza?" Ted asked, giving her a hand onto the dock.

"A pizza sounds *great!*" she said. "Real American food!"

Earlier, Ted had spotted a hole-in-the-wall pizza place a few blocks from the dock that had been giving off marvelous smells as they began their day's baking, and it was there they went. Basically a take-out place, it had three two-person tables along the wall opposite the counter, none of which were occupied, this being only noon. The place was definitely not geared for the tourist trade. The plump, flour-dusted man behind the counter seemed delighted to see them, but he spoke no English, and the one-sheet menus were in Greek. Fortunately, there were color photos on the wall behind him. Ted and Alix pointed at what appeared to be the everything-on-it special and got two Cokes from the glass-fronted refrigerator. The counterman rubbed his hands together, wiped them on his apron, and got happily to work, whistling away.

"Sorry to steal your thunder," Ted said as they settled with their Cokes into kitchen chairs at one of the oilcloth-covered tables, "but I'm afraid I already know about this unexpected development of yours."

"You do?"

"Yiorgos called Panos, and Panos told us about Donny. The question is: How do *you* know about it?"

"I was with Yiorgos when he got the call. In the speedboat."

His brow wrinkled. "You were . . . never mind; I don't want to know. The main thing is, you're right. The kid's death complicates things, especially if it turns out not to be an accident—which Yiorgos strongly suspects."

"I know."

"You know that too?"

"Sure, he told me."

Ted shook his head, smiled, and leaned back against the chair. "You know, I'm starting to think you just might be a natural at this kind of work after all. You sure know how to be in the right place at the right time—or in the wrong place, which is just as good if you don't get killed—and you do have one hell of a knack for getting information out of people."

"Maybe I ought to apply for a full-time job."

"Maybe you should. Want me to write you up a recommendation?"

Was he kidding? She didn't know, but then she wasn't sure she'd been joking either. Doing a little fishing, more likely.

No glasses or straws had been offered with the cans so they popped the tops and took their first swigs.

"Ted, a minute ago —I said 'developments,' not 'development.'"

He winced. "There's *more*?"

Alix told him about Christoph Weisskopf: that he had almost certainly been the forger of the Manet, and that he had recently been murdered.

Ted sat up straighter. "Whoa, where did *this* come from? How do you know this? How do you find *out* these things?"

She told him about the e-mail from her father and their earlier conversation, expecting him to express at least a little skepticism about the information, considering its source, but instead he listened thoughtfully, nodding once or twice.

"I know all about Weisskopf. He's a legend. We took a shot at nailing him once. Put a lot of legwork into it and never laid a glove on him. I can believe he's the one who forged it, all right." He surprised her by suddenly smiling. "Oh, I didn't tell you. You were right; it is a forgery. I hereby apologize for any doubts I may have had. Congratulations."

"Jamie come up with something?"

"Jamie came up with some good photographs, which were what I was hoping for. Let me show you. Do you have your telephone with you? Do you have a copy of the auction catalog on it?"

"Yes and yes." She went through her "kleptomaniacal" routine, smooth as glass this time, and navigated to the catalog.

"Go to the picture of the Manet," he said as he got out his own phone. "Zoom in on some relatively light part that doesn't have a lot of color variation—oh, the more distant part of the lake, for example."

"All right." She showed him the result. "Good enough?"

"Not as good as it'd be on a computer monitor, but it ought to do the job. Now . . ." He fingered his own phone and showed her the screen. "Look at this picture. Same area, right?"

"Yes. Not the same photograph, but yes, it's the *Déjeuner.*"

"Compare the two. Anything wrong?"

She peered at them.

"No, don't study them," he said. "Just take a quick look. See anything wrong?"

"Nope, not a thing. They're the same."

"Sure?"

"Positive. Am I missing something?"

Instead of replying, he said, "Okay, let me show you another one now." He brought it up. "Now compare this one with yours."

She did as he asked, comparing it to the image from the auction catalog that was on her phone and was puzzled. "Ted, I don't know what you want me to tell you. It's the same painting . . . no, wait. . . ." She took his phone from his hand and held it side by side with hers. "There's something about this one. . . . There's something different. . . ."

"Very good, but what?"

She shook her head. "I don't know, but there's *something.*"

"Yes, there is. Gotta hand it to you, kid. I am really impressed. That connoisseur's eye of yours is the real thing. I'll never doubt you again."

"Ha, I doubt that, but I appreciate the sentiment. But, you know, I'm still not seeing what it is about it. . . ."

He laughed. "That's because you're looking in the wrong place. You're looking at the painting."

"Well, of course I'm looking at the painting. What am I supposed to be looking at?"

"The *craquelure.*"

"The—?" She stared at him for a second then turned her attention to the network of fine cracks that ran over the surfaces. She looked quickly from one photo to the other.

"The *craquelure*—it's not the same!" she exclaimed. "These are two different paintings!"

"That's it," Ted said, smiling. "The greatest forger in the world and Weisskopf would be a prime candidate—might be able to duplicate every color and stroke of a painting, but there's no way he could possibly reproduce those thousands of intersecting networks of cracks. And . . . he didn't."

He explained that the photograph they were looking at now, the one in which the *craquelure* didn't match the auction catalog's version, had been taken more than half a century ago, in 1947, when the painting had been lent by its then-owner to the Jeu de Paume Museum in Paris to celebrate its reopening after the war, following its years as a storage house for Goering's looted art. The first photo, the one that *did* match the one in the catalog, had been taken only last year, when the Papadakises' St. Barts home had been the subject of a photo spread in *Architectural Digest.*

"In other words—" Ted said.

"In other words, sometime between 1947, when Panos didn't own it, and 2011, when he did, the real one was replaced by a fake. Ted, that's absolutely brilliant—the *craquelure.* I've never heard of a fake identified that way before."

"Thank you. I read about somebody doing it years ago, but this was my first shot at it. The thing is, it's almost never something you *can* use. The original has to be an old painting to start with, old enough to develop the cracks, and the fake has to be a copy of that specific picture, not just a painting intended to look generally like the work of some artist, and—this is the hardest part: There have to be high-quality photographs of both the original and the copy. Once you have all that, it's easy."

"Well, I'm still impressed. But what we still don't know is *when* the real Manet was replaced with the copy. It might have been after Panos had it, but it might also have been before then—anytime between 1947 and when he bought it, which we think was in 1997. Fifty years."

"Wrong; we do know. Jamie turned up a few other photographs, one of which is from another catalog—2002—when Panos put it up for sale at a Bern auction house but withdrew it when he didn't get his reserve price. And that photo *doesn't* match the one in our catalog, which means it's still the original. So . . ."

Again she finished Ted's thought for him. "So the substitution wasn't made until 2002 or later, well *after* he bought it. Wow, we're getting someplace. Okay, next question: Did Panos himself have it faked for some nefarious motive, who knows what, or was he himself the victim of some slick forger who'd taken it away for cleaning or restoration and returned the fake in its place?" (Someone like You Know Who, she thought but didn't say, although she knew Ted had to be thinking the same thing.)

He didn't say it either. "Well, being that Panos is Panos, my money is on his being the doer. Some people just aren't the victim type."

"That I agree with, but whoever did it, what I keep asking myself is how it's possible that the lab in Lyons didn't spot a fake of a hundred-and-fifty-year-old painting. They're the best there is. Could somebody there have been, what do you guys call it, 'compromised'?"

"Beats me; I don't have an answer to that either. Yet."

"And there's something else that doesn't hold up for me, Ted. How much would Panos have made from auctioning off the fake? Maybe ten million dollars, right?"

He nodded. "A mere pittance."

"But that's my point. For Panos it *is* a mere pittance."

He had been slowly rotating the Coke can on the table, but now his eyes came up to meet hers. "Why would you say that?"

"Well, everything about him. The yacht alone. It's a palace. He paid fifty-nine million dollars for it, so he must—"

"Not exactly. It *cost* fifty-nine million, which is a different thing. Panos has managed to pay seven-and-a-half million so far. And his payments are currently five months in arrears. The bank is threatening to take it back."

She blinked. "Oh. But the toys—that speedboat, the staff, the man's whole lifestyle . . ."

"That's the problem, his burn rate. He's spending way more than he's taking in."

"All right, what about all those multimillion-dollar homes he's supposed to own? In St. Barts, in New York, in—"

"He doesn't own any multimillion-dollar homes, he owns four multi-million-dollar mortgages. The one home he does own is a stone two-roomer in his home village, and he inherited that. And that fabulous art collection of his? He's underwater there too; he owes more on it than it's worth. From what we can tell, every single painting he does own outright is in this auction—and maybe some that he doesn't. He needs money, big-time."

This was such an overwhelmingly new take on Panos that it took her a few moments to digest it, and she still couldn't quite accept it. "Well, what about his big fractional investment scam? He's *got* to be raking in money on that. Why would he be doing it if he wasn't? And these are multimillion-dollar paintings they're investing in, aren't they?"

"Yes, they are, but at root the whole thing is a pyramid scheme, a Ponzi scheme, and it has the same flaw as every other Ponzi scheme. And in the end it's always a fatal flaw."

"You know, Ted, I hate to admit it, but I'm still not altogether clear on the ins and outs of this scheme. What's the fatal flaw?"

Panos's idea, he told her patiently, was to sell "shares" in a painting that he would wisely buy and later sell for a supposedly sizable profit—generally

20 percent or so, he told his investors. Put in a million, get back a million two hundred thousand. And the man delivered again and again, sometimes in only a month or two. With that kind of result, most of his investors dismissed their misgivings about such consistently prodigious returns, took their profits, and eagerly left the principal, that original million bucks or whatever, in the fund for the next killing. So all Panos had to worry about ever forking out were the earnings that they expected; he still had the original million. Actually, he had a lot more than that because some of the shares they were buying didn't exist, except in Panos's mind and his bank account. That is, he would sell a 120 or 130 percent of each painting if he could get it, and, of course, keep the extra 20 or 30 percent for himself.

The catch, of course, was that it was impossible to keep this up indefinitely, so what Panos was doing, and this was the very essence of a Ponzi scheme, was using the principal from new investors to pay the older ones their "profits." As long as he could keep bringing in willing new suckers, things chugged right along, but when the economy sputtered and there weren't as many rich new suckers as before, he reached the stage of having too many older clients to pay and not enough new clients to cover them. And it all started to go bust.

"The fatal flaw," Ted repeated. "From what we've been able to put together, that's where he's at now and he's hoping this auction brings in enough at least to get him right with his investors so he can bail out before he gets caught. Otherwise he's headed for a Madoff-level fall and he knows it. So . . . an extra ten million bucks or so isn't chicken feed to him."

Alix had sipped her drink and listened carefully while he'd explained. "Wow," she said quietly. "I had no idea. You'd never know from looking at him, would you? He looks as if he's on top of the world."

"You wouldn't be much of a con man if you couldn't pull that off."

The counterman now showed up at the table with knives, forks, paper plates, and a wad of paper napkins, went back to the oven, shoveled out a pizza, deftly sliced it, not into pie-shaped wedges, but into squares, or as near as the pizza's curving rim would allow, and brought it to their table. He looked proudly down at his steaming creation, affectionately down at his customers, and used both arms to make an encouraging gesture. They smiled their thanks, but he remained waiting, whistling under his breath, until they each took a piece, tasted it, and *m-m-m*-ed how very good it was. Satisfied, he retired.

"It's . . . interesting," Ted said to Alix and sniffed at the slice he held. "Different."

"Different," Alix agreed.

"Anyway," Ted continued, "we now have a lot of things going on here, coming together. We have a murdered forger, a probably murdered purser, a slashed Manet, a forged Manet—"

"Correction, make that a forged, slashed Manet," Alix said. "There's still a real Manet out there somewhere, presumably unslashed."

"That's right, and let's not forget the faked Monet; that's another thing. And by no means let us forget the Ponzi scheme, rapidly shrinking in relative importance, that brought us here in the first place." He shook his head. "Alix, I've never claimed to have a connoisseur's eye, but I do have a pretty good record when it comes to sizing up situations and circumstances. There's no way all this is merely coincidental. It's all tied up together somehow, and if Panos doesn't have his finger in every piece of this pie, I'll eat my hat. Or turn in my badge; whichever comes first."

"You're not saying he's actually a murderer, are you? Or are you?"

"No," he said with a laugh, "I might be thinking it, but I'm not saying it. I need some evidence before I crawl that far out on a limb. I don't trust my intuition quite as unreservedly as you do yours. But I am saying he's involved, he knows what's going on, he's in the middle of it all."

That didn't compute for Alix. She could see why Panos—and probably quite a few others—might want to get rid of Donny, who knew too much and talked too much, but why kill Weisskopf, his bread and butter when it came to creating the forgeries? Had Weisskopf been blackmailing him, perhaps? No, Weisskopf was hardly in a position to go to the police or anyone else. She was just putting these thoughts into order and raising the Coke can to her lips when a thought came to her so suddenly that she set the can back down with a *clunk* that made the counterman jump.

"Ted, you're definitely right, at least about a part of it. I just realized. He *did* know the Manet was a fake! Before I said anything, I mean."

Ted put down the slice he'd had in his hand and gave her his full attention.

"I was talking to Edward just a little while ago," she told him. "He said that before the cruise started, when he'd begun to break the news to Panos that the lab identified the Monet as a fake, Panos had assumed he was talking about the *Manet*. Edward thought it was just that Panos couldn't keep the names straight, but I think—"

"So do I," Ted said with animation. "He knew it was a fake, all right, and he was planning to auction it as the real thing. And . . . I'm thinking out loud here . . . when Panos found out that you were raising doubts about it—"

"Probably from Edward; he was on his way up to the reception right after I opened my big mouth."

"Possibly so."

"He figured that he'd better get it out of sight before I came up with some solid evidence, and mutilating it was the best way of doing that right then and there."

"Yes. He loses money on the auction, but he still gets the insurance. And of course, he still has the original to sell too; that is, if he hasn't already sold it."

Ted was nodding along with her. "I like it. It adds up. But what I don't get is why he would've been in such a hurry. Why didn't he wait? I mean, I know he didn't want to leave it out there for you to scrutinize at your leisure, but why do it when you were standing right there and he had to deal with you? That was risky."

"Oh, that's obvious. I figured that out a long time ago."

His left eyebrow went up. "Did you now?"

"The reason he was in a hurry," Alix said serenely, "was so that it could logically be blamed on one of the reception people—and there were something like a hundred of them. If he'd waited till they'd left, it'd be down to the very few people still on the ship, which would include him."

The suspended eyebrow came down. "Okay, I like that too. But if you figured it out so long ago, would you mind telling me why you waited till now to mention it?"

"Well, all right, technically speaking, I guess I didn't exactly figure it out, but I did think about it as a possible scenario."

"All right, then, let me ask you about another possible scenario you may have thought about. You've gotten to know Mrs. Papadakis a little. What do you think the chances are that she knows about all this? That maybe she's involved?"

The question surprised her. "Gaby? Zilch. I doubt if she's even aware of the financial troubles he's in. Besides, I can't see Panos letting her in on it. This is a woman who wears her heart on her sleeve. She'd be rotten at being cagey and evasive and all. And I think, down deep, well, I just think she's a good person. Certainly not a crook. And *definitely* not a killer."

"Okay," Ted said noncommittally. He ate a little more, started to say something, thought again about how to say it, and finally got it out. "Alix, things have changed. People are getting killed now. So you need to understand that amateur time is over. As of now, you'd better consider yourself off the case."

"Is that an order, boss?" she shot back. "Don't I at least get a notice of separation?" That "amateur time" had stung. A few seconds ago, he was still interested in her opinions.

"Think of it as a favor," he said no less sharply and then softened. "I'm sorry. I didn't put it very well. You've done a terrific job already, more than we could have expected. You've been a huge help."

"Yeah, right."

"No, I couldn't be more serious. I mean it. But this has morphed into something completely different from what we started with. Forget the fractional investment thing. This has turned into a major international operation now, and to your credit, it all stems directly from your identification of the fake Manet."

"One fake makes a major international operation?"

"No, it's more than that—"

"You mean the Monet forgery too? What, is there some kind of . . . of international forgery ring? Are there really such things, and not just in the movies?"

He smiled and looked inscrutable. "You said all that, not me. I've said all I'm going to say about it, which is more than I should have, so please forget it. Let's just say it's bigger than you thought—or I did, for that matter—and at this point, the investment scheme is on the back burner. For the moment, I'm working on something else, and you're not working on anything. Just do what you're supposed to be doing for Panos and go along for the ride. Just—"

"Keep a low profile."

"Right."

"Tread carefully."

"Exactly."

"Ted, something else just occurred to me. Too bad I'm off the case, because it's something you really might want to put in the hopper."

"Well, since you thought of it during a meal the FBI is paying for, I guess, technically, you're still on. Let's hear it."

"It's this: Since Panos immediately jumped to the assumption that Edward was talking about the Manet when he told him there was a forgery, then can't we conclude, by implication, that he *hadn't* been aware that the Monet was a fake too? That it came as a surprise to him? In other words, that he's not the only one making forgeries of his collection?"

"That is a very good point," he said, chewing thoughtfully on a gob of salami, green pepper, prosciutto, and cheese.

"And, if you'll allow it, I believe I can solve another mystery for you." He waited.

"Cheese," she said.

"I beg your pardon?"

She waved a pizza slice. "It's feta, not mozzarella or provolone or anything like that. That's why it tastes different. And smells different."

"Ah," he said, "you're right. You did it again." He lifted the Coke can in toast. "The connoisseur's nose."

22

The rest of the day, her third aboard the *Artemis*, was blessedly unevent-ful. Edward was waiting at the start of her informal chat session with an offer to assist, and she happily delegated to him all questions about value potential, financial trends, and the like. They were now only two days from the auction, which was scheduled for the following night, on the way from Corfu to Rhodes, so interest in the paintings had increased. All of the guests showed up wanting to hear what she could tell them about one painting or painter or another, and most stayed the full two hours, follow-ing her around as she answered others' questions. Fortunately for her, most of the questions about the contemporary works fell into Edward's prov-ince, so she happily spent her time in the music room, talking about things she knew.

People continued to hang around and engage her well into the cock-tail hour, and it was only afterward, when she was dressing for dinner, that she realized what a welcome interlude it had been, a kind of minivacation from thoughts and theories and suspicions of murder and forgery.

On her way back to her stateroom to dress for dinner, she saw Ted and Yiorgos leaning on a railing, head to head. Now, what was that about— the undercover FBI agent powwowing with the Hellenic Police lieutenant colonel? Did that qualify as a "major international operation"? She jerked her head, refusing to waste her time thinking about it. Not her affair. She was off the case.

At dinner, the first sit-down meal she'd attended, held in the small-scale owner's dining room, it was harder to keep the morbid thoughts at bay, what with Panos ostentatiously presiding as jovially as if he had nothing on his conscience, or, more likely, no conscience at all. She couldn't take her eyes off him. Vulgar, petty, cunning . . . but a killer? Easy enough to see him as a crook, a con man, an all-around scoundrel; he would have been perfect in an old Errol Flynn swashbuckler as a fat, villainous *alcalde* or a rouged, scheming courtier, but central casting would have laughed him out of the studio at the idea of his playing a murderer. He just didn't look the type.

On the other hand, who did?

The bartender must have done a good business at the cocktail party because everybody was visibly loosened up, and there was plenty of laughter and chatter as they took their assigned seats. Alix's place card—like the others, in a holder the base of which was a silver model of the yacht ("Please accept this miniature *Artemis* as a memento of your voyage")—put her at a corner, between Gaby at the end of the table and Edward on her right. Panos was at the head, not easily in her line of sight, which was fine with her.

Dinner aboard the yacht was every bit as glamorous as she'd heard; every one of the men in black tie (God, Ted was truly gorgeous!), the two women in floor-length dinner gowns: Gaby's a tasteful, rose-pink, schoolgirlish confection with an Empire waist and a gauzy, pleated skirt; Izzy's a voluminous, eye-popping, leopard-patterned, jewel-belted caftan worn over silken harem pants and silvery slingbacks with four-inch stiletto heels. They both looked beautiful.

So did Alix. She'd taken her friend Chris's advice, gone back to Le Frock Vintage Clothing and emerged with a black, spaghetti-strap, knee-length cocktail dress for forty-five dollars, ultrasimple but classic. Blanche had even thrown in a pair of smoky glass pendant earrings to go with it. The outfit looked great on her and she knew it, but she took little pleasure in the evening. The conversation at the table seemed silly and shallow. The food was predictably wonderful—oysters, lobster bisque, Caprese salad—seven courses in all, each one perfectly prepared and elegantly served, and each with its own wine—but she had no heart for it. That "amateur time" crack had stuck with her. Until the moment he'd said, "You're off the case," she'd had a purpose, and she was doing something useful and engaging. Now it all seemed simply sordid, and she was a fifth wheel on the wagon, more of a hindrance than a help to Ted, just one more thing for him to worry about. Pointless. She should never have come in the first place.

She slogged through the meal, eating little, drinking more wine than she meant to, and hardly speaking to her table companions, and she left when the espressos were poured, which was as early as she could without calling attention to herself. Forty minutes later she was in bed with the TV turned to an old *Magnum, P.I.*

Three days to go. It seemed like a lifetime.

Tomorrow morning, Corfu.

23

*W*hat a long, strange road it had been. Or maybe not so strange. Maybe it was the family genes reasserting themselves. She'd killed two people now, one by proxy, you might say (thank you, Uncle Frankie), the other by her own hand. People said it got easier after the first time, and maybe they were right. Donny had been the second, and even though he was the one she'd done herself, it was true; it had been easier for her. Of course, when it came to eminently killable people, Donny was in a class by himself, so maybe that was the reason.

But that was behind her now, as were the miseries and humiliations of the last decade. Out the stateroom's window she could see the freighter-like ferry already loading cars for its nine a.m. trip to Albania. Less than an hour from now, she would be aboard, on her way, and she would never look back. A new life. A new, rich life.

There was one more person she wouldn't mind killing—who badly needed killing—before she left, but it was too late for that now. She had only a little time left and she needed to concentrate on the task at hand. She had already unscrewed the credenza from the wall and pulled it far enough away to give herself some elbow room. Now she was using a screwdriver to pry off the waist-level wainscoting on the maple paneling behind it, but it was harder than she'd expected. She was nervous, and she was making a mess of it, poking holes in the wall and chipping and scarring the paneling, not that it mattered. But she couldn't get the blade of the screwdriver deeply enough between wainscoting and wall to give her the leverage she needed to get it off. And the heel of her hand hurt from trying to use it to drive the thing in. Why hadn't she thought to get a hammer? A pry bar? She turned back to the credenza, looking for anything that might be serviceable, grabbed a heavy, silver-backed man's hairbrush and whacked away, putting dents in the hundred-year-old silver, but beginning to make progress with the wainscoting.

At one point she thought she heard someone approaching the door, and it was as if a lump of freezing mud filled her throat. Her breath stopped; her heart jumped. But whoever it was, if there really was anybody, kept moving down the corridor. She breathed again, a little dizzy now and trembling, angry with herself for being so panicky. Surprised too; she wouldn't have expected that in herself. One more slow, calming breath and back to the job, working more quietly and deliberately, although her fingers, so steady a minute ago, were shaking now. She had to get the screwdriver inserted in two places a couple of feet apart to successfully break the section of wainscoting free, but she finally managed it, and there it was: the opening, the "safe" she'd known was there but had never actually seen before. The all-knowing Donny had told her about it, a secret oblong recess, three feet wide and a couple of feet deep, built into the wall behind the wainscoting but not shown on any plan.

It was narrower and deeper than she'd expected, not so much a box as a slot, and she had to get down on her knees to see inside.

There was something there all right, rolled up in butcher paper deep inside. She reached eagerly for it. From the first day of the cruise, she'd known he had something cooking—she could read the son of a bitch like a book—something that he didn't want her or anybody else to know about. And with Panos, that had to mean money, in one form or another. At first she'd assumed it was just the paperwork for one of his fishy deals, but then, from a stranger-than-usual shiftiness in his manner, she'd begun to think it was something more tangible than that, and where would he have it if not in his (supposedly) secret safe? It had been sweet, innocent Alix London who had unknowingly told her what it was before they'd even left Mykonos, but it had taken until last night for what she'd said to hit home, and this was her first—and last—chance to see if she was right.

She tore at the paper wrapping, increasingly sure of what she would find. When it lay in shreds on the carpet, she peeled back a corner of the rolled painting that had been inside. She saw a grassy hummock on which a picnic had been spread on a white cloth. There was a wicker basket with a bottle of red wine sticking out of it, half a loaf of bread, some unidentifiable meats, the lower part of a seated woman, her full, robin's-egg-blue skirt spread over her legs and feet, and beside her, on the grass, a matching, folded parasol . . .

200

It was the bottom right-hand corner of Édouard Manet's Déjeuner au Bord du Lac. *She unrolled the rest of it, her heart thumping away. She knew it! There was no ugly slash. The canvas was whole and unmarred. She came near to whooping her triumph. This was the real one, the original! The bastard had known all along that the other was a fake. Had he been going to unload this one somewhere along the way? Do the same thing that she was planning to do with the Monet? No, no, even as coincidences went, that one seemed too far-fetched. Still, what else . . . She jerked her head. Who cared; what difference did it make? She was the one who held it now in her shaking hands, and she hugged it gingerly to herself. What was it that it was supposed to be worth? Ten million euros? Dear God! That was even more than—*

.   .   .

"Gaby!"

She froze. She hadn't heard the door open. "Panos . . ." she managed to get out before the gob of freezing mud stopped her throat again. Her mind raced, hunting for explanations, prevarications, and not finding any, not with the wall torn up behind her, the carpet littered with wrapping paper, and the painting right there in her hands.

"What the hell are you doing?" he screamed.

"Panos . . . not so loud, people will—"

"What do I care about people, you thief?" He stomped furiously toward her. "Thief!" he yelled even louder, straight into her face. "My wife, the thief!"

"Panos . . ."

"THIEF! THIEF! TH—"

Later she would say honestly that she had no memory of picking up the heavy, silver-backed hairbrush again. But she couldn't deny what happened next. She aimed for his face but hit him squarely on the ear. He was astounded. She had never struck him before. He looked blankly shocked for a moment, his mouth hanging open, and then his face swelled up, suffused with blood. Some people whitened when they were enraged. Panos turned red. He raised both fists, clenched and quivering, above his head.

She swung the hairbrush again, this time catching him over his left eye. It wasn't a terribly solid blow because he flinched back a step, but when he did his foot slipped on a clump of wrapping paper, and he fell heavily backward, catching his head on a corner of the credenza on the way down. When he hit the floor he lay without moving.

"Ahh . . . uhh . . ." he said. His eyes were open but unfocused. A rivulet of blood dribbled down his cheek from somewhere.

Gaby, thoroughly panicked, hurriedly rolled up the painting and ran for the door. When she flung it open, she screeched and reeled back. "Emil! What are you doing here?"

He was standing there looking startled and stupid, with his hand still in the air preparing to knock. "Gaby? What . . ."

A faint "uhh . . . nngg" reached them, and Emil's gaze swung past her into the room. "Gaby . . . oh, my God, what . . . what have you . . ."

A second ago she had been close to fainting, but Emil's stuttering feebleness brought out her formidable reserves of strength. She grabbed him by the collar (the closest she could come to the scruff of his neck) and jerked him, flabby and unresisting, into the corridor. Behind them, Panos's heels thrummed on the carpet.

"Gaby, wh—"

"Shut up. Let's go. We've got a ferry to catch."

. . .

There had been a time when Emil had seemed to her a godsend. Over a year ago it was, when he'd been staying with them for a few days at the house on St. Barts, as Panos's clients sometimes did, and she'd caught that randy gleam in his eye. He'd seemed more attractive back then (as so many men do before you know them), and they'd begun an affair that was still sporadically in effect. Eventually, when she'd seen how little he respected Panos, she'd told Emil about the satisfying deception she'd practiced on her husband by having forgeries made of two of his paintings and then selling the real ones off while the fakes went back into his collection. And Panos never once batted an eye. She'd done it with works by Odilon Redon and Émile Bernard. She'd been afraid at the time to mess with any of the biggies.

What made it especially delicious was that the idea had come from Panos himself, via (of all people) Donny. She'd been having an on-and-off fling with Donny too—he was, after all, a beautiful specimen, and when he stopped preening and prattling about himself and got down to business, he was a surprisingly good lover, probably a matter of pride with him. Lounging around after one such episode Donny had told her about the weirdly costumed man he'd seen more than once on the yacht when it was in port and not in use by Panos or anyone else. He'd spend four or five long days in front of an easel, painting and painting and painting away, copying one of Panos's pictures. The copies were so good that Donny, no genius but sharp when it came to spotting angles, had arrived at a vague notion of what might be going on and had tried a little friendly blackmail on the artist, Christoph Weisskopf, who readily proved he was working for Panos, not cheating him.

For Donny, that had been the end of it, but Gaby saw opportunity there. She'd made Donny her intermediary in getting in touch with Weisskopf, who saw no problem in knocking off a picture or two for her without informing Panos. The two copies had been made, setting her back a total of $14,000. Donny himself had been glad to sell the originals for her to some scummy fence he knew for $20,000 apiece. His reward had been $1,000 and a few extra favors from Gaby. Gaby's profit had thus been $25,000, which she'd thought was pretty good, but when she'd told Emil about it, he'd scoffed. He had connections that could have brought her twenty times that. Next time, he'd said, come to him and he'd prove it.

She'd replied by informing him that, as a matter of fact, she'd recently had Weisskopf make a third copy from Panos's collection, this one a big step up from Redon and Bernard: a *Rouen Cathedral* of Claude Monet's. So here was Emil's chance to put up or shut up. Donny had told her his contact was offering a hefty $60,000 this time and Donny thought he could get him up to $75,000. Could Emil do better than that?

A few days later he telephoned with his answer. Sit down, he told her, and then said that, assuming that it passed inspection, the buyers were ready to pay €2,500,000. In cash, full payment on delivery, said delivery to be made in Saranda, Albania, on the morning of May 25, when the *Artemis* would be docked a ferry ride away in nearby Corfu. How did that sound to her?

As he'd expected, she was floored, but not so floored that half an hour later she didn't suggest to him that if two and a half million was their opening offer, didn't he think he might charm them up to a nice round three?

Emil had laughed. "These people you don't charm."

Mafia, he meant, but she hadn't said anything. Emil had a way of forgetting—or choosing not to remember—that half of her male relatives were or had once been mafiosi—not with some wannabe Albanian mafia either, but with the real thing, *Mafia* with a capital *M.*

It wasn't long before the two of them realized that the Monet meant more than a giant payday; it was their ticket out of lives they both despised. They could escape—Gaby from Panos, Emil from his wife, both from their stunted existences. What if they didn't return to the ship from Saranda? What if they rented a car instead and headed to Croatia, to Zagreb, where Emil had been born and claimed he still had useful connections, where Gabriela had sung several times and was still much esteemed, and where two and a half million euros would go a long, long way?

That had been the plan. When Panos had discovered the Monet forgery just before the cruise there been a brief period of terror on Gaby's part. If Weisskopf were to tell him that it was she who'd had it commissioned, he would throw her out, cut her off, and probably bring charges. Her life would be over. For the first time she took advantage of her doting Uncle Frankie's repeated, unambiguous offers of his "services" if she ever needed them. All she had to do was ask. She asked, he delivered, and Christoph

Weisskopf was no longer a problem. That was another loop out of which Emil had been kept. He'd never known about Weisskopf at all. She kept waiting for him to ask where the forgeries had come from, but he never did. At root Emil was an insecure man, easily shaken, and he didn't go looking for trouble. As a result, there was a lot he didn't know and she meant to keep it that way.

The plan remained in effect.

. . .

"I cannot *believe* it," Emil said through stiffened, barely parted lips. They were alone on the windy aft deck of the ferry, and he was staring fixedly down at the slowly spreading wake of the ship rather than looking at Gaby. "I can *not* believe it." He had recovered his manly self-assurance and sense of command as soon as the ferry had cleared the breakwater and was safely into the strait that separated the Greek island of Corfu from Albania. "How could you *do* such a stupid thing? There were a *hundred* other things you could have done. What were you *thinking*?"

What Gaby was thinking was that this guy was really starting to get on her nerves. She was sick of the constant negativity, of his bossiness, of the endless carping and nagging and after-the-fact "advice." And was his overemphasis of a word in just about every sentence something new or a habit that she had, for some inexplicable reason, never noticed? Whichever, it was making her grind her teeth now.

"Emil," she said without expression, "just stop talking for a while, all right? Can you do that?"

"Christ," he muttered. "I had everything *so* worked out. But no, *you* had to—" But when she turned to look at him, he read something in her face that made him think twice. "Oh, hell, I'm going to take a walk around the deck. I need to think."

Good, she needed to think too. It was only in this last hour or so that she'd concluded once and for all that when Emil's part in this was over, he had to be gotten rid of. Not killed, there was no need for that (as far as she could see at the moment), but dumped. She needed him to finalize today's all-important transaction and get the money, and she needed him to get her safely to Zagreb, and, once in Zagreb she needed his protection and help in getting her set up with the documents and connections she would require to get back to civilization. Brazil, maybe, or Ireland.

Then he could be dumped. A year, no more. She could last that long, even in Croatia.

. . .

Alix woke with something that wasn't quite a hangover but was definitely on the wrong side of happy, healthy, and fit. Instinctively, she groped for the bedside phone to call for coffee, but changed her mind and asked for orange juice instead.

She'd barely gotten into her robe when there was a *tap tap* at the door. In came Artemis, as crisp and fresh and smiling as ever, pushing a rolling table with a glass pitcher that held enough orange juice for four, a pot of coffee, and a basket of warm pastries topped with two of the buttery croissants that Alix had so quickly come to look forward to. Not this morning, though. Looking at them made her gag a little. She reached for the orange juice, but Artemis beat her to it and poured a glass for her. As Alix had come to expect, it was as fresh as could be, foamy and thick with flecks of pulp.

"May I serve you anything else?"

"No, thank you, this is more than enough."

"Are you planning to go into Saranda today, Miss London?"

"Into where?"

"Saranda. Albania. You can get there by ferry."

"I didn't know that. Don't I need a visa or something?"

"Technically, yes. Actually, no. Your passport is all. Saranda is, shall we say, quite informal when it comes to such things."

"Okay, thanks for mentioning it. I might do that."

"The reason I ask is that there are only two sailings a day, and most of our guests who were going there were on the nine o'clock—"

"What? It's after nine?" Alix hadn't slept that late in years. She was an early morning lover. On those few occasions when she missed the dawn, her day was never as good as it might have been.

"It's nine forty-five, I'm afraid. But there is also a hydrofoil, smaller but much quicker, that leaves at ten thirty."

"Oh, I don't see how I could make that. Wouldn't I have to take the launch into port, then—"

"Not at all, we're already in port. Here in Corfu it's possible for yachts of our size to berth in the marina." She pointed to the window, out of which Alix had yet to look this morning. "And there is your ferry, not fifty meters from here."

"Thank you, Artemis, I might do it at that," Alix said without conviction, but after the chief stewardess had left and she'd had some more wonderfully restorative juice (but not so wonderful that she wanted to tackle the coffee or the croissants), she decided it might be a good idea. Remaining on the *Artemis* all day didn't hold much appeal, and as for Corfu Town, she'd seen its moderately interesting sights when she'd been here on Uncle Julian's yacht. But Albania, that would be someplace new. The last time she'd been here it was still the People's Socialist Republic of Albania, reclusive and paranoid, and visitors were not encouraged. Certainly there had been no public ferry from Corfu.

What the hell, she thought, why not? A quick shower, a sundress and sandals, and she'd be off.

⋆　•　•

The Hotel Porto Eda is generally thought to be one of the better hotels in Saranda, which isn't saying much, but its solidly middling three-star rating, its location only steps from the marina, and its price (forty euros, breakfast included)—good value, but not cheap enough to bring in the backpackers—combine to draw most overnight foreign visitors, of whom there aren't all that many. A pink building of four balconied stories, with potted palms on the roof and a giant, peeling Tuborg Beer billboard looming over them, it boasts a tidy little lounge area, clean and modern, with faux-leather sofas and armchairs and glass-topped coffee tables, where guests meet other guests or wait for transportation or drink the excellent coffee or tea that is served there.

At 11:15 a.m. on this particular Friday it held the usual six or eight people having their midmorning coffees. Among them was Gabriela Papadakis, sick to her stomach with tension; opening nights had been child's play compared to this. She was so stressed she kept forgetting to breathe. And when a friendly male tried to engage her in conversation, his first good look at her manic eyes scared him off before he'd gotten out the first sentence.

Had they found Panos yet? Could he still be alive? He'd looked as if he were dying, but why hadn't she made absolutely sure? Emil, damn him, had panicked and his panic had infected her, and they had run.

The cleanup crew knew better than to enter their stateroom before one p.m., but still. . . . She had no clear memory of pulling the door closed when she and Emil had left, but surely she must have. Mustn't she? Anyway, didn't they close automatically? She couldn't even remember that. Everything was so muddled. She wished now she'd never gone looking for that safe. Whatever the value of that damned Manet, it wasn't worth *this*. Her eyes had been fixed on the hotel's glass-door entrance for half an hour; she expected to see the police barge in to arrest her at any second. *What was taking Emil so long?* She couldn't sit there very much longer without screaming.

They had arrived in Saranda at 10:45. Emil had openly carried the two paintings, the Monet and the newly found Manet, into the country in a tubular leather map case. There was no interest in them at customs, as he'd promised her there wouldn't be. (Still, she'd made sure to be well behind him in the exit line.) They'd asked him to open the tube and pull out the rolled-up contents so they could take a desultory look for drugs or weapons, but pictures? Why would the bored Albanian customs officers care about pictures coming into the country? Or going out, for that matter? The inspector had stifled a yawn and motioned him through with a waggle of his fingers.

Gaby still didn't understand what he planned to do with Panos's *Déjeuner au Bord Du Lac*, and she thought he wasn't too clear about it himself. She didn't blame him for this; she had dumped it in his lap only two hours ago. But when he'd said that he planned to try to sell it in addition to the Monet that had already been agreed upon, she'd exploded.

"Are you crazy? You think these gangsters have brought along an extra few million dollars just in case you happen to bring another painting with you? They'll kill you for it and keep the money and keep *both* paintings."

"No, they won't," he said. "I'm their source for this kind of thing. They've done business with me before and they'll want to do it again. They know they can trust me, and that's worth more to them than any two paintings. And I trust them. They—"

"You trust them? You *are* crazy."

"Please, Gaby, I'll work something out with them. It'll be all right. Would it kill you to just trust my judgment for once?"

Just about, but what choice did she have? So now she sat in the lounge, an untouched cup of espresso on the coffee table in front of her and a leather tube worth approximately five million dollars, even at black market rates, clutched in one hand and clamped between her knees for extra assurance. Emil was up in room 204, talking to the buyers. This sort of thing was done in two steps, he'd told her. Making sure they had the money while she remained here, in a separate place, with the paintings, was the first. In the second step, having seen the money, he would come back down to get the paintings and bring them up to exchange for the money. And that was it, there was no third step. With the money in hand they would hop in the car they'd rented, and it was off through Montenegro and Bosnia and

Herzegovina, to Zagreb. Nobody in the world would know where they were, and what a thrilling, freeing thought that was. *But what was taking him so long?*

"It's on," he said, so suddenly and so close that it started her on a hiccupping fit. He'd come up behind her while her attention had been focused on the doors. "Give me the tube, Gaby. We'll be out of here in twenty minutes."

She was so consumed by the hiccups that he had to pry it out of her hands, and even then her fingers wouldn't let go. "Wait . . ."

"Damn it, Gaby—"

She got her hiccups enough under control to gasp, "They're . . . giving us the . . . two and a half million . . . for the Monet?"

"Yes, I just counted it. Now all they need to do is see it." He tugged harder.

She held on. "What about the Manet?"

"They'll give us five hundred thousand now if they like it and another amount later, to be determined—"

"So they *had* an extra half-million euros with them. I *told* you they would have paid you that for the Monet alone. You idiot—"

He dug his fingernails—they were well manicured, but on the long side for a man, in her opinion—into her wrist. "You're making a scene!" he whispered harshly. "There are people here. What's wrong with you? Everything's going fine."

"I . . ." Out of the blue, a complete surprise, she was crying. "I don't know, it's all so . . . oh, Emil, what's wrong with me? I'm sorry, I just want us to get out of here, I just want it to be over."

"Well, it never will be if you don't let go of the damn thing."

Her fingers released their grip, and he pulled the tube safely out of her range and sat on the sofa beside her. "You have to stay strong for me now, Gaby. We're almost there. Wait'll you see it; it's beautiful, the money." He was speaking softly, almost singing the words, and stroking the back of her hand the way one would to calm an hysterical five-year-old. "Sixty beautiful little stacks of five-hundred-euro bills; can you imagine? And it all fits in a duffel bag, can you believe it? And guess what it weighs. Fifty pounds? A hundred? No, just fourteen pounds. Didn't you think it would be much more? I thought—"

Abruptly she snatched back her hand. "Stop babying me; I'm all right. It was a momentary . . . I don't know what it was, but it's over now and you don't need to worry. It won't happen again."

He gave her hand one more pat as he rose. "There, that's more like it. That's my—"

"I said stop it! Now get the hell back up there and let's get this over with."

He grinned, only a little nervously, leaned over to plant an abstracted kiss on her forehead, and headed for the elevator.

24

Watching Albania's shoreline glide by from a window seat in the fifteen-row, airliner-like interior of the hydrofoil, Alix couldn't imagine it looking any more unwelcoming in its People's Republic heyday than it did right now. She'd read the *Artemis*'s two-page pamphlet guide while waiting for the ship to get going, and it had told her about the "thousands of gun-emplacement pillboxes" she would see on her way to Saranda. So she'd been ready for them. They were, according to the pamphlet, the legacy of Enver Hoxha, the xenophobic Communist leader of the republic for the forty years following World War II.

Still, she hadn't been prepared for their astounding density. She'd taken it for granted that "thousands" was hyperbole. It wasn't. Concrete, beehive-shaped gun emplacements, each with its ominous black opening facing the sea, were lined up along the shore for miles. Sometimes arranged in rows, sometimes in irregular clumps, they might be separated by as much as a hundred feet or as little as ten. Surely, she thought, there were more than enough to hold the entire Albanian army. For twenty solid minutes, she continued to pass them.

They were deserted and gunless now, but all the same it didn't give her a good feeling about the country, and Saranda itself didn't help. Seen from the pier, it seemed to be mostly composed of boxy, 1960s-style apartment buildings in various stages of decline. Nowhere in view was there anything resembling a commercial or historic downtown of interest to a visitor. By the time she'd gotten through customs (a ten-second process), she was wondering what she was going to do all day; there were no return ferries until evening. There were some modern, nice-looking beach resorts visible at the south end of town, but she wasn't in the mood for beach resorts.

What she *was* in the mood for was another chance at the coffee at which she'd so blithely turned up her nose earlier and maybe a little something to go along with it. According to the pamphlet, Albanian coffee was strong and tasty, and the nearest place to the dock where it could be gotten was the *kafe* in the lobby of the Hotel Porto Eda, where English was spoken, after a fashion, and euros were accepted. That settled it. She didn't have any Albanian currency, and the only word of Albanian she knew was *kafe*.

The Porto Eda was right in front of her as she left the ship, practically on the dock, and she made straight for it. As she pulled open the glass doors, a puff of air from inside carried the welcome scent of coffee to her. Unfortunately, it also blew a speck of something into her eye. Blinking, pressing a hand over the eye, she asked one of the two receptionists at the desk for the ladies' room and was pointed toward the back of the building, near the elevators. To reach it she had to walk through the café, sensuously inhaling the thick, unmistakable aroma of Turkish coffee, although she was betting they probably called it "Albanian coffee" here, the same way—

"Alix, is that you?"

She turned her one functioning eye toward the voice and through the tears saw Gaby sitting there on a white leather sofa.

"Oh, hi, Gaby, I—"

Gaby had risen halfway up. "What are you doing here? What's happened?"

Alix was confused by the strain in her voice and on her face. "Why, nothing's happened. I just came in for some coffee. Is something the matter?"

"No, no, I was just . . . . It's just that . . . no." She sat back down, looking as though she were restraining herself from saying anything more.

"Gaby, may I join you? In a minute, though. Give me a chance to rinse something out of my eye first."

"Oh, but I'm only going to be here another minute. Emil will be . . . that is . . . Sure, I suppose so. If you want." She seemed to realize the way she sounded and appended a sunny, friendly smile. "Sure," she said again. "Can I order you something in the meantime?"

"You bet, please, a cup of Turkish coffee. A double, if they have them."

Flushing the speck out of her eye proved difficult, taking a good five minutes, and when she was done the eye was red and stinging, but at least she could keep it open. Lusting for the coffee that she hoped was waiting for her, she used the towel roll to dry off and went to the door. Before it was fully open she knew that something was wrong, but it took her a second to figure out what it was: There was no sound, no clinking of cups, no scraping of utensils, no murmured conversations. She stepped out into the café.

Gaby was gone; everybody was gone. The coffee Gaby had ordered for her was on the table, fresh and steaming, and half-finished coffees and pastries littered the other tables. The three stools at the bar were empty. The barista had disappeared, as had the clerks behind the reception desk. She was alone in the noiseless lobby, a *Twilight Zone* moment. A slow chill rolled up between her shoulders and spread out on the back of her neck. She jumped at a rustle behind her and to her right, and when she spun around she saw two armed, blue-uniformed men in black body armor— Albanian policemen; there had been another one on the pier—at the back of the building, near the rear exit. They were facing away from her, closely watching the fire door to the stairwell, their bodies tense.

Weapons, body armor, and jumpy Albanian cops. Whatever was about to happen, she preferred not to be there when it did. The quickest route to the front entrance was around the corner of the café and through a small atrium that held the elevator. She had barely stepped into the atrium when the massive form of Yiorgos materialized from around the far corner. She had never seen him anything but self-possessed and unruffled, but now he was agitatedly waving his arms and yelling at her. In Greek.

Startled, she stood rooted to the spot. "Wh—"

"Dammit, Alix"—This time, surprising her even more, it was Ted doing the materializing, and he looked every bit as upset as Yiorgos. — "didn't you—"

He never got to finish the question because that was when the elevator door on Alix's right whooshed open and all hell commenced breaking loose. Out came two men, one svelte and neatly bearded, wearing a business suit over a tieless white shirt buttoned up to the collar, and the other, bull-necked and swarthy, dressed in hey-look-at-me-I'm-a-gangster mode: tan, mirrored aviator sunglasses and a supple, blatantly expensive, chestnut leather bomber jacket straight from Fendi or Armani. At the same moment, four Albanian cops converged on them, two from around the same corner from which Ted and Yiorgos had come, and two, plus a man in street clothes, from where, she didn't know. Everybody—Ted, Yiorgos, the good guys, the bad guys—was shouting and gesticulating, and most of the police had their handguns out—old-fashioned snub-nosed revolvers of the kind that American police forces had stopped using decades ago, but still plenty intimidating when they were waving around a foot from your head.

Smack in the center of all this stood Alix, dumbfounded and frozen, not knowing whether to run or duck or just say her prayers. A policeman reached for her to pull her out of the way, but the leather-jacketed man got there first, catching her neck in the crook of his arm and jerking her up against him so that her body shielded his. Alix struggled, batting at his arm and face, but her back was to him and she couldn't get enough weight behind her fists to do any harm. And he was strong, as a quick, hard squeeze of her neck between his forearm and his biceps showed, shutting off her air. With his other hand he was brandishing a thick pipe or bar just a few inches from her face. That served to get her attention too, and she stopped struggling. He eased the pressure enough for her to pull in a couple of shallow, strangled breaths.

Everyone except Ted was still yelling. She caught a glimpse of him off to the side, looking stricken and speaking urgently to Yiorgos, who was busy bawling at the bad guys. Leather-jacket started dragging her backward, toward the hotel entrance. He was screaming louder than anyone. She couldn't understand a word but from the faces of the police, she had no trouble grasping the point he was making: *Keep away or I'll kill her.*

She knew he could do it too, and easily. It had taken him—what, two seconds?—to completely cut off her air and turn her into a rag doll. She could see that the police knew it too. They had stopped shouting and were now dithering, looking to the plainclothesman for guidance. Ted, standing a little away from the others, began sidling around to one side, but Leather-jacket saw him and squeezed again, harder. Alix had been struggling to breathe as it was—his eye-watering cologne didn't make it any easier—and little starbursts now exploded behind her eyes. Ted stopped at once, lifting his hands to show he'd gotten the message. The pressure was eased once more. Her knees, which had given way without her realizing it, braced themselves again.

The other man who had been on the elevator, the man in the suit, had been left behind, and with no nearby body to grab for protection, he was in trouble. Wild-eyed, he reached under his jacket and behind him with one hand, but was stopped cold by the almost simultaneous cocking of four revolver hammers—*snick snick snick snick*—none of them more than six feet away from him. Meekly he held both hands out well away from his body and one of the cops spun him around and pulled out the gleaming black semiautomatic pistol he'd been after. Then he angrily held it up to show to his fellow cops. He was mad, Alix thought, because the guy had a newer and better weapon than they had. It made her giggle and she realized she was getting muzzy and stupid. Lack of oxygen?

One of the Albanian cops roughly handcuffed the second man, pinned him by the back of the neck and frog-marched him off. The others slowly began advancing toward Alix and her captor. Leather-jacket, still dragging her backward, speeded up. One of her heels caught in the carpet, momentarily slowing them, and he punished her by tightening his hold again. More stars. Twisting her head to the side allowed her to suck in a little air but made her dizzier, brought her to the brink of blacking out. Something about pressure on the carotid arteries? Her mind seemed to be floating away from her, out of her reach. She wanted to turn her head forward again, preferring gasping to fainting, but it was impossible. She had both hands on his arms now, trying without success to give herself a little more room before she did faint. When he readjusted his grip to keep it tight, his wrist pressed against her cheek. With a huge effort she managed to twist her head the two inches she needed to sink her teeth into his wrist. She felt tendons grind under her teeth and tasted blood. He howled, but rather than loosen his arm he tightened it again, savagely this time, and took a backhanded swat at her with his other hand. When he did he almost lost his hold on what she now realized wasn't a bar or pipe at all, but a long mailing tube—no, it was made of leather; a map case then?

The case wobbled on the tips of his fingers for a moment, and it took a frantic swipe for him to pluck it back out of the air. When he did, the arm that held her slipped enough to let her take in something close to a full breath, the first she'd had since he'd had her; but in another second he'd adjusted and she was clamped more firmly than ever in the vise of that thick, leather-sheathed arm. But that one lungful of air had instantly sharpened her mind, and what she was thinking was how desperately he had lunged for that case, and would surely lunge for it again if she . . . if she . . .

Behind her eyes, the starbursts started silently popping again, tiny fireworks, and her thoughts began to lose shape, to fragment and to fall away. If she didn't do something now, right now, she'd black out in seconds and be dead not long after. She let her knees go soft again and sagged, making herself a dead weight, as if she had already lost consciousness, and when he was forced to readjust for this, loosening his hold on her throat a little, she was able to gulp another quick breath and use the brief spurt of energy to snatch at the map case with both hands, get her fingers around it, and yank it out of his hand.

He fumbled for it with his free hand, still struggling backward with her. She dug in her heels again to make it harder for him, managing to hold the case at arm's length in front of her, where he couldn't reach it without letting up on her neck. They were only a dozen feet from the door now and moving toward it fast. His hold had retightened, but before the constriction could affect her she jerked the case up, as if at his head. It was a feint and it worked. He flinched, bending to the side and giving her the freedom of movement she was after. They had stumbled into, and almost tripped over, a steel-framed chair near the door, and it was down onto the metal back of this that she smashed the map case. The case was sturdy; it dented only a little. He was babbling frantically to her now, or rather *at* her, wild with desperation. She took heart from that and whacked the case against the metal frame once more. The dent was now a crack, and the case had given way and bent almost double at its center. And Leather-jacket was nearly hysterical.

But she was losing strength—the starbursts had given way to wavering black spots that grew and shrank and moved in and out of focus. The world began to tilt. Nausea roiled deep inside her. She was able to raise the case yet again but neither her muscles nor her mind would cooperate in bringing it down on the chair, and she could only hold it there, just out of his grasp, her fingers numbed, her vision darkening. Leather-jacket uttered a kind of low moan and grabbed for it with both hands. Alix let go—she couldn't have hung on to it any longer anyway—and as he clutched at it, her eyes rolled up, the world went red and then black, and she collapsed to the floor.

The next instant the police were on him and it was over.

25

"**W**ell, I can't say it was easy, but I finally got my coffee," Alix said, thirty minutes later, as she started on her second cup with a happy sigh. A fabulously, wickedly sweet, sticky Albanian pastry had already been consumed and two more waited in the basket, but not for long.

Ted smiled at her across the table, hands circling his own cup. It had taken him a while to loosen up, but now he seemed relaxed. Some of the police were enjoying similar snacks at other tables. The Porto Eda *kafe*, not yet reopened to the public, was providing free refreshments for them all. ("To thank because we don't shoot up the place," Yiorgos had said.)

Ted was just finishing up a brief explanation of what she'd stumbled into—the "international operation" he'd referred to earlier. It had gotten its start only a few hours after he'd arrived on the *Artemis*. He'd gotten word through the FBI grapevine that an Albanian mafia bust had been in the works for a while, in which the police there hoped to take down some top-level mafiosi on customs violations (in much the same way that Al Capone, having successfully eluded conviction on murder, prostitution, and Prohibition-related charges, was finally jailed for tax evasion). At the center of the planned bust was an illegal importation of paintings to take place a couple of days hence at the Hotel Porto Eda in Saranda. Since a couple of days hence was the very date that the *Artemis*, practically bulging with masterpieces, would be calling at Saranda, it didn't require massive brainpower to figure out that there might be a connection between the two.

Knowing that Yiorgos was on leave from a colonelcy in the Hellenic Police, Ted had guessed correctly that he was the representative from the

Greek side. He'd told Yiorgos who he was and, with the Bureau's go-ahead, had offered his help. Yiorgos had been quick to accept. What exactly was going to happen they didn't know, but the Albanian police had set up a surveillance van near the hotel that morning and had been tuned to room 204 ever since. Yiorgos and Ted had been brought over in a police boat at eight a.m. They had assumed that Panos would be at the heart of it and were surprised when he didn't show up on the nine o'clock ferry, but their puzzlement ended when Emil and Gaby walked off it carrying the map case and headed straight for the Hotel Porto Eda. They had then—

Alix, her mouth filled with a chunk of pastry number two, had practically choked.

"*Gaby*? Gaby was . . . was dealing with the mafia?"

"Oh, yeah."

"So she and Emil—"

"Alix, I don't have all the details yet, or anything close. We had a nice, neat theory all constructed around Panos, and now, with this, instead of a theory we have dozens of bits and pieces, and we don't know how they fit together yet."

He finished what was left of his coffee, grimacing when some of the grounds apparently went down with it. "Look, I have to get back to Yiorgos and the others. For you, the cruise is over; we're sending you back. You've had a tough time of it, and, frankly, there's really nothing for you to do anymore."

He waited, probably expecting a fight, but Alix shrugged; she couldn't argue with what he'd said. Besides, she was ready to be done with the *Artemis*.

"Your luggage is on its way here from the yacht. Then we're flying you to Athens, and from there to DC tomorrow, where we'll book a hotel room for you for a couple of nights—three, if you want them. You would have been spending them on the cruise anyway—"

"DC? Why?"

"You'll have some paperwork to take care of, and being there will make it easier. Besides, it won't hurt for you to relax for a day or two, take a little time to decompress and see the sights—on us; you earned it."

"Uh-huh. And of course you're flying me business class. Or will it be first?"

He laughed. "Sorry, kid, Panos isn't paying for this, the Bureau is, so you get to go civil-servant class, otherwise known as K class, otherwise known as common-rabble class."

"You're staying with the cruise?"

"Sure am, but only till tomorrow. You know, the auction is scheduled for tonight at sea, and then tomorrow morning the yacht's supposed to make a quick stop at one of the islands, Kythera, I think, where Panos is planning to get off and fly back, to St. Barts. The guests are welcome to stay with the cruise to Rhodes and then back to Mykonos if they want, but I'm going to get off with Panos. Get some more face time with him, maybe have lunch together while we're waiting for our flights."

Befriend and betray, Alix thought.

"Anyway, I'll be back in DC the day after tomorrow myself. Let's get together for lunch."

"Now where have I heard that before?"

"Trust me, this time I'll be there, and I'll have more to tell you by then. Let's say one o'clock at the Garden Café in the National Gallery. You know where it is?"

"The National Gallery, sure. The Garden Café I'll find."

"It's a nice place to eat, and it's only three blocks from HQ. Oh, one more thing. The paintings that were in the case? They're fine; you didn't damage them. I thought you'd want to know."

She was confused. "What difference does it make? They're forgeries; aren't they?" She frowned. "*Aren't* they?"

"No, why would you think that?"

"Because you told me it was a forgery ring."

"The hell I did. *You* said it was a forgery ring."

"Yes, but by not contradicting me, you led me to believe . . ." She gulped. "They weren't?"

"No, ma'am."

"They were . . . they were . . . oh, God, the real Manet? And the real Monet? And I was just whacking away . . . ?"

"Yes, ma'am. *Le Déjeuner au Bord du Lac*—the authentic, unslashed one—and a Monet *Cathédrale de Rouen,* equally authentic and even more beautiful, in my opinion." He grinned. "Cat got your tongue?"

She nodded dazedly. "If this was a kiddie cartoon, this is the part where my eyes would spin around like pinwheels, and I'd go stiff as a washboard and fall over in a faint."

"I don't recommend it." His laugh mellowed into an affectionate smile. "Good job, Alix. A little unconventional maybe, but a good job. Okay, kiddo, you wait here. Have another cup of coffee. When your luggage shows up the cops will get you to the airport. Your flight's not until four. See you in a couple of days. Have a good trip."

26

The luncheon buffet served in the National Gallery of Art's elegantly porticoed, classically columned Garden Court is periodically rethemed to reflect a particular kind of cuisine, and this month the theme was American, which, as usual in culinary circles, meant meaty, heavy, unpretentious, and big on gravies and starchy vegetables. Pot roast, turkey pot pie, and a salad of glazed turnips, carrots, and beets were among the dishes on the buffet table. After four days of Continental fare, nothing could have suited Alix better, and Ted must have felt the same way because both of them filled their plates on their first trip to the buffet table, Ted with the beef, Alix with the chicken, and both of them with the root vegetable salad, buttermilk biscuits, and a wedge of Monterey Jack cheese.

"Don't you want to go back and get something else?" Ted asked as they returned to their table alongside the fountained pool that was the court's centerpiece. "I can still see a tiny little space on your plate with nothing on it. Right there, see? Between the roll and the cheese."

"That's more empty space than I can see on yours, pal," Alix said. "Besides, I'm saving room for dessert."

"Don't be ridiculous. How can you not have room for Georgia pecan pie with caramel sauce?"

Alix arranged her napkin on her lap and poured herself a glass of the Pale American Ale they had ordered from the drinks waitress. "So, I have a million questions. Tell." She buttered her roll and waited.

"Mm, the pot roast's exactly like my grandmother used to make," Ted said. "Done to death, fatty, gristly . . . just delicious. American cooking at its finest. All right, I'll start at the beginning." He had to stop and think, though, to determine where that was. "Okay, the Manet. Or rather, the two Manets."

While they ate, he explained. The copy, the one that had been slashed, had been commissioned by Panos from Weisskopf a year earlier, and had been among the auction pieces until it was slashed, as Alix and everyone else knew. But what Alix and just about everyone else didn't know was that Panos had brought the original aboard too, and hidden it in the Papadakises' stateroom, his intention being to sell it to the mafia in Saranda, as he'd done several times before with other paintings.

"I'm already lost," Alix said. "It was Gaby and Emil who were selling it. How did they get their hands on it? Surely, Panos didn't—"

"No, he didn't. Gaby stole it, if you want to be literal about it."

"What do you mean, if I want to be literal? Did she or didn't she?"

"Oh, she took it, all right, and she gave it to Emil to sell, but what she didn't know was that Emil knew about it from the start and was already planning to take it across and sell."

"Now I'm really lost."

"Well, there's more to Emil than meets the eye. Turns out he has mob contacts all over Eastern Europe, and he was Panos's emissary to the Albanians. When Panos had something to sell, it was Emil who'd arrange the deal, and when the yacht called at Corfu, he'd carry the painting, maybe two paintings, across to the Albanians, bring the money back to Panos, and take a not-so-modest commission for his efforts."

"Not this time, though?"

"No, this time the plan was to screw Panos, take off with the money to Zagreb, where he comes from, and live happily ever after."

Alix picked reflectively at her food. She'd eaten the velvety turkey and the carrots and now had only the peas—not a favorite—to work with. "Okay, what about that Monet? Where did that come from?"

"That's still being worked on, but it looks as if Gaby did exactly what Panos was doing: had Weisskopf make a copy for her—without Panos knowing about it, of course—and substituted it for the one that was supposed to be in the auction. Emil, meanwhile, had arranged to sell the *real* one, the one it'd been copied from, when they got to Saranda—along with the one he was supposedly selling for Panos."

"And then they would both take off with the money and live happily ever after in Zagreb?"

"That was *her* plan. His plan was to screw Panos *and* Gaby. See, she didn't know about his arrangement with Panos any more than Panos knew about his arrangement with Gaby. You know where the cops grabbed him? Tiptoeing out the back door all by himself, to the car they'd rented. With five million euros in cash."

"He was just going to leave Gaby in the lurch?"

"That was the idea. True love. Gaby was foaming at the mouth when she heard. They had to put him in a separate car to make sure the poor guy got to the station in one piece. What would you say to another go at the buffet?"

"You read my mind." At the table Alix spooned herself another portion of the turkey pot pie, and Ted tried it this time as well, and both got some candied-walnut-and-grape salad to go along with it. The drinks waitress was hailed, and they ordered another bottle of ale to split between them.

Alix didn't quite have a million questions, but she had plenty, and over the next half hour he did his best to answer them with what had been learned so far and with surmise for what hadn't.

"I can't believe it," she said at one point. "She actually tried to *kill* Panos?"

"That's what he says, and he's got the lumps to prove it. The hairbrush is being analyzed, and the specks of blood on it are his, all right. And if the freshest fingerprints—the most superficial ones—on it are hers, which I think they will be, than at least we'll know she walloped him with it."

"Walloped, I can see. Stealing his paintings, running off with Emil, I can see. She's hurt, she's vulnerable, she's got some . . . issues. But murder? Uh-uh, there you're wrong."

"Sorry, but I don't think I am," Ted said, pouring the beers for them. "I don't think Panos would even have been her first victim. I think she had Weisskopf killed too. She has a family full of mafiosi, you know. A discreet phone call to Uncle Icepick or whomever . . ."

"Oh, guilt by association, is that it? Yeah, I've had a little experience with that myself. You want to tell me what possible reason she would have for murdering Panos's forger?"

"Because we're pretty sure that he was *her* forger too; that he made the Monet for her, and that Panos was on the verge of finding out, and that was something she couldn't let happen."

"Oh, brother, talk about speculation."

"I also think she murdered Donny," Ted went on, with an edge to his voice now. "So does Yiorgos, and so does just about everybody on the crew when you press them for ideas. The two of them have been the subject of gossip for years. He visits her in her—"

"I don't believe this." Alix was growing more heated. "This is how the FBI works? *Gossip*, for God's sake? Ted, what evidence is there that Donny was murdered at all? What makes you think he didn't drown out there, trying to make off with the petty cash? He was going to be put off the boat the next morning; he had the money on him—" She realized that she was rapping on the table to emphasize each point—lecturing him, really—and made herself stop.

"Finished?" He waited without expression for a few seconds. "As a matter of fact, he did drown, according to the medical examiner."

"Well, then—"

"He also had a blood-alcohol level of .08, which isn't all that terrible as long as you're not behind the wheel of a car, but he was also filled to the gills with what is rapidly becoming the drug of choice for your sophisticated date rapist. Mix enough of it with enough alcohol—it doesn't have any taste—and your date is practically a zombie. Anything's doable. Rape, robbery . . . or, to pluck a wild example out of the air, throwing some all-but-unconscious person off the deck of a yacht without having to go through a struggle."

Alix's heart constricted. "What's the name of this drug?"

"I don't remember. Mostly, it's used by vets—aldimine, cavatene, something like that. What difference does it make? The important point—"

"Ketamine," Alix said miserably.

He stared at her. "That's right. How do you know that?"

Alix sighed. "She was using it as a sleep medicine. She told me."

Ted uttered a brief, appreciative laugh and sat back in his chair with a sigh of his own. "Damn. You do have your uses."

"I can't believe it," Alix said. "She was so open—I was so sure she was—" She grimaced. "Some connoisseur's eye I have."

"Hey, don't look so downcast. That's not the way genius works. It's usually a one-trick show. Einstein had trouble tying his shoelaces. Arthur Conan Doyle believed in fairies. You, you're murder on sizing up paintings, but maybe people aren't your métier. And remember, the celebrated FBI—well, me—didn't do that well either. I never suspected her of anything."

"I guess," Alix said, nodding "yes" at the waitress who had come with the coffee pitcher. "Sheesh."

"And now there's something else I want to talk to you about," Ted said with the air of someone who had the world's most wonderful gift all wrapped up in a red ribbon under the table and ready to hand over.

"No, wait, just a couple more questions."

What would happen to them all now, she wanted to know—to Gaby and Panos and Emil. This was one of those "surmise" answers, Ted said, but his best bets were these: Gaby and Emil, now in Albanian custody on customs charges, would be easily cajoled or threatened into serving as material witnesses against the mafiosi in exchange for their release, but Panos would surely see to it that they faced charges in Greece; both of them for their theft of his Manet and Monet, and Gaby for assault by hairbrush.

"I'm guessing Emil will talk his way out of doing any serious time by blaming it all on Gaby, but Gaby's in serious trouble. The Greeks will come up with a murder charge on Donny's account, and if the New York District Attorney can put together a case, they'll want to try her for Weisskopf's murder as well."

"And what about Panos? What happens to him?"

Ted shrugged. "Nothing, as far as I can see."

"Nothing! But how can that be? What about the Manet forgery? What about the fractional investments?"

"Forging a painting isn't a crime, Alix—not until you try to sell it as the real thing."

"Yes, I know, but he *was* trying to sell it. It was in the auction."

"But he pulled it before it came up for sale."

"Sure, but that was only because I spotted it as a fake and *he* slashed it to—"

"The 'because' won't matter. His lawyer will simply point out that he did pull it before the auction itself, and he'd pulled the Monet as well as soon as he'd gotten the news that it was a fake too. As for the slashing, no law against destroying your own property."

"What about knocking me silly—isn't that a crime? And I'm more than willing to testify in court—"

"To what?"

"To . . ." She slumped. "Oh, I see what you mean. I didn't really see him, did I?"

"Not from under that shawl, you didn't. And as to the fractional investments, well, Panos cleared almost fifty million dollars on the auction; Mirko alone bought eight of them—twenty-nine million bucks' worth—for his hotels. We think Panos will use the money—plus the money he's bound to get for the original Manet and Monet, both of which will naturally be returned to him—to make his investors whole, close the operation down, pull in his lifestyle and expenditures from filthy rich to just plain rich, and disappear into the sunset. He's ready to call it a day."

"And you're going to let him?"

"Don't look so shocked. Once his investors have their money back—and their profits—I don't see them having much interest in seeing that he goes to court. Nor would we, frankly."

"Huh."

"Meaning?"

"Well, it hardly seems fair, does it? The point of the whole operation was to go after Panos. And he winds up sailing off scot-free. It was a waste of time."

"That's not the way to look at it, Alix. A lot of good things happened, and we were a big part of them. The sale of a major forgery was prevented, a murderer and a crook are now facing charges, as are a couple of mafiosi overseas, and two beautiful paintings have been kept out of the bad guys' hands and are still in circulation, as opposed to being used for dishonest purposes and going down into some deep, dark vault where nobody ever sees them again. Not too bad for three or four days' work. And fairness? Sorry, that doesn't enter into it. That's just life."

She was nodding along with him. "Okay, yes, you're right, it's just . . ."

"I understand, but that's the way it works out sometimes. Personally, I think we did great. Now, what I really wanted to talk to you about? Listen . . ."

There was a new case brewing, he told her, involving a consortium of five Miami dealers who were selling fraudulent Old Master paintings to gullible buyers. These were not forgeries, but they were also not what they were supposed to be. Seventeenth-century artists like Rembrandt, Rubens, and Van Dyck, as Alix knew, ran large-scale workshops in which the apprentices were taught to paint by scrupulously copying the methods of the master, and some of them did it exceedingly well and continued doing it for decades after. As a result, there were a great many "school of" paintings floating around, some of them quite good. What this consortium was doing was selling the works of the students but charging for the works of the masters. A few hours spent erasing and replacing the artist's signature, and, presto chango, *Bearded Man with Black Velvet Cap* by one Govaert Teuniszoon Flinck became *The Apostle Matthias in Meditation* by Rembrandt Harmenszoon van Rijn, thereby increasing its asking price from $300,000 (at most) to $15,000,000 (at least).

Alix had a pretty good idea where this was leading. "And you're telling me this because . . . ?"

"In October I'm going to be spending a week down there getting to know them—schmoozing, I guess you could say—and looking over what they have to offer."

Befriend and betray, Alix thought.

"They claim they'll have two Van Dycks, among others. It'll be an undercover thing, of course."

"The return of Rollie de Beauvais?"

"Nope, this time around I'm Sandy Chambers, leveraged-buyout boy genius. And I will have with me my trusted personal assistant and guru in all things cultural, Valerie Swann, whose opinion I value enormously."

"And that's me, Valerie Swann."

"That's you." He lowered his chin to his chest and dropped his voice a couple of registers. "If you choose to accept this mission."

Alix shook her head. "Ted, are you out of your mind? I'm *terrible* at this. Tell me, how much help have I been on *this* mission? I came up with no information at all—not a smidgen; I got myself knocked on the head and caused a whole lot of commotion and confusion, thanks to my wonderful connoisseur's eye; and as to the mafia thing, exactly what was my contribution? Blithely waltzing into the middle of an international bust and almost wrecking it, meanwhile nearly getting myself killed and destroying a couple of masterpieces in the process."

He was laughing. "I admit there were a few bumps in the road, but, honestly, nobody in our unit has ever seen anyone like you for looking at a painting for five seconds and tossing off a snap judgment, and—this is the important part—getting it *right*. They're starting to call you the Art Whisperer."

"That's flattering, but—"

"Look, there's nothing you did wrong that a little training and practice wouldn't fix, and the paperwork for it is already in the pipeline. You're tentatively written in for a July first through eighth course at Quantico."

"No."

"Not a problem; there's another session in September."

"I'm sorry, no."

"Look, Alix, no offense, but you really do need to be trained for this. Anybody does."

"I didn't mean no, I don't want the training; I meant no, I don't want the job."

Ted wasn't the kind of person who would let a shock show in his face, but he had no ready response and for a few seconds, the only sound was the gentle purling of the fountain. "You don't want . . . ? But why?"

"I'm just not suited for it."

"Oh, come on—"

"Let me finish, Ted. You know, when you said to me the other day that I was off the case, my first reaction was, well, basically, resentment, and I was in a rotten mood for the rest of the day. But after a while my little snit passed, and I realized what a relief it was to be done with spying on anyone—even a slime ball like Panos—or sneaking around collecting gossip and hearsay and reporting it back to you or anyone else."

"You certainly don't make the work sound very appetizing," he said with a crooked smile.

"It's not a question of 'appetizing;' it's a question of . . . do you remember where Wittman writes about how you either have the skills for undercover work, or you don't? Well, I don't. This 'schmoozing' first and then dropping a ton of trouble on them—I just can't do that, crooks or not, and to tell the truth . . . well, you're such a decent guy, I honestly don't understand how you can do it either." It was more than she'd meant to say, and she was immediately sorry.

Ted didn't seem to take offense. He looked at her soberly, even a little ruefully. "It is hard sometimes," he said quietly. "Well, it's your decision, of course, and I won't bug you about it, but I'm not going to deny that we're disappointed." He shoved his chair back from the table. "I'm going to get my pecan pie. Can I bring you anything?"

"Sure, I'll have a slice of the apple pie."

"With ice cream?"

"Of course."

She watched him walking to the buffet table, stylish and attractive in a beautifully tailored pale-blue linen sport coat. Or maybe not beautifully tailored. Ted had the kind of wide-shouldered, narrow-waisted build that would make an off-the-hanger jacket from the men's section at Walmart look as if it had been sewn especially for him by a Savile Row tailor. Once at the buffet and facing in her direction as he sliced pie, he looked up at her and smiled: a sweet smile, appealing, and genuine—seemingly genuine, but with Ted, who knew? When it came to what he was feeling, the man was a cipher, and as far as she could see, it was habitual. *I'm not going to deny that we're disappointed.* What kind of a reaction was that? Mightn't he just as well have said *I'm disappointed*? But no, as usual, he'd censored himself when he was in danger of actually giving away something personal.

Or else there was nothing personal to give, his interest in her was strictly business, but that she doubted; she'd picked up too many signals. Either way, it didn't . . .

Halfway through the thought, she realized what she was doing. She was building a case, working her way to a conclusion: However many desirable qualities he might have, however much she sensed the "buzz" between them, Ted was someone with whom it was impossible to imagine a satisfying long-term relationship, and the thing for her to do was to stop trying. It was a conclusion she'd been resisting without knowing it, but now she felt suddenly lighter, more her own person. Life moves on, chapters close (or in this case, never really open). Now what was on her mind was getting back to Seattle and resuming her real life, and she was raring to get on with it.

He returned with the pies and set them down. His smile was as friendly as ever, and as unreadable. "Now what are you looking so happy about?"

She returned the smile. "Must be the apple pie," she said, digging into it. "Smells great."

After a couple of mouthfuls, she set down her fork. "You know, I could still see myself doing some short-term work for the art squad once in a while, if there's a use for me. In fact, I'd like that."

"Such as?"

"Oh, such as taking a look at a suspect painting when what you need is a quick, right-now opinion because there isn't time for a lab analysis. But no going undercover."

"Being our art whisperer, in other words."

"That's about it."

He chewed for a while, considering, then nodded. "I could live with that."

I could live with that. Now there was Ted for you, in a nutshell. Alix went back to her pie, trying not to laugh.

27

"**M**y goodness," Geoff said mildly. "And here I thought I'd lived an adventurous life."

"That's it?" Alix said. "No admonitions, no caveats, no fatherly warnings for my own good?"

"I wouldn't think of it."

Alix had just told him about the cruise, and his lack of parental advice was uncharacteristic but not surprising, since she'd left out an inessential detail or two that even the Culture Guru, let alone the general media, had no way of knowing about and blabbing about: the facts that she'd been working for the FBI, that she'd gotten herself knocked out almost the minute she boarded the *Artemis,* that she'd sauntered into the middle of an Albanian mafia bust and damn near gotten killed, and, oh, possibly a few other trivial items of no import.

She *had* been surprised, however—surprised and appreciative—when she'd gone down to the baggage area after flying in from Athens (it had been even worse than she'd feared; with her late booking, she'd been assigned a middle seat between two corpulent men, one of whom snored almost the entire way) and found Geoff waiting to welcome her and give her a lift into the city.

Driving with her father had its own set of problems: He drove too fast, he followed too closely, he made you nervous just by the way he sat so upright and tense behind the wheel, like whichever meerkat had been assigned guard duty. And his vehicle was a tired, sad 1994 Nissan compact that looked as if it had never enjoyed a single night under a roof. The only thing that held its bumpers on, she thought, was the rust.

Still, it was toasty inside—outside, it was damp, with a cold, pearly mist—and she was glad to be back and glad to be with Geoff. The warmth was making her sleepy, and she snuggled her shoulder comfortably into the corner, against the window.

"I wouldn't do that, child—lean against the door."

She pulled away from it. "You mean it could open up on me?"

"Sometimes it opens by itself; sometimes it won't open at all."

"Well why don't you have it—"

"Other times it won't close. It's very mysterious. Oh, my, hold on!"

Whenever Geoff had to brake suddenly it was more exciting than when other people braked suddenly, because he almost invariably stamped on the accelerator and not the brake pedal in his excitement. She had to prop her hands against the glove box to stay upright until he found the right pedal, which always took a second or so. They screeched to a typically exciting fishtailing halt a few yards to the rear of the pickup truck that had prompted the action.

"That was not my fault," he said before she could say anything. "He slowed down without any warning. You saw that, didn't you?"

She tugged on her seat belt to make sure it was secure. "I'll tell you what the most adventurous times of my life are, Geoff. When I'm driving with you."

"Now that was hurtful," he said cheerfully, "and I think I shall change the subject. I was speaking with an old associate of mine—did you just make a face?"

"No. I was thinking about it, but I didn't. How would you know, anyway? You're not looking at me."

"No, but I know you, so let me clarify. By 'old associate,' I did not mean some fellow miscreant—"

"Geoff, I didn't—"

"I meant an associate from my days as a conservator, Marie-Élise Audet, who in times past was a conservation and scientific research technician at the Met and is now the head of oil painting evaluation at the *Laboratoire Forensique Pour l'Art*."

Her sleepiness evaporated. She sat up straight. "Oh?"

"As you might guess, our conversation centered on Papadakis's sham Manet and how it was that it managed to get by the laboratory's evaluation process. And . . ." He turned briefly away from the wheel to flash a self-satisfied grin at her. ". . . I believe I have come up with the answer." He waited for her response.

"I'm impressed. Let's hear it."

"As you know, the *Laboratoire*'s signature analytical method relies on drilling a core sample from the painting. Well, when Marie-Élise reread their contract with Papadakis, she found that he had put in an extremely unusual proviso: that the sample be taken not from the visible face of the painting, but from the extreme margin of the canvas, the part hidden by the frame."

"But why would that be unusual? I'd think no one would want a hole drilled right through the face of their painting."

"For several reasons. It costs the owner more, it takes more time, and, given the amazing techniques employed by the *Laboratoire*, it isn't necessary. They are able to work with a core sample that is less than the breadth of a human hair—the hole is a mere pinpoint, quite undetectable."

"Ah. And so that made your friend suspicious?"

"Not at the time, no. In working with art collectors, one soon learns to expect some very strange conditions, provisos, and demands. But when I heard about it, it made *me* suspicious. Now, the forgery itself is back in Panos's hands and I don't believe there's any legal way of obtaining it to check on what I'm thinking—it's his property, after all—so what I'm about to suggest is entirely speculative, but I believe someone with Christoph's skills could certainly have managed it. I think he—"

"Geoff, you don't want to turn off here. This is the way to your place, not mine."

"Sh, stop interrupting. What I think he did was to cut the original painting, the one from which he'd been copying, out of its frame, leaving the canvas's margin where it was, beneath the frame. Then he glued the fake painting in its place, first *extremely* carefully matching the edges. And then he glued a new lining to the back, thus covering any signs of what he'd done from that side. So . . . when the laboratory took its core from the part under the frame, they *were* drilling into the original canvas. Unfortunately, it happened to be the only part of the original canvas that was left."

"Mm."

He looked at her, lips pursed. "You perceive a problem?"

"I perceive two problems. First, when they analyzed their core, it would have shown immediately that the lining was new, not old. Second, Weisskopf might have been good enough to hide the telltale signs of cutting and gluing on the front from the average person, but from the lab? I don't think so, no matter how 'extremely careful' he was."

"Oh, really?" Geoff said smugly. "Well, first, for your information, the core is used to analyze layers from the canvas *up*—the canvas itself, sizing, ground, paints, glaze, varnish. Not the lining, if there is one. An analysis of the lining would contribute nothing to the determination of authenticity, since most paintings this old have been relined more than once, often many times. As you know. Second, those 'telltale signs,' even if present which I doubt—would be underneath the frame, and would be apparent only if the frame were removed and they were specifically looked for, which there was no reason to do in this case."

Alix thought about it and slowly nodded. "Geoff, I humbly apologize; that makes a lot of sense." But then, a second later: "Wait a minute, though, we think Weisskopf did Mrs. Papadakis's fake Monet too, and yet the lab *did* catch that. Why would that be?"

"Probably because Christoph did not go to all that trouble—and it would have been a lot of trouble—with the Monet. You see, any good forger-for-hire would have a wide range of prices for a wide range of services. My guess is that Mrs. Papadakis did not go top of the line. It may be that she had no knowledge that such services could be commissioned, or perhaps the additional money was not available to her." He pulled into a parking space, turned off the engine and smiled at her. "There. Everything tied up nicely and neatly to your satisfaction?"

"As far as the paintings go, yes, but I hope you won't be offended if I point out that this is not the curb in front of the building in which I live; this is the parking lot in front of the warehouse in which you live."

"Yes, of course it is. You're coming upstairs to dinner."

What with the ten-hour time difference between Athens and Seattle and the miserable flight home, it had been a long and fatiguing day for her, and all she wanted to do was to get to her own private, personal, homey space and sack out. This was not the day to face Geoff's living circumstances for the first time.

"I'm kind of tired, Geoff. I think maybe next—"

"Absolutely not. I've gone to considerable trouble in preparing the meal, and 'no' is not an option."

"*You're* preparing dinner?" She had never known his food preparation to go beyond opening a can of soup or (less frequently) heating a frozen dinner, the kind that came with everything in one box, separated into little compartments, dessert included.

He swiveled slowly in his seat. "You find that improbable?"

"No, not at all, just wondering what we're having, Campbell's Tomato or Campbell's Split Pea."

Up rolled his eyes. "'How sharper than a serpent's tooth' . . . No, I thought we might enjoy a stroll down memory lane. I have all the ingredients for what used to be your favorite beach picnic in those long-ago days at Watch Hill. You probably don't remember—Laughing Cow cheese—"

"— fish fingers, cherry yogurt, chocolate milk, and ham and cucumber sandwiches cut into eighths. No mayo."

"You remember. I'm touched," he said lightly, but she could see that he was. It warmed her heart.

"That sounds wonderful; I would love it," she said and meant it.

But her enthusiasm waned when they opened the metal entrance door and stepped into that dank and depressing corridor of raw concrete with its two naked bulbs hanging from the ceiling. Then through the austere cubicles that constituted the "offices" (the sign on the frosted glass now down to *Of s*). Beyond this, she had never been. They came to a roomy old freight elevator with torn and soiled padding, which they took up to the second floor. Facing them was another formidable steel door, not as banged up as the one below, but bad enough with its peeling, dirty-white paint that showed the old, underlying green. Geoff tapped in a security code, turned the doorknob, stepped back, and offered a little bow.

"Welcome to my castle," he said.

Alix took a breath before stepping in. *Tell him it's nice, tell him you really like it, tell him—*

"My God," she burst out, "it's spectacular!"

She had seen one or two nicely done warehouse lofts in New York's SoHo district, but none like this. Like the New York ones, this was a single cavernous room separated into living areas by head-high, freestanding walls, furniture groupings, and metal support elements, but what a room! The movable interior walls were covered with beige fabric, the exterior walls either painted a creamy off-white or paneled with woods that wouldn't have been out of place on the *Artemis*. Windows, of which there were more than might have been expected, were frosted on the street side—the view would have been of similar drab buildings across the street—but clear and large on the back side, from which the downtown Seattle skyline could be seen above the nearby roofs. Glass doors opened onto a small deck overlooking a surprising brick-walled garden below, with benches, a little dining table, and a brick path that wandered among shrubs and small trees. On that side of the loft, the north side, were his workroom—she could see the equipment, smell the glue and shellac—and a tiny kitchen, minimally equipped but with handsome granite counter-tops. On the south side were his bedroom and bath, partially shielded by the largest of the partitions. The living room, where she now stood, ran from one side of the loft to the other. Except for the tiled kitchen, the floor was a gleaming expanse of satiny cherrywood.

She was so relieved, so pleased, that she could hardly speak. "Geoff . . . this is . . . this is . . . it must have cost . . ."

He beamed at her. "Well, the boys helped quite a bit, you know, and you'd be amazed at what one can find on Craigslist, but it's true; I've had a very good year, child. In fact, I'm about to provide employment for another new worker."

Ah, she thought, *another old friend must have gotten out of jail. Well, that sort of thing was certainly working out for him so far. Tiny and Frisby were both great.*

"Now go and sit over there"—he pointed to a white leather Scandina-vian armchair, part of a grouping that faced a propane fireplace with a cheerful fire already going—"while I do the finishing touches on our meal; there's a good girl." He began to busy himself in the kitchen but then poked his head around the partition that separated it from the living room. "Would you like a glass of wine while you wait?"

"I'll wait for the chocolate milk," she said, heading for the indicated seat, but the warmth from the fire felt so good that instead she went to sit on the hearth that had been constructed around it, basking in the heat that went a long way toward unknotting her neck and shoulders. It was going to take her a while to get reused to the weather in Seattle, where a fire was a welcome thing the third week in May. Facing in this direction, she could see more directly into the workroom, where there was an old table littered with tools, tubes of glue, segments of picture frame, and what looked like bases and pedestals for the gimcrack frippery that constituted Venezia's inventory of objets d'art.

"Looks like you're keeping busy enough," she called. "Working on anything interesting?"

"Oh, yes, very much so. I'll show you later. Alix, was I supposed to thaw the fish first? And how long am I supposed to—oh, never mind, there are directions on the package. It'll be ten minutes. Are you keeping yourself entertained?"

"Sure," she said, getting up and going to the workroom to have a look for herself. Once inside, she saw that there was a nook in one corner that couldn't be seen from the living room, almost as if it had been arranged that way on purpose, so naturally that was where she went.

One step into it, and she came to a halt. "Oh no, don't tell me . . ." she murmured. "Please let this not be what it looks like. Please let there be a simple explanation."

She was standing before an easel on which was a handsome oil painting about two feet by three. On the fabric-covered wall facing it were pinned-up reproductions of similar paintings, most of which she knew and which any serious student of art history would know. All were by that much-loved darling of forgers, the mid-nineteenth-century French painter Jean-Baptiste-Camille Corot—of whom Tiny had joked, "painted almost two thousand paintings just in the last ten years of his life. Three thousand of them are in the United States, a thousand of them are in Asia, and the rest of them are still in Europe."

The Corot-like painting on the easel was without doubt a forgery, and a brand-spanking-new one at that, which it didn't take a connoisseur's eye to discern. It was only half finished, and the smell of the paint was still strong. She shook her head with disbelief as she looked at it. *This was his 'new venture'? God help us; here we go again.*

It wasn't a copy of an existing picture, like Panos's Monet and Manet had been, but part invention, part pastiche, as most forgeries are. The pictures on the wall had been used as guides to come up with a completely new painting, but one that was unmistakably in the style of Corot. This was not Corot's late style, though—the sketchy, loosely painted pictures of nymphs

241

and cherubs in blurry gray-green dells that were so easy to fake; this was early Corot, Corot at his masterly best—the Piazza San Marco in Venice, exquisitely exact, with needle-sharp outlines, meticulous brushwork, and so clear a definition of every object, architectural detail, and person in it that you had to look twice to be sure it wasn't a photograph. This was a style that only a crazy person would think of trying to duplicate.

A crazy person or Geoff. No wonder the three of them had found the Corot story so hilarious, damn them.

When she turned to stamp out to the kitchen and confront him she found him standing right behind her smiling broadly.

"What do you think? Not too bad, eh? I haven't quite—"

"Oh, Geoff, how could you? After all you've put us through . . ." Her throat constricted. She didn't know whether she was feeling anger or pity, but whatever it was, it was intense.

His expression was as blank and surprised as she had ever seen it, but after a moment it cleared. "I think," he said with a smile, "that you may have gotten the wrong idea."

"What, you didn't paint this?"

"I did paint it."

"And it's not a fake Corot?"

"It is a *genuine* fake Corot, or will be when I've finished."

A couple of beats passed. Geoff continued to smile. "Is there something I'm not getting here?" Alix asked.

For answer, he went to a file cabinet in the outer part of the workroom, came back with a glossy, fold-over pamphlet, and put it in her hand. Cautiously, suspiciously, wary of being hoodwinked, she began to read.

GENUINE FAKES

from

Geoffrey London

A "much-respected museum conservator" (New York Times), *a "gifted forger"* (ArtNews), *and an "utterly delightful man"* (People),

Geoffrey London spent years in prison for concocting and executing "the most brilliant string of forgeries of the decade, perhaps of the century" (The Atlantic). Having paid his debt to society, he is now on the right side of the law and is putting to happy and legitimate use his extraordinary ability to meticulously bring to life the styles—and actual methods and (to the extent possible) materials—of the world's great artists from Jan van Eyck to Jasper Johns.

Whether you would like to own your own scrupulously reproduced favorite painting by Renoir or Picasso, or a "new" one specially painted for you, Genuine Fakes will be happy to provide it. Or how about a portrait of your spouse "done by" van Gogh or Modigliani?

All paintings are signed by Mr. London and are framed in a manner appropriate to the artist and the time. If you prefer your older paintings aged and crackled, this can be done for a small additional fee.

Costs vary depending on the work involved, but are generally in the $5,000 to $15,000 range, averaging about $8,000. Turn the page for images of sample paintings and their costs. More information can be found at http://masterforger.com.

Alix looked up, shaky with relief, but not sure whether to believe it. "This is really true? This is your 'new venture'?"

"This is it."

"I thought . . . I thought . . ."

"I can see what you thought, but being the forbearing person that I have learned to be when it comes to you, I choose not to take offense."

"But Geoff, do you think people are really going to pay you ten or fifteen thousand dollars for a fake?"

"Not only going to but already have. Alix, dear, I've been open for business less than two months, and already I've fulfilled two commissions, with three more in progress or waiting to be started. This painting here, the Corot? Fifteen thousand five hundred, since she's ordered the *craquelure*. I have the boys helping me with things, and they are having the time of their lives. Making an honest living by forging paintings, what could be better? It's almost as if I'm running a seventeenth-century workshop, just like—well, modesty forbids."

"I don't recall it forbidding you before," Alix said, laughing. "Geoff, this is wonderful. I admit I'm amazed that you're actually getting customers, but I couldn't be more pleased."

"Ah, but you could, and I'm about to prove it. Come with me."

They went back out to the living room, and on a low glass table near the fireplace was a small porcelain flower vase with a single fresh rose, against which now leaned an ordinary white business-size envelope. *For my darling daughter* was written on its face.

Alix didn't know whether it was the words or her relief or her pleasure in the new outlook for Geoff's future, but she was suddenly close to tears.

"Open it," he said. "Sit down first."

What now? She sat. She tore open the envelope and took out a check. "Pay to the order of Alix London," it said, "$35,368.75."

"I don't . . . what—?"

"First installment," he said, looking happier and somehow lighter, more buoyant, than she'd seen him since before he'd gone to jail.

She was utterly at a loss. "Of what?"

"Of the four that you have coming to you for the sixty thousand dollars—your entire remaining college fund—that you gave up to help me through my time of tribulation. Assuming ten percent interest over nine years, it comes to a total of $141,475—four payments of $35,368.75 each, although of course the next three will be recalculated to reflect additional interest."

"Geoff . . . you *knew*? Leonard swore to me you'd never find out where that money came from." Leonard Arliss had been the family attorney at the time of Geoff's 'tribulation,' and had assured Alix that there was no way that her father could possibly learn that she had been the source.

"Oh, don't blame Leonard; it didn't come from him."

"Then how—Geoff, I . . . this is wonderful of you, but, really, I can't—" She held the check out to him.

He put his hands behind his back. "Of course you can. Now stop being silly."

"But—"

"Now you listen to me. That is your money, not mine. Please don't deny me the pleasure of repaying you for what had to have been a tremendous sacrifice on your part. A simple thank-you and a gracious acceptance would be nice but not required. And if you force me, I can be just as tricky as you are and see to it that it comes to you some other way." That familiar twinkle glimmered in his eyes. "Although I really would prefer to take credit for it, if it's all the same to you."

The tears that had been building turned to laughter and she sank weakly down into the armchair. "Thank you, Geoff . . . Dad."

A signal beeped in the kitchen. "Dinner is served," he said and went to get it. In a few seconds he returned with a tray that held everything and carefully placed it on the low table.

He looked doubtfully at it. "Fish fingers . . . chocolate milk," he said uneasily. "I'm not sure this was such a good idea. After the meals you must have had aboard the *Artemis*, this must seem rather, well . . ."

She reached up to grasp his wrist. "Geoff, this has got to be the most wonderful dinner I've ever had or ever will have."

Acknowledgments

Our thanks to Bill Campbell, retired San Diego Police Department Detective Sergeant and former security consultant, for cheerfully filling us in on the ins and outs of day-to-day security operations on a world-class superyacht. Our thanks as well to Dr. David L. Black, founder and CEO of Aegis Sciences and clinical assistant professor of Pathology, Microbiology, and Immunology at Vanderbilt University, for setting us straight on a key question of toxicology.

ABOUT THE AUTHORS

With their backgrounds in art scholarship, forensic anthropology, and psychology, Charlotte and Aaron Elkins were destined to be mystery writers. Between them, they've written thirty mysteries since 1982, garnering such awards as the Agatha Award for the best short story of the year, the Edgar Award for the year's best mystery, and the Nero Wolfe Award for Literary Excellence. The pair revels in creating intensively researched works that are as accessible and absorbing as they are sophisticated and stylish. Charlotte was born in Houston, Texas; Aaron in New York City. They live on Washington's Olympic Peninsula.